Tea for Three

A Mulberry Lane Novel, Volume 1

Melissa Crosby

Published by iHeart Press, 2020.

Copyright

ISBN - 978-0-9951379-1-2
Print ISBN 978-0-9951379-2-9

About This Book

Three women
Three cups of tea
Three new beginnings

Sarah Gardner's husband went to sleep one night in November and never woke up. At forty-years-old, the new widow is left to care for their three children, all of whom are under the age of five.

Twenty-five-year-old Filipina, Kate Morgan, thought she had met the man of her dreams during what was a perfect summer vacation. Now married to the handsome American who had swept her off her feet, and over 8000 miles away from home, Kate soon realizes that her mother was right: vacations end and people change.

Louise Delaney couldn't ask for anything more. At fifty-nine, she had enjoyed almost four decades of blissful marriage to Warren—may his soul rest in peace. But Louise's seemingly perfect world is upended when she gets a visit from a sixteen-year-old who says she is Warren's daughter.

Three exceptional women—each of whose hearts are broken into a million pieces—come together in this extraordinary tale of life, love, and true friendship.

A Letter to You

Dear Friends

I'm so glad that you have chosen to read *Tea for Three - A Mulberry Lane Novel*. Those of you who have read my romance novels in the past will know that this book is slightly different. This time, I wanted to write about women and how truly amazing we all are—each and every one of us.

As I explored the issues and hidden burdens that many women carry as daughters, mothers, wives, and partners; I found myself drawing a lot from my own experiences. In fact, my own Filipino heritage has helped me to develop Kate's character.

It has been a true joy for me to write the stories of Sarah, Kate, and Louise. I love how, even in their darkest moments, they lifted each other up; never failing to share their own strength, hope, and faith.

Life can be tough, but I believe that with unwavering faith in God, and family and friends like Sarah,

Kate, and Louise by our sides, we can overcome anything.

So, I hope you have a great time in Carlton Bay; and that you enjoy getting to know these incredible women of Mulberry Lane.

Hearing from my readers is one of the things I most enjoy about being an author. You can contact me through my website at www.melissacrosby.com

Kind wishes

Melissa ♥

Acknowledgements

To Wayne, my forever love; thank you for always believing in me.

To Rev Ben Johnson-Frow, for your guidance.

In no particular order, thank you to my amazing readers Genna Marshall-Dunn - Gold Coast, Australia, Shan Ko -Vermont, USA, Michaela Hofer - South Dakota, USA, Fleur Wilkinson - Christchurch, New Zealand, W. Shan Ko-Putnam - Vermont, USA, and Kim P, - NC, USA. Thank you for answering all my questions, no matter how silly. And for sharing your opinions on some of the hard topics in life.

Until the next book,

Melissa ♥

Prologue

Sarah Gardner

Three weeks earlier, November 23rd

Sarah watched as a white butterfly landed on her husband's casket as it was lowered into the ground. She couldn't believe it. Adam was dead. His heart had failed him in his sleep and he never woke up.

The butterfly idly flapped its wings—one, two, three—before slowly taking flight. Sarah sat up straight and rubbed her left wrist with her hand. She felt for a pulse and breathed a sigh of relief when she'd found it.

Sarah could still remember the feel of Adam's skin when she rolled over for a cuddle. The morning alarm was yet to go off and she'd woken from the sun's rays pushing through the curtain. His skin was cold—like ice. Only it didn't melt like ice.

Just the year before, Adam had insisted on planning their funerals. The idea came after their youngest child was born. He thought it the prudent thing to do. *"We don't want to burden the kids with having to make decisions about our funerals,"* he'd said. It was what Adam had to do when his own parents died ten years ago. It was a car accident that took them; sudden and unexpected. He didn't want Liam, Noah, or Zoe to go through that. So the Gardners met with their insurance company, updated their wills to include funeral arrangements, and even went as far as choosing their caskets. Well—Adam did. Not Sarah. It felt macabre and unnatural to her.

It came as a surprise to Sarah how easily one could buy a casket. She ordered Adam's online from *Costco.* During the planning phase, Adam had scoured the internet to find affordable, but 'stylish', caskets and showed Sarah the *impressive* range that Costco had online. *"See?"* he had boasted. *"Take a look at this one, Sarah. It's perfect. I told you! People waste money when there's just no need to. We all still end up six feet under—fancy casket and all. Those funeral guys are all crooks!"*

Adam meticulously jotted all the details down in the *Moleskine* notebook she'd bought him for Valentine's Day earlier that year. If Sarah had known he was going to use it for that specific purpose, she'd have just given him a stack of cheap composition notebooks.

He'd kept the notebook in the top right-hand drawer of his desk. *"If anything ever happens to me,"* Adam said, *"open this drawer and you will find everything you need."* So when the time came to plan his funeral, Sarah opened the top drawer. There it was—just as he said it would be. Adam was always so organized. So much more than she ever was.

Sarah flicked through the pages and ran her fingers over the ridges of Adam's heavy handwriting. Item 1345273 - *The Hampton Casket by Prime - Costco.*

She turned the computer on and went on the *Costco* website. On the search bar, Sarah typed in the item number and hit enter. Sarah's eyes stung as she read through the product description. For the price of $999.00, Adam would be buried in a casket made of Poplar wood finished with a mahogany gloss. Tears streamed down her face as Sarah continued to read. The casket had a light cream velvet interior.

It had started with a small chuckle. Sarah wiped her tears and smiled. Trust Adam to find a casket that had an adjustable eternal rest bed (both head and foot) and included a matching pillow and throw. Her chuckle turned into a laugh. Hours later, she was still laughing. And when the babysitter returned home with the children, she'd found Sarah laughing hysterically in the study—on the floor. The poor girl called her mother, who then called 911.

The event must have been traumatizing for the babysitter, because after the funeral, she resigned. *Immediately* after. *"There's no good time to tell you,"* she'd said. *"So I'll just go ahead and say it."* And so she did. She'd said it and ended with, *"I'm so sorry for your loss, Mrs. Gardner."*

That night, Sarah found herself without both a husband and babysitter. One might joke that they'd ran off with each other; sadly, that wasn't the case. It was funny, but not funny. No.

Despite her mini-breakdown, however, Sarah had to give it to Adam. His forward planning had helped her get through the toughest challenge of her life to date. The funeral had been well-attended and if Adam could see how many people were at his own funeral, he'd have been pleased and would have given a toast. *Thank you all for coming.*

Back at the house, everything was perfect—as far as funeral receptions went. From where she sat, Sarah looked around for her children. She had no idea where they were. But she could hear them and took comfort in knowing there were, at the very least, safe at home.

Charlotte, Adam's cousin and their closest family member in the county, had catered the event. She was the owner of a small cafe in Willow Oaks, which was the next town up from Carlton Bay. If it wasn't for Charlotte, Sarah would not have known how to cater for a funeral reception. *"I wouldn't have it any other way,"* Charlotte had said when Sarah told her that Adam had specifically wanted her to cater at his funeral. Sarah had even asked if she wanted to read his notebook. Charlotte—bless her sweet heart—had declined.

With everything being managed by Charlotte and her staff, there wasn't much that Sarah had to do. She performed her widow duties as best as she could by sitting, listening, and nodding when people offered their condolences even if they all said the same things. *"He will be missed. Adam was a great guy. Everyone loved him."* Unfortunately, to Sarah, none of what they said mattered. Adam was gone. He didn't run away with the babysitter. He died and left them for good.

Kate Morgan

KATE'S HUSBAND, EVAN, supplied all of Adam Gardner's needs when it came to eggs and milk. Adam was the deceased. Adam didn't buy a lot, mind you; but that was one of the things that the locals of Carlton Bay liked about Evan. He was happy to cater to the needs of anyone, whether they were a big business or a small household.

Adam liked to support the local businesses and farmers alike, and those were the people who'd turned up to his funeral. Kate imagined that they were all thinking the same thing, wondering if they had lost another client—or if the bereaved wife would continue the business relationship.

Being new to the town—and the United States—Kate didn't really know anyone at the funeral reception. For better or worse, she had gotten used to standing around and being ignored at these small events that her husband, Evan, took her to.

Kate turned around at the sound of her name being called—or shouted. Shouted was the more accurate term.

It was Evan who was calling her, of course. In fact, she'd become rather sick of hearing him butcher her name. Besides, no one else knew her enough to yell out across the room for her. She spotted him and made her way to where he stood among, she guessed, a group of other farmers.

"Have y'all met my beautiful wife?" Evan pulled her close to his side. "This is Kate. She's from the Philippines" he said proudly of his *imported goods.*

When Kate agreed to marry the charming man holidaying in her home country, she hadn't anticipated that her whole life would be placed on hold and that she would be someone's—for lack of a better term—trophy wife.

"It's nice to meet you, honey," one of the guys said.

"Oh, she's a beauty, isn't she?" another said, as one might say of their prized cattle.

"Do you have a sister that looks like you?" joked another.

"My uncle has a Filipino girlfriend," said the tall one. "You might know her, she's from the Philippines too."

"Do—you—speak—English?" someone asked slowly, several decibels higher than normal.

Yes, Kate spoke English. She had also graduated with a degree in Hotel and Restaurant Management and worked at one of the top hotels in Manila. However, to the tall one's dismay, she didn't know every single one of the 110 million Filipinos in the world. But she didn't say all that. Gosh, no. She wouldn't have dared. Every time she opened her mouth to speak, people made it perfectly clear that they didn't understand (or appreciate) her thick, foreign accent. So she had learned to keep things short and simply answered with a yes or no.

She felt Evan kiss the side of her head, leaving a trail of goose pimples down the back of her neck. Daily threats of divorce and calls to immigration had left her less than enamored with her older husband. But she smiled at him—smiled at them. She had learned to. In just six months, Kate had been trained to sit, stand, and do, like a good ol' American farm dog.

Never in her life had she felt so alone.

"Don't do it," her mother had warned in Filipino. Kate could still remember the disapproval in her face. *"What could you possibly have in common with a man twenty years your senior? You haven't known him long. People change when the va-*

cation is over! I forbid it!" She ended her sermon with a mighty "tsk!"

But, always the believer in love, fate, and happily ever-afters, Kate brushed off her mother's caution and followed the man of her dreams. Everyone knew that when life beckoned you as a twenty-five-year-old, you answered. *"I'm an adult, Ma!"* she had argued. *"I'm doing it and you can't stop me."*

It disappointed her to the innermost depths of her broken heart to learn that her mother had been right. Evan turned out to be, not the man of her dreams, but of her nightmares.

"I'll just go and help Sarah with the children," Kate said when she noticed the three butter-blonde Gardner kids running around in the backyard. It was the perfect excuse to get away from the awkward conversation she'd found herself in with Evan and his farmer friends. And when the guests had started leaving, Kate told her husband that she had offered to stay the night to help Sarah with the kids.

"Good idea, darling," Evan said, his voice deep. "You make sure you keep her happy. We don't want to lose her as a customer."

Kate nodded.

That night, when the sun fell and only darkness filled the sky, Sarah approached her. Kate was on her hands and knees picking up the children's toys, which had been scattered everywhere. "Thank you," Sarah began, "for your help." She looked drained.

"You don't need to thank me. I'm happy to help." Kate knew that Sarah had no idea who she was. The truth was, she hadn't properly met Sarah. But it was an excuse to take a much-needed break from her controlling husband, so she jumped at it, thinking she would deal with the consequences later. "Why don't you get some rest," she said. "I'll put the children to bed."

"Oh, I couldn't let you do that." Sarah's eyes spoke of sadness.

Kate stood up and offered a hand to Sarah. "I'm Kate," she said. "Evan Morgan's wife. He's the one that delivers your milk and eggs."

Once a connection had been established, Sarah's face relaxed.

"You go and have a nice bath and I'll put the children to bed." Kate placed a hand on Sarah's arm. "When you finish, I'll have something ready for you to eat."

Sarah stood motionless for a second before a tear escaped from her eye. "My babysitter quit."

"I know," Kate said, though she hadn't, really. She had been to many funerals in the Philippines before. It was always a weird, but nice, family gathering of sorts. Wakes were held for nine consecutive days before the funeral. Friends and relatives stayed and surrounded the grieving family. They sat and kept watch over the dead, never leaving the bereaved alone with their grief, offering to do everything for them, come hell or high water. "I'll stay with you. You're not alone."

Sarah bit her lips. She was fragile and weak.

"I've got you." Kate meant what she said. She would be there for this woman whose heart, like hers, had been broken into a million pieces.

Louise Delaney

THE DAY AFTER ADAM Gardner's funeral, Louise got up early. She'd decided the night before, that she would go over to check on the wife, Sarah.

The funeral reception was held at the Gardner's house and while Louise had been sitting admiring the French country style sofa, she'd heard two women talking. She hadn't turned around, but from the conversation itself, she surmised it was the babysitter. From where she sat, Louise could feel the pain of both women—pain that emanated from the one doing the breaking up and pain that came from the one broken up with. The dumper and *dumped*.

She knew exactly what poor Adam's wife was feeling. It had been three years since her own husband died, but not a day went by that Louise didn't think about Warren. With three children under five-years-old, she had no doubt that the young widow had her hands full.

Louise didn't know her very well, but she lived two houses down from the Gardners. It made sense to her that she should go and see what she could do to help.

Louise knocked on the bright red door of 603 Mulberry Lane and held her surprise when an Asian woman answered the door. "Good morning. I'm Louise Delaney," she'd said, a hand to her chest. "I live in number 607. I thought I'd come and see if Sarah needed a hand with anything today."

"Come in, come in" the woman said. "I'm Kate. I'm just helping Sarah out too." Her accent was not from this part of town, Louise could tell. She'd lived in Carlton Bay for a very long time, and she thought she knew everyone in the small seaside town.

"Thank you." Louise stepped into the house. "How's Sarah?" Louise followed Kate through to the living room where Louise could see she had been vacuuming.

"She's still asleep, and so are the children. I thought I would get a start on tidying up after last night's reception. Were you there?"

"Yes, I came by, but I didn't stay for very long." Louise took her jacket off and hung it on the coat rack on the corner. "Should I get some breakfast going for when they wake up?" It was 8:30am and it wouldn't be too long before Sarah or at least one of the children woke up.

"Okay, sure," Kate said as she turned the vacuum back on. She was obviously not one for conversation.

Louise went to the kitchen and looked in the fridge to see what she could cook. From her own experience, food was the last thing she thought about. The morning after Warren died, Louise couldn't bring herself to eat anything. The smell of food made her retch, and she recalled how their daughter, Madison, made sure that she ate something—anything—to get some kind of nutrition inside her. But Madison was thirty-years-old when Warren died. The Gardner kids were all still so little.

She looked in the pantry to see what she could prepare. Oatmeal was something that both Sarah and the kids could eat. She pulled some bread out in case they preferred something like peanut butter or jam on toast. Or both.

Louise considered herself a very lucky woman. She had married Warren when she was just nineteen, and they remained married and perfectly happy for thirty-seven years. The 'perfectly' part of their marriage came with hindsight though, she admitted. It wasn't unusual to appreciate something until you've lost it. But they had Madison. And Madison was the love of her life.

It was through Madison that Louise learned about unconditional love. Before Madison was born, Louise only knew love as that between a man and woman. Or love for family. Friends. That kind of love. With Madison though, she bore for her child an immortal kind of love. A love that would never die. A love that would never hurt and never falter. Not when Madison first told Louise she'd hated her—Madison was ten-years-old at the time. Or that time when she'd said Louise embarrassed her, and blurted, "*why can't you be like other mothers?*" Not even when Madison had her first boyfriend and was never home. And most certainly not when Madison decided to get married and fly across the world to live in New Zealand. No. Louise's love—a mother's love—withstood all kinds of hurt, disappointment, and pain.

After Madison left for New Zealand, Louise made a conscious decision to look after herself. She wasn't dead. No. In fact, she had plenty of life in her yet.

It all happened one day. She'd gone to church, just like every Sunday—only that time, it was a Wednesday—and she prayed. She'd asked God for a sign; something that would tell her what she should do.

Her fervent prayers had been answered when one afternoon, as she strolled the dockside along Lighthouse Road, she entered the Carlton Bay Bookstore—which unsurprisingly was the only bookstore in Carlton Bay. As usual, it was empty, bar maybe one or two customers. She browsed the shelves and talked to Edna, who owned the shop, asking her about any new releases that may have come in.

What she'd learned instead was that Edna wanted a change. *"I'm too old for this,"* she'd said. *"And I'm thinking of closing up at the end of next month. It's time that I retired."*

Four weeks later, Louise signed the dotted line and found herself the owner of the only bookstore in Carlton Bay. She had renamed the store, Chapter Five.

Chapter one represented her youth.

Chapter two was for the next phase of her life as a married woman.

Becoming a mother took Chapter three.

Chapter four marked the death of her husband and the beginning of her life as a widow.

And chapter five was—well...it was *her* chapter. The chapter that revolved around no one else, but herself.

"Louise?"

Louise looked up from the pot of oatmeal she'd been stirring. "Sarah," she sighed the name with a smile. Louise turned the pot off and walked across the kitchen, arms extended, to where she stood. "How are you feeling this morning?"

Sarah opened her mouth to speak, but no words followed.

"I know, darling, I know..." Louise comforted. She took Sarah by the shoulders and led her to the breakfast nook, where she pulled a chair out for her. "Have a seat and I'll pour you a coffee."

Sarah didn't fight her. She had let herself be led and sat down. "You don't have to do all this," she said softly.

"I want to." Louise smiled warmly. She knew what it was like to lose a husband.

Winter

Now I lay me down to sleep,
I pray the Lord my soul to keep.
If I should die before I wake,
I pray to God my soul to take.
~Henry Johnstone

Chapter 1

Sarah Gardner

Sarah woke to Zoe crying hysterically. She rubbed her eyes and sighed as she stood up from the yellow armchair—her favorite. She made her way up the stairs when she was overcome by a dizzy spell. Sarah leaned against the wall to steady herself.

Sarah went into Zoe's bedroom to find her sitting up in bed. Her normally wispy golden hair was a rat's nest and snot ran down from her nose. Sarah opened her mouth, but no words came. Sarah stared at her two-year-old daughter. *How can such a loud, invasive sound could come from someone so small?* Sarah narrowed her eyes. *Please shut up, Zoe. Please. Please. Please!* Sarah took a deep breath in. "Zoe, honey,"—Sarah said as she sat next to her little girl—"what's the matter?"

Instead of answering however, Zoe's cries only grew louder.

"Please, Zoe..." Sarah could feel a headache coming. Sarah picked her up and rocked her in her arms, when Noah marched in with his pudgy hand inside an open jar of peanut butter. "Oh my goodness, Noah! Where did you get that? Can you please come here?"

Like his little sister, the three-year-old did not give his mother an answer. He put the jar under his arm and began opening and shutting Zoe's drawers, smearing peanut butter everywhere.

"Noah, don't do that. You'll get—"

As one would expect, Noah shut the drawer with such force that he'd accidentally slammed it on his own finger.

Sarah stared at him, shocked.

Noah wailed, and Zoe joined him.

The only thing that kept Sarah from joining them was the realization that her oldest son, Liam, was not there. Without saying a word, she pulled Noah close and kissed his finger. "Liam?" Sarah called out.

"It hurts, Mommy," Noah said with tears as large as the peas he refused to eat the night before.

"I told you not to do that," she said to Noah. "Liam!" Sarah called out once more. Firmer, louder.

Sarah put Zoe down, which only prompted the toddler to cry again. "Stay here," she said. "Noah, stay with your sister." Sarah stumbled down the stairs to the living room. There was no sign of Liam. She went into the kitchen. "Liam!"

Sarah stopped in her tracks. She had no idea where he was. Liam was missing.

"Mommy,"—Noah came up behind her—"Liam's not letting me play with him."

"Where is Liam?"

"He's not letting me play." Noah said.

Sarah got on her knees to face him. "Noah, I need you to tell me where Liam is."

Noah took Sarah by the hand and led her to the garden. Liam had covered some hedges with a blanket to build a fort.

Sarah kneeled by the makeshift entrance and lifted the corner of the blanket. "Liam?"

"Get out!" Liam screamed.

"Liam, I was worried about you. Please come inside."

"Mommy, I want to play in too," Noah cried.

"Noah—get inside!" Sarah didn't mean to snap at him, but she did.

Noah cried and stormed off into the house.

Sarah let out a breath and lifted the blanket again. She put a hand on Liam's leg. "Honey, please come—"

"Go away!" Liam kicked her hand.

"Ow! Liam, so help me—" Sarah got up and brushed her knees. She couldn't do this. She just couldn't.

Sarah returned to the house and headed straight to the fridge and scanned the notes posted on the door. Then she saw it; a yellow post-it square which had the numbers of Kate and Louise. Sarah grabbed the note and looked for her phone.

She did the only thing she could think of. She sent them a message.

HELP!

Sarah sent them a text, even if she didn't know the women well. From the little she had managed to pick up, Kate was the one who had stayed over the night of Adam's funeral. And Louise was a neighbor—Sarah had seen her around before—who had come the morning after and made them breakfast.

The two women had continued to go around to Sarah's every day after that. And grateful as she should have been, the day came when Sarah started turning them away. She stopped answering their phone calls. And when they rang the doorbell, she hid.

After that, Kate and Louise did the next best thing. They slipped notes under Sarah's front door, asking if she needed anything—a break, a meal, a shoulder to cry on. They'd also left casseroles and cooked meals on the doorstep. But for Sarah, none of it mattered. The dust had settled. Everyone had gone back to their own lives. It was then that it hit her—and it hit her hard. Adam was dead. He was never coming back.

The truth was, Sarah had been spiraling. It felt as if she was falling down a deep, dark well—reaching for a rope or a hand—but no one was around to pull her up. She'd spent that last three weeks sleeping on the yellow armchair in the living room. It was her favorite. The yellow fabric brought a pop of color to the otherwise beige room. She hadn't had a decent rest, waking up several times each night.

But it was the only thing she could do. Sarah couldn't go back to the bedroom she'd shared with Adam. No. Never. It was where Adam had died.

It happened sometime around 5:30 or 6:00am. The alarm hadn't yet gone off. Sarah turned over and laid her head on Adam's chest, expecting him to take her into an embrace, like he always did. Only this time, he didn't. Instead, the icy touch of his skin slapped her awake.

No, she couldn't do it. It would hurt too much.

The day times weren't quite as bad. Sarah moved purposefully. Or she tried to. With three children under the age of five, she had to—even if she didn't want to.

They say that time waits for no man. While it may be so, Sarah had learned that grief too waited for no one. It overwhelmed her at every turn and every point of every day. And as soon as the sky turned dark and Sarah had fed, bathed, and changed the children, she would allow grief to finally take her.

Within the space of fifteen minutes, both Kate and Louise stood in Sarah's living room—or what remained of it.

It would have been obvious to anyone that Sarah hadn't picked up a broom, dishcloth, or rag in three weeks. She hadn't vacuumed either. Nor had she showered.

"I'm so sorry about the mess," Sarah said.

"Don't you worry about the mess," Louise said. "Why don't you tell us what we can do to help."

Sarah told them what had happened that morning. She'd given up pretending she could do it all. "Now Liam's out in the garden and refuses to come inside. Noah and Zoe are upstairs," she said. "That's them crying...of course. Noah hurt his finger. I can't...I don't think I can do this." The flatness in her own voice surprised her.

"Okay," Louise said. "Kate, why don't you go and see if you can coax Liam in and settle the kids?"

"Of course." Kate nodded and headed out the back.

Louise then turned to Sarah. "Do you have any trash bags? And some *Lysol*?"

Sarah stared at Louise. "You have the most beautiful eyes I have ever seen," she said. "Are they brown?"

"Thank you, dear. They're hazel," Louise said, obliging her.

"What color are my eyes? I really like your eyes. They're very beautiful." There was no rhyme or reason for what Sarah had just asked. She said the first thing that popped into her mind—the first thing that didn't relate to the children, or cleaning...or death.

"Sarah, dear, why don't you go and take a shower, and I'll take care of cleaning up here."

Sarah suddenly felt very vulnerable. She was embarrassed. Embarrassed about the mess that her house had become. Embarrassed by how she looked. Sarah worried that she probably smelled a bit rank too. That's probably why Louise was telling her to take a shower. For the first time in three weeks, Sarah saw her life through the eyes of an outsider and she burst into tears.

"Okay—let's see." Louise took Sarah by the shoulders and led her up the stairs. "Come with me."

Sarah did as she was told. Unblinking, she followed Louise into the bathroom and watched as she turned the water on. "You'll feel much better after a nice bath," she said.

It had never ever crossed Sarah's mind that one day, a perfect stranger would be bathing her. But there she was, in a bath drawn by her nice neighbor with hazel-colored eyes.

"How does that feel?" Louise asked as she scrubbed Sarah's back.

The gentle touch brought tears to her eyes.

"You know," Louise said, "when my Warren died, I went through the same thing."

"Who?"

"My husband, Warren. He died three years ago."

"I'm sorry for your loss," Sarah said. "My husband died three weeks ago."

"I know, darling. It's been a difficult time for you."

"I wish I had known your husband." Apologies spilled from within her. Sarah felt bad that she didn't know her neighbors. Or that one of them had died. They'd moved to Carlton Bay six years ago. She felt ashamed for not knowing that someone so close was grieving.

"He was a good man," Louise said. "And not a day goes by that I don't think about him fondly."

Sarah stared at the water in front of her. "I don't want them to take my babies away." Her voice was croaky; all but a whisper.

Louise stopped what she was doing. "Who's taking your babies away?"

"Social services." The fear had been hanging over Sarah since she'd first recognized she was incapable of handling Adam's death. Although she tried, a part of her knew that she wasn't giving her children the best version of herself. "I'm scared that they'll say I'm unfit."

"Sarah, no one is going to call social services," Louise said as she poured water over Sarah's hair. "And no one is going to take your children."

Sarah held her head back and let the warm water spread over her like an undeserved embrace. "I'm a failure...I've failed them. Adam will never forgive me."

"You have not failed anyone. This is just a setback." Louise squeezed shampoo into the palm of her hand.

Sarah closed her eyes. She could feel three weeks of dirt and grime lifting as Louise massaged her scalp.

"Is there anyone that can take care of the children while you take some time for yourself?"

Sarah shook her head. "Adam has a cousin in Willow Oaks."

"Grandparents?"

"Adam's parents died ten years ago in a car accident," Sarah said. "Both my parents are gone too."

"That's how Warren went—a car accident." Louise rinsed the shampoo off Sarah's hair and applied some conditioner.

Sarah closed her eyes and breathed in the clean smell of grapefruit and mint. "I'm sorry to hear that."

"Don't be—it was an accident," Louise said. "This cousin of Adam's—in Willow Oaks—do you think they can help?"

Sarah didn't think she could bring herself to ask Charlotte for help. She had children of her own and a business to run. "I can't ask her to do that. She's much too busy."

"Well...you don't ask, you don't get," Louise said with certainty. "Now, don't get me wrong here, but I think that we should go and see your doctor."

Sarah hung her head down and laid it over her knees. She didn't want to see a doctor.

"There's no shame in asking for help. And with what you've been through, I'm surprised you haven't gone sooner. I'd be happy to go with you."

"He's just going to put me on medication," Sarah mumbled.

"So what? People take medication for headaches—why shouldn't we take some for depression?"

Sarah looked at Louise. "Do you think I'm depressed?"

Louise shrugged. "I fell into depression when my husband died."

"I'm a mom—I have kids. I can't get depressed."

"You're a mother and that's probably why you have depression," Louise countered.

"Are you saying the kids depress me?" Sarah's mouth curved into a smile.

"We'll make an appointment for tomorrow." Louise got up off her knees. "Can you get up okay?"

Sarah pushed herself up, and Louise proceeded to dry her with a towel. "I've never stood naked in front of another person before," she said.

"There's a first for everything."

"I'm sorry. This must be so weird for you."

"Not any weirder than it must be for you," Louise joked. "Besides—it is what it is."

Like a child, Sarah followed Louise into the bedroom. She watched her pick out a sweater from the closet and, after opening a few drawers, a pair of yoga pants. "Louise?"

Louise looked up from the drawers. "Hmmm?"

"Thank you."

"For what, dear?"

"For being here with me."

Chapter 2

Kate Morgan

Kate had managed to calm Zoe down with a bottle of milk and cuddles. She'd also kissed Noah's boo-boo better. Liam, she'd found, was in a makeshift fort behind the trees in the back of the garden. The four-year-old was angry, but when Kate asked if she could come into his fort, he'd agreed. She was glad he hadn't asked for a password.

Kate herded them into the boys' bedroom and one by one, sponge bathed them with warm water. Their clothes were dirty and food stains had crusted over. They would have been relieved to get changed in to some fresh clothing.

It broke her heart to see them that way, but she knew that no one could ever blame their mother. Sarah had been through a lot in the last few weeks. Having to care for three little kids solo after the death of one's husband was a lot to ask of anyone. She was glad that Sarah had messaged her.

When Kate got the text message, she didn't hesitate. Regardless of how little she knew Sarah or the other woman, Louise, she knew that she needed to help. And besides, it was better than spending another day at home waiting for Evan.

"Kate?" Louise knocked on the door.

"Come in," she said, putting a t-shirt over Noah's head.

"If you're done, maybe you can come down and we can get these guys to eat something."

Louise was a beautiful woman in a mousy kind of way. Her light hazel eyes, covered with an overgrown dark brown fringe, glowed with kindness. Kate wondered how old she was. "We won't be long," Kate said with a nod.

When she finished dressing the children, she carried Zoe on her hip and led the other two down the stairs and through to the kitchen where Sarah sat blowing into a cup of hot tea.

"Hi kids," Louise sang when they'd filed in.

"Mommy!" Noah cried when he saw his mom. "I hurt my finger."

Zoe wrestled herself off Kate and ran to her mom's side, crying once again.

Kate glanced at Louise. "I think we need to give Mommy some time to have some breakfast," she said. But her words were ignored, and the crying grew even louder when Liam hit Noah on the head.

"Do you have Charlotte's number?" Louise asked Sarah, who pointed to a list of phone numbers on the fridge. "Is she the woman that owns the Strawberry Fare Cafe?"

Sarah nodded.

"Oh, that's my favorite cafe." Louise lifted the phone off the cradle and proceeded to make a call.

"Who wants some cereal?" Kate asked the children, copying Louise's enthusiasm.

"Me!" Liam raised his hand.

"No," Noah countered his big brother, "*I* want cereal."

Zoe remained in Sarah's lap, sucking her thumb. Her nose and cheeks were bright scarlet.

"There's plenty of cereal for everyone," Kate said. "Can we all move to the breakfast table, please?"

Kate sighed in relief when the boys did as they were told. She opened the cupboard and grabbed the boxes of Cheerios and Cornflakes. She set a bowl each in front of the boys and asked what they wanted. After she'd filled their bowls, she turned to Zoe. "Do you want to eat anything, honey?"

Zoe buried her head in Sarah's neck.

Kate felt powerless. She didn't really know how to look after children. She'd hoped they couldn't tell just how out of her element she was. She wasn't made of parent-material. It was just as well that Evan didn't want children. She shuddered at the thought of the kind of father Evan would make...and the kind of mother she would be.

"Okay," Louise said as she returned to the kitchen. She set the phone back down in its cradle and turned to them. "Charlotte says that her husband Ben will be here in thirty minutes. They can take the kids for as long as you need."

Kate was relieved that Louise had taken charge. Had they been in the Philippines, she might have been of more help. She would have been able to offer more solutions. But in Carlton Bay, Kate felt like she was just a child herself. She was as reliant on her husband as the kids were on Sarah.

Being in Carlton Bay—married to Evan—was like depending on her parents all over again. She did whatever Evan told her to do, just as she did with her parents when she was younger. She cried in the bedroom whenever they'd get into an argument, also as she did when she was a teen. And she waited for him to give her money when she needed to buy something—exactly how it was when she was still at school.

Her life, as she knew it, had regressed.

She had regressed.

Chapter 3

Louise Delaney

It broke Louise's heart to see Sarah waving her children goodbye, but she knew it was for the best—as least for the time being. Charlotte and Ben had two children themselves—twins; so that was a comfort. And it was sweet of Ben to have made the effort of telling Sarah that it would be fun for the children. She hoped he was right.

"Are you ready?" Louise asked Sarah, who'd nodded. She took her by the arm and led her to the house.

Back inside, Louise saw that Kate had begun tidying up. She had unraveled a roll of black trash bags and was walking around tossing things in—used paper plates, plastic cups, candy bar wrappers, loose sheets of drawing paper. It was three weeks' worth of trash that had piled up. It wasn't a pretty sight, but she knew better than to make any unnecessary comments.

"I don't know how to thank you both." Sarah's voice trembled as she spoke.

"Well," Louise said, "let me tell you now that you don't need to."

"Sarah, we're happy to do it," Kate said. "I'm glad you reached out to us."

"Why don't we stop for a break—coffee or tea, maybe?" It was just after noon and Louise could feel the beginnings of a grumbling stomach. "I can make us some sandwiches."

When the three women sat down to lunch, Louise poured them each a cup of tea.

Sarah picked her cup up. Her hand trembled, causing the tea to spill.

"Are you okay?" Louise asked.

Sarah nodded and replaced the cup on the table. "Just a little tired, I think."

"Fair enough. You've been through a lot." Louise took a bite of her grilled cheese sandwich. There wasn't much in the fridge and she'd made a mental note to do some grocery shopping for Sarah. "Eat up."

"You know, my Auntie Ness had the same thing," Kate said nodding towards Sarah's hand which continued to tremble. She dabbed the spilled tea with a napkin. "She was a very stubborn woman. In the Philippines, we have this term—*pasma*."

"What does it mean?" Sarah asked.

Kate paused for a moment. "I don't think there's a direct translation for it in English, but it has something to do with shakes and tremors. Mostly in the hands. Like, when you work really hard and then you feel like you're shaking involuntarily. I think you might call it a spasm."

"So her hands shook because she was stubborn?" Louise asked with a slight amusement in her voice.

Kate chewed thoughtfully. "Stubborn in the sense that she would iron and wash her hands."

Louise frowned. "She's stubborn because she ironed laundry and washed her hands? I don't understand."

"No, she suffered from *pasma* because she washed her hands *after* ironing clothes," Kate said matter-of-factly, yet with an intonation that made it sound as if she was singing. "I don't know—I know it sounds weird. Filipinos have a lot of weird beliefs," she said, waving a hand in front of her.

"What other beliefs do Filipinos have?" Sarah asked with some interest.

Louise was pleased to see Sarah smile, and she could see that encouraged Kate, too.

Kate paused to think. "Oh, I have one!" Kate exclaimed excitedly. "At birthday parties, you always have to serve some kind of noodle dish. Or pasta."

"Like lasagna?" Louise offered.

Kate shook her head. "It has to be long noodles—like spaghetti."

"Why's that?" Sarah asked.

"Because long noodles represent long life."

"What if you cut the noodles?" Louise asked.

Kate wrinkled her nose. "I don't know, I never tried it."

"We didn't have spaghetti at Adam's last birthday," Sarah said quietly.

Kate looked up from her plate, obviously horrified by what she'd said. "Oh, Sarah, I'm so sorry. I mean, it only matters to those who believe it."

"No, don't be." Sarah began to chuckle. "I probably should have cooked more spaghetti," she said, now laughing.

Louise tried to stifle her laugh, but when Kate began to giggle, there was no way she could keep hers in.

"Too soon for jokes?" Sarah asked, laughing.

Poor Kate couldn't seem to understand why they were laughing.

"I'm sorry, I shouldn't be laughing," Louise apologized. Kate was very sweet, and Louise would hate for her to think that they were making fun of her.

Sarah cleared her through. "Me too—sorry, Kate. We're not laughing at you."

"Don't be sorry. I'm glad to see you laugh," Kate said.

"And darling," Louise placed a hand over Sarah's, "it's never too soon to start laughing." Louise had seen more death that she'd wanted to admit. She knew a few people who had been diagnosed with one awful thing or another. It seemed that at her age, there were more people sick than healthy. "It's certainly better to die having lived a life of laughter, then it is to die having lived a life of pain and worry."

"I think Adam had lived a good life," Sarah said wistfully. "We were always laughing." She wiped the corner of her eye with a napkin. "He was my best friend."

Louise nodded. "Warren was my best friend too."

"How old was he when he died?" Kate asked.

"Well, let's see," Louise paused. "I'm fifty-nine—"

"You're fifty-nine?" Kate asked. "Sarah, what about you?"

"I'm forty-one," Sarah replied.

Kate's eyes widened. "I thought you might be older than me, but not by so much."

Sarah laughed again. "What are you, Kate? Twenty? Twenty-one?"

"Twenty-five," Kate said as she sat up a bit taller.

"It's the Asian beauty," Louise said. "You will probably keep your youthful looks years to come." Louise smiled. These days, at fifty-nine, she was—more often than not—the oldest one at gatherings she attended. When Warren died, she'd found herself lacking in social contact. They'd been married thirty-seven years, and they were each other's company. Sure, they had friends, but over time, even they'd disappeared. Louise learned that having a loved one die wasn't the hardest part. It was the *after* part.

In some twisted way, Warren's funeral had been a time to catch up and reconnect with people. She hadn't had time to cry. How could she? Everywhere she turned, there was someone there. Someone telling her how much they had missed her and Warren. Or someone sharing a funny story about her dead husband. It was a day to remember the good times and smile.

So it wasn't *immediately* after his death that was difficult. It was after—after everyone had gone and returned to the lives of the living.

The nights were especially difficult for Louise. The number of times she'd unconsciously slid her leg over to Warren's side of the bed was far too many to count now.

It was the same each time. Expecting his warm body next to her, she would instead be met with a cold, smooth sheet.

The empty side of the bed. It made her shiver. Each time reminded her that she was alone. And yet, she did it—over and over again.

Even cooking meals hardly ever seemed worth it anymore. She tried to cook complete meals in an attempt to keep some normality in her life. But she ended up with left overs—months and months' worth of leftovers. As it was, her freezer was filled with meals that she would *one day* eat.

So yes, she definitely had some idea of how Sarah must have been feeling and her heart broke for the young widow.

"This is nice." Sarah sighed. "I'm really grateful that you both came over. I didn't know who else to reach out to. I guess I'll need to get used to it just being me and the kids."

Louise studied Sarah's face as she looked out the window. She was too young to know such pain. "It gets easier. After three years of Warren being gone, I've gotten somewhat used to having an empty home. Are you married, Kate?" Louise asked Kate in an attempt to lighten the mood. When Kate nodded, she asked, "Where's your husband today?"

"He's at the farm as usual," Kate said in a melodic singsong tone. "He's always at the farm."

"Did you tell me before that Evan Morgan is your husband?" Sarah asked.

Kate nodded and took a sip of tea. "Maybe I should get a dog."

"Evan Morgan," Louise mused. "There was a rumor around town a few months back that he'd—" Louise stopped mid-sentence and covered her mouth.

"I know," Kate said. "That he got a mail-order bride?"

Louise briefly looked away. “I’m sorry, Kate, I didn’t mean—”

“It’s okay. I’ve seen the way people look at me. And I’ve heard the whispers at the grocery store.”

“Kate, that’s terrible!” Louise was aghast.

“To be honest, it’s starting to feel like that. Like I’m the mail-order-bride everyone says that I am. He changed from when we’d first met.”

“Do you wanna talk about it?” Sarah asked.

“Today’s not about me,” she smiled.

They’d spent the rest of afternoon cleaning up. Despite the circumstances, Louise was glad to have met the two women and felt a warm connection to them.

As she walked back home, Louise thought about how she was glad that she’d left the bookstore when Sarah messaged. Her assistant Olivia was there, so Louise felt comfortable leaving the shop in her hands. They had begun putting Christmas decorations up, and Olivia could carry on in between customers.

She’d decided one day that it was time for her to start saying ‘yes’ to things, no matter the consequences or where it might lead her. Louise thought that perhaps it was Warren’s way of giving her a nudge to step outside of her bubble that was the bookstore and home. In the years since he’d died, she’d kept to herself and her routines, thinking it was enough. Today, she realized what she’d been missing...friendship.

Louise walked up the path to her front door and was surprised when she was met by a young girl wearing a dark hoodie, carrying a backpack over one shoulder. "Oh, you startled me!" Louise brought a hand to her chest and chuckled softly.

"Are you Mrs. Delaney?" the girl asked.

"Yes—can I help you?" Louise unlocked the front door and pushed it open.

"I'm Abby." And when Louise showed no recognition. She added, "Abby Delaney. I'm Warren's daughter."

Chapter 4

Abby Delaney

Abby knew it was a dumb move to go and see the woman who'd been married to her father. Abby was the other woman's child, and she knew it. There was no denying that. But she didn't have anywhere else to go. She couldn't stand to be around her mother for one minute longer. And besides, her own father had suggested it. Long before he died in that stupid car accident. He'd told her during one of his rare visits. "If something ever happens to me, I want you to go and see my wife, Louise. She's a good person and she will make sure you're looked after." Then he'd given her a piece of paper with their home address and information, along with an envelope containing a letter for the wife.

At the time, Abby scoffed at the suggestion. But it didn't take long for her to realize why her father had done it. Abby's mother was a loser, and Warren had known it. Children are always the last to know that their parents are assholes. In any case, her father was right. Louise Delaney was a good person. Not many people would do what she did.

When Abby turned up at her doorstop and told her that she was Warren's daughter, the poor woman's face had crumbled. Abby could see it. Sure, she was only sixteen, but it didn't take a genius to put two and two together. It took all of a quick minute for Mrs. Delaney to realize that, all these years, her beloved had been cheating.

"Is this some kind of joke?" Mrs. Delaney had asked her.

"No." What more could Abby say?

"Who put you up to this?" The accusation in Mrs. Delaney's voice was rife, looking around as if waiting for someone to jump up from behind the bushes yelling, 'surprise!' But it wasn't a joke. There was no one behind any bushes.

Mrs. Delaney had invited Abby in to the house and offered her a cup of tea. And when Abby had said she didn't drink tea, she was quick to offer an alternative. "Hot chocolate?"

Abby nodded gratefully. She was thirsty and hungry. It had taken her over six hours to get from Portland to Carlton Bay. It would have been quicker to fly, but she didn't have that kind of money. So Abby had taken the train and two buses. She'd never been outside of Portland, and it had taken Abby all her courage to walk away from everything she'd known.

"First of all," Abby said when Mrs. Delaney had placed a mug of hot chocolate and a ham and mayo sandwich in front of her, "I want you to know that Dad—I mean, Mr. Delaney—"

"He's your father, Abby, so you should be able to call him dad."

Abby took a bite of the sandwich and chewed quickly.

"Take your time," Mrs. Delaney said. She was a lot shorter than Abby had expected. And nicer looking—like a real mom.

"I want you to know that Dad wasn't cheating on you." Abby wiped her mouth with the back of her hand. "At least not after I was born."

Louise held on to her own mug and simply smiled—not with her teeth showing, though. It was the kind of smile one gives when you see someone on the street. The one that formed a line across one's mouth. Her smile was wide. She looked very different from her own mother.

Abby continued. "He didn't really have a relationship with my mom—like, they didn't have sex or anything like that. He'd said that he was only there for me." Abby looked at Mrs. Delaney. She could see why her dad had chosen her over Abby and her mom. Mrs. Delaney was beautiful and calm. She was very polished, like those women you'd see on TV—like in Desperate Housewives, except older. And it didn't look like Mrs. Delaney was desperate. She was probably also a very good wife.

"Would you like another sandwich?"

Abby shook her head. "No, I'm all good."

Mrs. Delaney got up from the table. "Perhaps I should take you up to the spare room then."

Abby couldn't hide her shock. "So...I can stay?" She wasn't sure what to expect when she'd made the decision to find Mrs. Delaney. But she was glad to be welcomed. She followed her dead father's wife up the stairs and down the hall.

Mrs. Delaney opened a door and showed Abby through. "You can stay here tonight," she said. "Make yourself comfortable. I'll just be downstairs."

"Mrs. Delaney?"

"You can call me Louise."

"Louise." Abby felt the heat rise to her cheeks. "He chose you."

"I'm sorry?"

"Dad—he chose you," Abby said. "And he was right."

Mrs. Delaney pulled her cardigan around her. "About what?"

"You're a good person." Abby put her bag on the floor and unzipped it. "And I have something for you." But when Abby turned around to give Mrs. Delaney the envelope her dad had given her, she'd already closed the door behind her. She shoved it back in her bag and zipped it up.

Abby turned around and studied the room. She put her backpack on the bed and picked up the picture frame on the nightstand. Abby traced her finger around the frame that held a photo of her dad, Mrs. Delaney, and a younger woman.

Abby gently set the frame back down, realizing at that moment that she had a sister.

Chapter 5

Sarah Gardner

Surprised as she was, Sarah was grateful for how quickly both Kate and Louise dropped what they were doing to be by her side.

As she'd learned Kate had only just moved to the Bay. Sarah really liked her. Kate was funny without trying to be, and she was quite a sweetheart. It would be difficult for anyone not to like her. There was something so real and genuine about her that was refreshing. Sarah hated to think that Kate was stuck in an unhappy marriage.

And Louise—Sarah was disappointed that they hadn't properly met until then. Sarah had been to her bookstore twice before. The first was to buy a new book that Adam had wanted. She wasn't much of a reader. Not like Adam, who devoured the written word. The next time she went to Chapter Five was to buy Adam's *Moleskine* notebook—the one he'd written all his funeral plans on.

That afternoon, after both women had left, Sarah mulled over the suggestion Louise had made about her seeing a doctor. As much as she hated to admit it, Louise was right. There was something going on with herself and she needed some help.

So Sarah called her doctor and made an appointment for the next morning. After that, she called Adam's cousin, Charlotte, to thank her again for agreeing to take the kids. *"Who knows what might have happened to them if they'd stayed with me another day?"* she'd said jokingly.

She remembered what Louise had said: You don't ask; you don't get. So she put her coat on and walked over to Louise's house. Afraid of what she might learn at the doctor's the next day, she hoped that Louise would be able to go with her.

Sarah closed the door behind her and buttoned the top of her coat. As far as beautiful winter nights went, the evening air was crisp and perfect. It had been weeks since Sarah had stepped outside of her house. Winter had eased itself in without her having noticed. It felt about forty-or-so degrees with no sign of rainfall, which was a good thing. Sarah didn't much enjoy the rain, and yet Carlton Bay was notorious for its rainy winters.

She knocked on Louise's front door and stammered rather nervously when she opened it. "Hi again, Louise. I'm so sorry to bother you."

"Sarah, hi, come in," Louise stepped aside to let her in. "You're no bother at all. Is everything okay?"

Although Louise had smiled, Sarah felt that there was something off about her manner. "I didn't catch you a bad time, did I? I can always come back tomorrow."

"No, not at all. Come, I'll make us a cup of tea."

"I just wanted to firstly,"—Sarah followed her through the living room and into the kitchen—"thank you for being there for me today. And second, I called my family doctor and made an appointment to see him tomorrow." Sarah glanced around and noticed how clean the house was, with everything in its place. It was just as one might imagine of someone like Louise. "I wondered if you wouldn't mind coming along with me as a—I don't know—a support person?"

"Of course, anything you need," Louise said absently.

"Thank you so much, Louise. I really appreciate everything you're doing for me." Sarah babbled on for at least another minute before she noticed there was someone else in the kitchen. "Oh, hi!" she glanced back at Louise. "I'm so sorry, I didn't realize you had company." It was a young girl—fifteen, maybe sixteen.

"That's quite alright, Sarah. You weren't to know," Louise said calmly.

Sarah turned to face the girl. "I'm Sarah. I'm sorry to barge in, I just needed to talk to Louise for a bit."

The girl cast a glance at Louise as if she didn't know what to say.

"Sarah," Louise said, "this is Abby."

"Hi," Abby said, raking her thick, black curly hair with her fingers. Her rosy cheeks rose when she smiled. "I was just helping Mrs. Delaney make dinner. I can leave if you guys would like some privacy," she said, speaking more to Louise than to Sarah.

"No, Abby, that's fine." Louise pulled a chair out for Sarah. "Here, Sarah, make yourself comfortable and I'll boil the kettle for us. Abby is Warren's daughter, by the way."

"It's so nice to meet you, Abby. I didn't realize Louise still had a teenager in the house."

Louise set three mugs on the table. "Abby is Warren's daughter," she said again.

As soon as Sarah realized what Louise was saying—that Abby was not her daughter, but Warren's—she felt the heat rise up to her face and behind her ears. "I see. So Abby is your stepdaughter?"

Louise looked at Abby. "I guess you could say that."

The air in the room was awkward. Sarah wondered if they were fighting before she'd come. "That's nice," she said. She wanted to run out the door. She couldn't handle awkward—not right then. Somehow, she'd forgotten the social cues; how to be an adult—a normal, functioning adult capable of making small-talk and reading the room. Instead, she smiled and crossed her ankles together.

"Mrs. Delaney didn't know about me," Abby offered—as if things weren't awkward enough. "Until now."

Sarah then realized—she couldn't have come at a worse time. She wanted to kick herself. "Oh, dear...Louise, I'm so sorry. I should have—"

"It's okay. Abby and I are—we're trying to figure things out," she said with a smile.

"I think I should just leave you guys," Abby said, as she got up from the table. "I'll be in the bedroom if you need me."

"Thank you, dear. I'll let you know when dinner is ready," Louise said.

Chapter 6

Louise Delaney

Louise watched as Abby disappeared through the doorway, into the living room, and up the stairs. Her heart was heavy, and she felt a pain she had never felt before. A pain was far more intense than when Warren died. She felt a hand cover hers.

"Are you okay?" Sarah asked. "Do you want me to go?"

Louise blinked back the tears that had been building up in her eyes. She didn't want Sarah to go, but she also didn't want her to stay. "Would you mind staying?"

"Of course." Sarah smiled behind her own troubles.

It shouldn't have been that way. Louise was always the one who offered help—not the other way around. She wasn't a needy person. Never had been. But this was different. What did someone do in this situation? Louise hadn't noticed that the kettle had whistled until Sarah got up and filled the teapot with the boiling water.

"Do you want to talk about it?" Sarah's voice was soft, tender.

"She looks just like him." Louise's eyes betrayed her as tears escaped past her lids. She wrung her hands until they hurt and shook her head. "You know, she has his smile? She's got his blue eyes and curly hair. She looks just like Warren." Louise buried her face in her hands. Her shoulders shook as sobs of anguish overcame her.

Sarah got up from her seat and moved to the seat next to Louise. She placed an arm over her shoulders. "Louise...I know that nothing I say will ever make it better, but for what it's worth, I am sorry."

"You didn't do anything." Louise smiled.

"You really didn't know anything?"

Louise shook her head. That's what everyone was going to ask her—how did you not know? She'd asked herself the same question—*how did I not know?* She felt like a fool. Abby was sixteen—that meant, at the very least, that Warren had been cheating on her for sixteen years. And she never suspected it.

"Do you know why she's here?" Sarah asked.

Louise tucked her legs underneath her and cradled the mug of hot tea. "We were married for thirty-seven years," she said absentmindedly and shook her head. "For thirty-seven years, I gave my life to...to..."—she couldn't find the words— "that snake." She felt her anger rising.

"Is there anything I can do?" Poor Sarah probably had no idea what she was getting herself in to.

"But you know what?" Louise wiped her tears and blew her nose. "He wasn't a bad man." She took a sip of her tea. "Warren was the love of my life." She smiled as her dead husband's face crossed her mind. "He was warm and gentle; so loving. Good in bed too," Louise said with a chuckle.

Sarah listened. Dear, Sarah. She listened, so Louise continued.

"You know, I was convinced that God had blessed us with the perfect marriage? Right to the very end. And when Warren died in that car accident three years ago, I put all my faith in God. I wasn't sure if he'd remember me, but I prayed to him, anyway. I asked him to grant me the strength to get through the pain. And he did." Louise nodded absently. "What God would do this?" Her voice shook. "What God would send me this—this girl who claims to be Warren's daughter? In what world is it acceptable for a widow to look after the product of her husband's indiscretions?" She licked the tears that salted her lips.

Chapter 7

Kate Morgan

Kate had dinner ready at six o'clock, just the way Evan liked it. She'd made Evan's favorite—grilled the chicken pieces marinated in homemade barbecue sauce. It was one of the few Filipino dishes that he enjoyed.

"Honey, I'm home," Evan called as he came through the front door.

"I'm in the kitchen." Kate had set the table and plated the chicken, served with corn on the cob, green beans, and roasted potatoes. For her own meal, instead of potatoes, she scooped a cup of steamed jasmine rice. After that, she smoothed her hair and undid her apron. And when Evan came through, she smiled at him and motioned for him to sit. She was genuinely pleased to see him. When it was just the two of them, Evan was wonderful—but when it came to anything that had to do with the *outside world*, he became very possessive.

"How's my favorite girl?" Evan asked.

"Fine," Kate said. "I've got dinner ready." Kate knew she'd pleased Evan when he glanced at the table and grinned.

"You sure know how to please a man, darling." Evan planted a kiss on Kate's cheek and took his seat at the table.

"I had a good day today," Kate said cautiously.

Ethan cut into the chicken and took a bite. "That's good to know—what did you get up to?" he asked, his mouth full.

"I got a message from Sarah this morning." Kate carved the corn on to her plate. "She needed some help. So I went across to her house. Louise was there too." Kate brought a spoonful of rice to her mouth. "They were so lovely. I think I've made some new friends."

"That's good to know. Are they stay-at-home wives too?" Evan held clear beliefs that the place of a woman was in the home. "This,"—he pointed to his plate of food—"is delicious, honey. You've really outdone yourself."

Her barbecue marinade was a simple mix of banana ketchup, soy sauce, sugarcane vinegar, brown sugar, and *Sprite; b*ut it was always a big hit. "Just like my *Lola* taught me," Kate said with a smile, remembering her grandmother. "Anyway, you know Sarah—Adam's wife. She's a stay-at-home mom, and she has three children. I'm not sure if you know Louise, but she owns the bookstore on Lighthouse Road—it's Carlton Bay's Main Street."

"I know where Lighthouse Road is, Kate," Evan laughed.

"Of course you do. Silly me." Kate was relieved that he had laughed. It was better than the times Evan would grow condescending. "She says she knows you."

"I know her—Warren Delaney's widow."

It annoyed Kate that her husband defined women by their relationships to men. To her, Louise was *our neighbor*, or *the bookstore owner.* But to Evan, Louise Delaney was Warren Delaney's widow.

"She really should find a man and settle back down. It's not good for her to be out there running the bookstore all on her own. She needs a good man to look after her and manage the business." Evan paused to have a drink.

"She seems to be doing well."

"Just wait until she gets robbed or scammed." Evan scoffed. "Women should stay at home. Running a business is a man's job."

Kate studied her husband. What did she ever see in him? She dared not disagree with him. It was with those kinds of issues that Evan was especially stubborn.

"But for now, we should try to support her. Have you gone to buy anything from her store? Buy local, I always say."

That was true. He did always say that. A farmer by trade, Evan was a businessman at heart. She was always left in awe whenever she witnessed him handle difficult business situations—not that she'd seen him in action a lot. She supposed that was what made him so successful.

Evan had his eyes set on expansion and growth. That's why he was always looking at purchasing new land and business ventures. Adding to his crop farm, he also had investment stocks in farming and agriculture dotted across the whole country—North and South Carolina, Alabama, Louisiana, Texas, Arizona, Wisconsin. You name it and you could be sure that Evan had a stake in it. He liked to dabble in all sorts of agriculture and horticulture. Pigs, cattle, poultry, livestock, fruit and vegetables.

A self-made man, Kate was humbled by the wealth that Evan had amassed. He had two houses—one on the farm and the one they were living in. He also had three vehicles and there was nothing that he couldn't have. Kate, on the other hand, grew up in a regular middle-class family. They weren't poor by any means, but they were certainly not rich by Filipino standards.

Growing up, Kate's father had worked as an engineer. He'd built subdivisions—gated villages with large cookie-cutter houses, which Filipinos paid an arm and a leg for. He too had been a self-made millionaire—until the day he no longer was. A crash in the financial markets had sent his company to the ground and life as the family knew it had been turned upside down.

Kate's mother was a PE teacher at a private, all-girls Catholic school. She quit her job after a disagreement with the school principal who had opposed her use of neon leotards for gym wear. It didn't help that Sister Mary Ann also put a dramatic stop to her use of aerobics videos of *Jane Fonda* and *Cher* by marching into the gymnasium and pulling the plug of the large screen projector.

According to Kate's mother, the devout principal had fundamentally rejected her right to freedom and self-expression. Kate's mother had worked a couple of times, here and there after that; but for the most part, it was Kate's father that put food on the table.

"Would you like to come with me sometime?" Kate asked Evan.

"Huh?"

"To the bookstore," she said. "I also need to go downtown to find us a new teapot."

Evan frowned. "What happened to the one your grandma gave us for our wedding?"

"I'd accidentally chipped the spout while washing it," Kate sighed. It was always the same thing. Wealthy as he was, Evan tightened his belt at any expense he viewed as unnecessary. And to Evan, anything that Kate asked for was an unnecessary expense. "You know, I was thinking—maybe it's time for me to look for a job. Something to keep me busy and earn a bit of money."

Still chewing, Evan wiped his mouth. He looked Kate dead-straight in the eyes. "Are you saying that I don't provide enough for you?"

Oh, no. Not again. "That's not it, Evan. It's for me to have something of my own. To wake up with a purpose in the mornings. To be able to buy things like...like"—Kate stammered as she struggled to find the words— "your birthday, for example!"

"What about my birthday?" Evan leaned back into his chair.

"I'd like to be able to buy you a gift without having to ask you for money. I just want to have a bit of independence in my life. Is that so hard to understand?" Familiar feelings of resentment and regret rose within her. "Evan, when you met me, I was working. You knew that. And we've talked about this." Kate could hear herself pleading. She hated pleading.

"You're right. We have talked about this." Evan folded his napkin and laid it next to his plate. "So, there's no reason to talk about it further. A wife's place is at home. There's plenty for you to do here. And if you need to buy something, we have plenty of money for whatever you need." Evan got up from the table. "Thank you for dinner. Your cooking's getting better." And with that, he walked away.

Kate looked the other way. She didn't want him to see that he'd gotten to her yet again. Evan was a sweet man. But it was times like these—when he was blunt, stubborn, and patronizing—that she held no tenderness for him. Kate bit her lips and clenched her fists. "Buffoon," she mumbled under her breath.

And yet, as unimaginable as it seemed, she loved him.

Chapter 8

Sarah Gardner

Sarah got up early the next morning. She hadn't had much of a sleep and there was no point to lingering under the blanket. It was going to be an important day, and she needed to be in tip-top shape if she was going to see her family doctor. "He's going to tell me I'm crazy," Sarah mumbled under her breath as she folded the blanket and laid it on the yellow armchair. She pulled the curtains open and sighed at the sight of a beautiful winter morning.

In the car, Sarah buckled her seatbelt. "I can't thank you enough for coming with me today." She turned to face Louise. Despite everything that Louise was going through, she'd still kept her word about accompanying Sarah to the doctor. "I know you've already got a lot on as it is. And we really didn't have to take your car. I could have driven us here," she said quickly.

"Nonsense," Louise brushed off Sarah's concerns with a wave of her hand. "I'm happy to go with you. Besides, if I hadn't come with you, I'd probably just end up wallowing in self-pity."

"What about the bookstore?"

"We keep shorter hours in the winter. My assistant Olivia can look after the shop for a while." Louise hummed softly to herself. "It's good for me to get out from time to time."

Sarah looked around. Winter in Carlton Bay was slower than in other parts of the country. Stores and restaurants closed earlier than usual as not many bothered to venture out in the cold and rain that came with the winter nights. Even Lighthouse Road, the Bay's busiest strip, remained quiet as fishermen retired for the season. "What about Abby?"

"What about her?"

"Is she home? Is she going to be okay on her own?" Sarah felt a twinge of guilt for taking Louise away from her.

She kept her eyes on the road. "She's sixteen and she's quite capable of looking after herself."

To Sarah, Louise looked different. The lines on her face appeared deeper, and her bright eyes looked dull under the dark bags under her eyes. Sarah didn't know if she was imagining it, but it was as if—all of a sudden—the grays in her hair had started to show. Louise had aged overnight. Finding out that the love of your life had been cheating on you all along would do that to anyone. Sarah's heart went out to her. "Did you get to talk a bit after I left last night?"

"A little. I asked for her mother's details—just in case."

"That's a good idea. Her mother must be worried sick." Sarah was grateful for the time with Louise. She sensed a strong connection to her and felt that they could truly be friends. "Have you called her?"

"No, I haven't. I'm not really sure how to go about things just yet."

"I can understand that. It's a lot to take in." Sarah looked out the window. The beautiful morning sky she had woken to was gone. The sky was darkening, and it looked like rain. "I called Charlotte this morning to check on the kids."

"How are they?"

Sarah took a breath and held it in. "I miss them terribly," she said. "But I know there's something wrong with me right now."

"I know it must be hard for you, but you're doing the right thing," Louise said. "They'll be home soon."

"Can I tell you something?"

"Of course."

"No, maybe I shouldn't," Sarah hesitated. She was worried about what Louise might think of her.

"You don't have to tell me—but I want you to know that you can if you want to. I'm here to listen; no judgement."

Sarah sighed. "There are other things going on."

Louise didn't say anything. She listened.

"I've been...forgetting things."

"How so?"

Sarah shifted in her seat and turned to face Louise. "Like—you know—I'd go into the kitchen to do something, but then I'd forget what it was I wanted to do."

"Mm-hmm...that happens to the best of us," Louise said, her voice comforting.

"But that's not all." Sarah twisted her lips. "There was this time, last week—I was changing Zoe's diapers when all of a sudden, I didn't know how to do it."

"Oh?"

"Seriously. I couldn't recall how to put a fresh pair on. And more worrying was when Zoe began to cry. Oh, Louise...I just stared at her. Then the boys started fighting, and I could feel my heart—it was just banging. Bang! Bang! Bang! Against my chest. I resented them, Louise. I resented my children," Sarah covered her eyes with a hand. "I was afraid I was going to hit one of them."

Louise reached for Sarah's hand. "Look—everything is going to be okay. That's why we're seeing your doctor. We're going to get you some help."

"It felt like I was looking at them from inside a fishbowl. Everything seemed wide, almost unreachable. Zoe's face—her tears, her wide-open mouth—I had wanted to hit her. I could have hit her." Sarah squeezed Louise's hand. "I'm so ashamed of myself. Adam and I have never believed in that kind of parenting."

"The important thing is that you didn't strike any of them. You caught yourself and recognized that you need help." Louise glanced at Sarah. "Go easy on yourself. Did Charlotte say how the kids are going?"

"She said they're doing well. Liam has been throwing a couple of tantrums—here and there. But Noah and Zoe are having a good time with their cousins."

"He'll settle soon enough," Louise comforted. "He just needs to know that you will come back for him. Know what I mean? That you haven't abandoned him. He's probably having a hard time understanding what's going on."

Sarah felt like she'd already abandoned them. "I just feel like I'm failing them. I mean, what kind of mother throws her kids off to someone else just because things are tough?"

"Okay," Louise said in a serious tone. "Firstly, you did not *throw* them off. Second, the kids are with family. Don't forget that. And third—and the most important one, I should say—before you can look after others, you must first be able to look after yourself. And that includes looking after your own children, Sarah."

Sarah knew Louise was right. But it didn't take away the guilt that increasingly weighed on her.

"It's been one day. Give yourself some time." Louise smiled at Sarah.

"I told Charlotte I was seeing a doctor."

"Oh? And what did she say?"

Sarah sighed. "She mentioned that her best friend, Jenna—I'm not sure if you know her, but she owns the theater company in Willow Oaks."

"Oh, yes. I know of her. I've been to a few of her shows. What about her?"

"Well, one of Jenna's brothers—Caleb, he's the middle one, I think. He's back in Willow and is sort of trying to figure out what to do with his life."

Louise nodded, listening.

"Apparently, he was over at Charlotte's place when Ben got back with the kids. He's good friends with Ben, you see."

"Mm-hmm..."

"Well, as it turns out he used to be a grade school PE teacher and youth soccer coach," Sarah continued.

"And what is it about him then?"

"Sorry—I mean—I know I'm going on in circles. I really haven't had time to process all of this, and I'm still trying to figure it out. Like, I don't even know why I'm telling you this—"

"Sarah," Louise said, "relax. You can tell me anything. Let's start again."

"Okay, so Caleb is back in Willow Oaks. He's trying to figure things out for himself, and right now, he's staying at his mom's place. Well, it's actually his older brother's place, but when the older brother got married and bought a house, the mom moved in."

"Sounds like a pretty crowded situation." Louise laughed as if to lighten the air.

"Right. Yes, exactly. Now, to make a long story short, Charlotte mentioned that Caleb was really good with the kids—especially Liam. It seems that Liam has responded well to him. He's been following Caleb around." Sarah took a quick breath in. "So, Caleb's been *in charge* of Liam."

"That's good that Liam has someone he feels he can trust."

"Yes, I agree. Now, Charlotte asked if I would be open to having Caleb move in with us—with the kids—to help out."

Louise looked over at Sarah and then back at the road.

"She thinks it's like a win-win situation. Caleb gets away from having to live with his mom and newlywed brother and his wife; and I get to...well, I get some help with the kids." Sarah paused. "I guess I wanted to know if you'd think me crazy if I considered it?"

"Interesting." Louise turned into Marina Bay Road and pulled in to a parking space in front of the family medical clinic. "What are *your* thoughts on it?"

Sarah sat and stared ahead at the one-story building in front of them. It looked about as tired and dreary as she felt. "I don't know." She had many thoughts. Too many, in fact.

"Well, we can talk about it later." Louise unbuckled herself and opened the car door. "Right now, let's get you to your doctor." Before getting out of the car, she asked, "Are you alright?"

Sarah nodded. "I'm a bit nervous."

"Everything will be fine," she said.

At that moment, Sarah wished she had Louise's confidence. She supposed it came with age. It seemed to Sarah that she was a long way away from being as self-assured as Louise was.

SARAH REACHED FOR LOUISE'S hand when Dr. Butler's nurse called her name.

"Do you want me to come in with you?" Louise asked, squeezing her hand.

Sarah nodded and together they followed the nurse into the patient room. Sarah had never liked going to see doctors. Not even when she was pregnant with the children. Being in hospitals made her feel vulnerable.

After all the niceties were over and Dr. Butler told Sarah how sorry he was about Adam's passing. "How are you holding up," he asked.

Sarah shrugged. "I won't lie," she said. "It's been difficult."

"And is that why you're here today?" When Sarah nodded, he said, "Tell me about what you've been feeling. What symptoms have you been experiencing?"

She fought her nerves and opened up. "I feel like I'm drowning," Sarah said. "Like I can't breathe. Or I forget to breathe." She told him about forgetting things and not knowing what to do. Sarah looked at Louise, who nodded gently as if giving her permission to bare all. Before long, the tears came. "And the children," she said, her voice trembling. "I can't stand to look at them. I'm afraid I'm going to hurt them."

"You've had a rough few weeks, Sarah," Dr. Butler said. "It's a lot for one person. And on top of everything else, you've got kids to look after—to feed, to keep safe, to entertain. It's no surprise that you feel like you're drowning."

Sarah studied Dr. Butler's face. He was like the male version of Louise. He was so patient, and his manner was calm and comforting. He had what people referred to as having a good bedside manner. Sarah was desperate to be calm and collected, like them.

"She thinks she's losing her mind, Doctor," Louise said, taking Sarah's hand in hers.

"Trust me, Sarah, I'd be feeling the same way if I were in your shoes." Dr. Butler's voice was certain, yet soothing. When Sarah closed her eyes, it felt a little like Morgan Freeman was reading her a bedtime story. "I'm going to prescribe you some medication to take." Upon seeing the worry in

Sarah's face, he quickly followed it up with, "It'll just be for the time being."

Sarah nodded.

"We'll see how you get on with these prescriptions over the next two weeks. Sometimes, it takes a bit of trial and error," he said. "If you can, I want you to take time for yourself. Even if it's just an hour in the bath or a walk by the water." Dr. Butler signed the white piece of paper and handed it to Sarah. "Do you have anyone to help you with the children?"

"We're considering her options," Louise said, when Sarah didn't answer. "She may have a friend who can come and help."

"Good," he said, "that's good. You should know, there's no shame in asking for help, Sarah." He clasped his hands together to signal it was the end of their appointment. "I'd like to see you again in two weeks."

"Thank you, Dr. Butler," Louise said on Sarah's behalf.

Dr. Butler led them to the door and held it open. "If you have any questions, or if you're worried about anything at all, you just give Marlene a call and she'll let me know straight away." He motioned to his practice nurse. "And remember—I'll see you two weeks."

In the car, Sarah mumbled softly. "Thanks for being with me, Louise."

"Of course." Louise put the key in the ignition. "Now, let's go get your prescription filled and then get some lunch. After that, I'd like to ask a favor of you."

Wide-eyed, Sarah turned to face her. "Anything!" In that moment, the fact that Louise was asking for her help meant the world to Sarah. This woman who she'd met less than three weeks earlier had already done so much for her. At that point, there was nothing Sarah wouldn't do for her.

"I need to go to Portland," she said.

"Portland?" Sarah asked, somewhat surprised. It was at least a two-hour drive to Portland.

Louise nodded.

"Let's go to Portland, then," Sarah said with a smile.

Chapter 9

Louise Delaney

Louise started the car and headed for the pharmacy. Before hitting the road to Portland, they went to the bookstore to make sure Olivia was okay and grabbed a couple of ham and cheese croissants for lunch.

Back in the car, Louise drove towards I-105 E to Portland. She'd had a sleepless night—the first since the early days of Warren's death. She gripped the steering wheel so much that her skin tightened and her knuckles jutted out.

Aware of the silence, Louise turned the radio on and Bonnie Raitt's voice filled the air. "*I can't make you love me.... You can't make your heart feel something it won't.*"

She had always loved that song and would sing to it when no one was around to hear her. This time, it stirred a whirlpool within her. The words wrapped itself around Louise like a big, weighted blanket.

The song continued. "*...then I won't see the love you don't feel when you're holding me.*"

Tears stung her eyes as the pain of Warren's betrayal washed over her once more.

"Here in the dark, in these final hours..."

"This song always makes me emotional," Sarah said, breaking the silence that hung like damp laundry.

"Me too," Louise chuckled as she tried to disguise her sniffling. She was grateful for the distraction and ability to still laugh. She still couldn't believe that Warren had fathered another child. There was a saying that the proof was in the pudding...well, the pudding had been served—all five foot six of her. And Louise struggled to swallow it down. She wondered what she would tell their daughter, Madison. Even if Madison was an adult with her own life, it would break her to learn that her father had an affair—and another daughter. Madison was a daddy's girl. The news would destroy her. It was just as well that Madison couldn't come over for Christmas. It had been a long time since she'd seen her only daughter. Maybe Madison was right. Maybe they were estranged after all. Accepting the status quo had always been a difficult thing for Louise.

"So," Sarah shifted in her seat to face Louise, "why are we going to Portland?"

Louise paused, glanced at her wing mirror, and merged in to I-105 E. "There's something I need to do." She saw from her peripheral that Sarah was looking at her.

"Are you sure you want to do this?" Sarah asked. She had no doubt already figured it out what Louise had planned to do.

"I need to do it."

When they got to Portland, Louise pulled over on the side of the road. She took her cell phone out and typed in the address of where they were going. She turned the GPS on and waited for the all-knowing voice to give her directions.

At the end of the road, turn right.

Louise put her indicator on and pulled out on to the road.

"Where does she live?" Sarah asked.

"Thank you for coming with me, Sarah," Louise said.

"No thanks necessary."

"She lives in the Marton district—Vancouver." They were just two hours away from Carlton Bay, and yet everything was so vastly different. Oregon Pine lined the streets, keeping the tired homes hidden from sight.

"In one-hundred and fifty meters, turn right onto McLoughlin Boulevard", the all-knowing voice said.

Louise turned right, and finally, left on to Winchester Street.

"Your destination is on the right." The GPS said. And once more, *"You have reached your destination."*

Louise parked across the road from a tan colored single-level unit. From where they sat, it looked to her that there were multiple units, each with a different colored door. She checked the address that Abby had given her. "It's that one," she said to Sarah, pointing at the middle unit. "Number 4586."

"What do you want to do?" Sarah asked.

Louise opened her door and got out of the car.

Sarah followed her across the road.

No Smoking signs were plastered on the walls of each unit. She walked up to the brown door. Louise took a deep breath and knocked three times.

Within a few seconds, the door swung open. "Whatever it is you're selling, I don't want it," barked a woman holding a lit cigarette in one hand.

Louise stared at the woman before her. Her blonde hair was streaked with rose-colored dye. And her eyes—Louise felt as if she was staring into her own. Her heart banged against her chest. Warren had an affair with a woman whose eyes were just like hers. *The snake!* "Are you Rachel?"

"Who wants to know."

The woman's aggressiveness was astounding. Louise couldn't believe how Warren could have been attracted to someone so...uncouth. "I'm Louise." She glanced at Sarah for some support. "Louise Delaney."

Rachel's eyes widened, and a frown quickly followed. She eyed Louise—up and down, and back up again. Rachel took a drag of her cigarette before stubbing it against the wall and tossing it to the side of the house. "What do you want?" she asked. "You wanna come inside? But let me tell you now, I don't have no fancy stuff like y'all must be used to."

"No, no. I'm alright here, thank you." Louise took a deep breath in.

"Suit yourself." Rachel crossed her arms over her chest.

"I just came to tell you that Abby is with me." Louise struggled to see what Warren had seen in her. The short denim skirt she wore was enough to make Louise shiver in the winter air. Rachel wasn't his type, nor was she anyone who would have been in their circles. *How did they even meet?*

"Oh—so she scurried off to you, huh? It figures." Rachel leaned against the door frame. "She'd always wanted to go live with her dad. Always thought he'd give her a better life. Guess she's your problem now. She *obvs* thinks you're the better mother."

Obvs? "Look, I'm just here to let you know where your daughter is and that she's safe. I don't want to start anything." Louise felt the blood rush to her face. "As a mother, I thought that you would like to know."

"Keep her," Rachel spat as she reached for another cigarette and lit it. "Saves me from having to look after her."

"Keep her?" Louise couldn't believe what she was hearing. "Saves you from having to look after her?" It was no wonder Abby had run away.

"Okay," Sarah put a hand on Louise's arm. "I think it's time to go."

Louise shook her head. "Unbelievable." She unzipped her purse. She pulled out a piece of paper she'd written on the night before. "Here are my details." She handed the folded sheet to Rachel and then added, "for when you remember that you have a daughter who needs you."

Rachel took the piece of paper from Louise. She crumbled it and threw it over her shoulder. "You took her in—you keep her. Now if there's nothing else, I'm busy doing my nails. I've got a hot date tonight."

Before Louise could say anything, Rachel stepped back inside her house and slammed the door shut.

"Are you okay?" Sarah asked, taking her arm.

Louise nodded. "I just—I can't believe..." She couldn't find the words she wanted to say.

"I know." Sarah put an arm around her and led Louise back across the road. "I know."

Chapter 10

Abby Delaney

Abby stayed in bed and scanned the bedroom. It was simple, but easily the prettiest room she'd ever slept in. The queen-sized bed was spacious and so comfortable. Even when she stretched out like a starfish, she still couldn't reach the corners. It was that big. The comforter was smooth against her skin and was over-sized and puffy. It was like sleeping on a cloud. Or cotton candy—without the stickiness of the sugar.

Louise had left early that morning. She knew because when she woke up, Abby spotted a note had been slipped under her door.

> *Abby,*
>
> *I've gone to Portland with Sarah to run some errands.*
>
> *There's cereal and oatmeal in the cupboards. If you prefer, there's some sliced bread in the fridge. Make yourself at home.*
>
> *I'll see you tonight when I get back.*

Louise

Abby smiled when she read the note. No one had ever left her a note before. She was well used to waking up to an empty house—sometimes for days at a time.

But as she reread the note, a wave of panic came over her. "What if she went to Portland to see Mom?" Abby twisted her mouth and chewed at the bits of skin that her teeth could catch. Just last night, Louise had asked Abby to write her mother's details down. She'd said it was in case of an emergency.

Abby jumped off the bed and ran down the stairs to where she'd seen Louise put the notepad she'd written on. She opened the hall table drawer. The notepad was there, but the sheet that Abby had written on had been torn off.

"Typical," Abby scoffed. She should have known that Louise would try to find a way to send Abby back to her mother.

Abby slammed the drawer shut and stomped back up the stairs to her bedroom, slamming the door shut behind her. "It's not even your bedroom," Abby cried, berating herself for how stupid she'd been.

"What was I even thinking?" she thought after she'd calmed down. "Girls like me don't get to live in nice houses, or sleep in pretty bedrooms. Or have nice mothers."

For Abby, life was unfair. Everyone had a mom and dad. They lived in nice houses, and had family dinners together. She, on the other hand, had an absent mom and a dead dad who, when he was alive, had only really gone to see her about once or twice a year. Abby lived in a small block apartment that she shared with her mother and whoever was the boyfriend of the month. The thought made her shudder. She didn't like the guy her mom was with. He was creepy and made her feel uneasy.

Abby pushed herself out of bed. She decided she needed a shower.

Just as she'd finished dressing, Abby heard the doorbell ring. She hung her towel back up and ran down to answer the door.

"Hi!"

"Uh—Louise isn't home," Abby said, knowing that the woman wouldn't be looking for anyone else.

"Oh, okay," she smiled. "I'm Kate—I live across the street."

"Uhm—I'm Abby."

"Nice to meet you. Are you Louise's niece?"

Abby wasn't sure what to say. She hadn't really discussed with Louise how she should introduce herself. Besides...what was the point? Louise had obviously gone to Portland to tell her mom that Abby was with her. They'd probably already made arrangements to send her back like some piece of property. "I'm—uh—her stepdaughter."

"Oh, I didn't realize she had a stepdaughter. But I'm new here, so there's a lot I don't know yet." Kate laughed. "It's so nice to meet you," she said again.

They stared at each other for a moment.

"Okay, well I better be going then—"

"Do you want to come in and wait?" Abby asked. "But, I mean, I don't think they'll be home for a while."

Kate smiled. "Sure, okay."

She had a pretty smile. Abby liked her warm, cinnamon skin tone. And she had a beauty mark on her left cheek just like all the classic beauties—Eva Mendes and Natalie Portman. Abby stepped aside to let her stepmother's friend in. "Do you want a cup of tea?" That was what Louise offered the other woman when she came over.

"I'd love one," Kate beamed.

"Okay—but you'll have to make it yourself because I don't really know how to make a good cup."

Kate laughed. "Don't worry, I can make it myself. I didn't really know how to make coffee or tea when I was your age either."

Abby led Kate to the kitchen. "I'll turn the kettle on. The cups are in the cupboard on the left. And there's like different kinds of tea on the bench."

Kate got to work. "So how old are you, Abby?"

"Sixteen."

"Wow,"—Kate said wistfully— "I remember being sixteen."

"How old are you?" It was easier to speak to Kate than it was to Louise. "I mean—sorry. That was rude, wasn't it?" The last thing she needed was Louise's friends complaining about her being rude.

"Well, I asked you first—so you're not being rude," Kate chuckled. "I'm twenty-five."

"I thought you looked younger than Louise." Abby shrugged. That's probably why Kate was easier to talk to. Abby recalled what Louise did when Sarah came around to the house the night before, and she tried to do the same things. She and her mom weren't really the entertaining kind. She pulled out a chair for Kate. "You can—uh—sit down if you like."

"Thanks!" Kate sat down and joined her.

"You said before that you were new here. Where were you before coming here?" Abby didn't know many people outside of Oregon.

"I'm actually from the Philippines. Do you know where that is?"

Abby nodded. "Southeast Asia."

"Very good! You know your geography. Not many people know exactly where it is."

Abby told her about the kids at school. There were a few Filipinos and Chinese. "Why did you move here?"

"I fell in love." Kate sighed and rested her chin on her hand. "Do you have a boyfriend?"

She shook her head. Abby had no time for boyfriends. Her mother had lots of them. A lot of good that did her. It was enough to put Abby off boys and relationships.

"You'll fall in love one day," Kate said.

"I don't want to," Abby blurted.

"Oh? Why's that?"

Abby hadn't intended on divulging her entire life to a complete stranger, but Kate was so easy to talk to. As Kate had a cup of tea, Abby had her hot chocolate and told her about her mother, the boyfriends, and the late nights that turned into days. "I don't think she ever really wanted to have me. She just got stuck with me."

"Oh, Abby, I'm sure that's not true."

Abby shrugged. "I know it is." Unfortunately for Abby, it was true. Her mother prioritized everything and everyone else over her. She'd spent the last half of her life trying to understand what she'd done wrong, that even her mother didn't love her. But she was done trying to figure it out. She was done, and she was never going back.

"So, you ran away from home?"

"I don't think you can call it running away if there's no one chasing after or looking for you."

"You know," Kate said. "I didn't have a very good relationship with my parents either."

"Really?" This surprised Abby. Her first impression of Kate was that she seemed to have it all together.

Kate nodded. "They were both busy with their own things. My dad worked all the time, and my mom hung out with her friends more than she hung out with us."

"Sounds like my parents," Abby sighed the words. "Dad was always away. I mean, of course he was...he had his *real* family. And Mom's always out looking for the next flavor of the month boyfriend. No wonder boyfriends never take her seriously."

It was a minute or two before any words were spoken. "Sometimes, we don't know why things are the way they are," Kate said gently. "The only thing we can really control is how we react to the situation we find ourselves in."

Abby nibbled at the skin around her fingernails. She had never been able to talk to anyone about her problems so easily; but with Kate, it didn't feel that way. "That's why I left. I want to take charge of my own life."

Chapter 11

Sarah Gardner

Sarah closed the door behind her and set her keys in the ceramic bowl on the hall table. It felt strange coming home to an empty house—the quiet brought with it some unease. She caught a glimpse of Adam's keys and picked them up. The key chain was the same one she'd made for him when she had first learned to crochet. It was sloppy, and the stitches were either too loose or too tight. They had joked that soon, everything in the house would be crocheted. Sarah put a hand on the hall table to steady herself. An intense pain throbbed in her heart as she gasped for air and struggled to breathe.

It had been a big day.

Going to see Dr. Butler had been overwhelming, but it was the right thing to do. Sarah fished for the brown paper bag of medicines in her purse and headed to the kitchen. She read through all the literature before drinking one tablet each of *Citalopram* and *Aleve PM,* which was supposed to help her sleep at night.

As Sarah prepared a cup of tea, her thoughts went to Louise and the day that she'd had. As far as mistresses went, somehow, Rachel wasn't what Sarah had expected. Not that she had any expectations, but she just wasn't what she...expected. Louise was such a proper and respectable looking woman. And Rachel was—well...how could she put it? Rachel was from the other side of the tracks, as they say. And when Sarah first saw her, she thought that Rachel was a prostitute.

She couldn't begin to imagine what Louise must have been feeling when she stood face to face with Rachel. But Sarah was glad that she could be there to support her new friend.

Sarah sat down and dunked a tea bag into her mug.

She looked around.

The house really was empty. It was nothing but a space of emptiness, devoid of the sounds of happy children, of conversation, and of laughter. Gone were the sounds of Adam yelling out answers (though incorrect) to the TV as he watched *Jeopardy*. Or when he'd pretend to be a scary monster chasing after the children. Never again would anyone come up behind her, as she washed the dishes, and whisper in her ears. Never again would she feel a trail of soft kisses planted down the length of her neck.

Sarah took a deep breath.

And another one.

And another one.

Biting down on her upper lip, Sarah got her cell phone from her bag and called Charlotte. She had an overwhelming, almost desperate, need to hear her children's voices.

"Hey you...how's it going?" Charlotte asked as soon as she picked up.

"Better today than yesterday," Sarah said, trying to keep a steady voice. "How are the kids? Are they giving you grief yet?"

"Oh, kids will be kids," she said. "And besides, Caleb has offered to stay with us so he could help out while I'm at the cafe and Ben's working."

Sarah sighed. Everyone was banding together to look after her kids because she couldn't. "I'm so sorry to put all of this on you and Ben."

Charlotte quickly cut her off. "Honey, you are family. And we look after each other."

Sarah wondered if she was still *family*. Technically, Charlotte was Adam's family. She was his cousin. Were in-laws still considered family after the connection is gone? "But Caleb—"

"Trust me, you're doing Caleb as much of a favor as he's doing for you."

"What's his story, anyway?" Sarah was curious.

"Well, like I told you earlier, he came back home a few months ago, and he's been staying with his brother. Caleb is one of the Myers brothers."

"That's right," Sarah said, recalling that Jenna was the only girl. "How is Jenna, by the way?"

"She's doing really well. The repertory theater takes up a lot of her time, and she loves it. Her kids are a little older now, so the less they need her...the more she puts into the business."

"That's good to know." Sarah had met Jenna a few times over the years when she and Adam would visit Charlotte and her family in Willow Oaks. Jenna was almost always there.

The pair of them—Charlotte and Jenna—were inseparable. As Sarah knew it, they'd grown up together and were best friends. "So, why is Caleb back?"

"Caleb is—how do I put it? Shall we say he's going through a mid-life crisis?"

"I am not going through a mid-life crisis!" A voice yelled in the background.

"I'm guessing that's Caleb?" Sarah asked with a laugh.

"Yup," Charlotte said. "I call it like I see it," she yelled back at Caleb.

"You guys are funny."

"He's a good guy," Charlotte said. "So anyway, he was a PE teacher and a soccer coach in New York. I think I already told you that. And somehow, he's decided that enough was enough—for now at least. He says he's looking for something else."

"So, he wants to come to Carlton Bay and be a nanny?"

"Well...I don't know if nanny is the right term."

"A *manny*, then?" Sarah joked.

"Yes! I like it!" Charlotte laughed out loud. "You should meet him. He's great with your kids."

Sarah paused. "I can't afford to pay him though."

"I don't think he wants money—or—I don't know. Hang on, let me go get him on the line for you. Just a sec—"

"No, Charlotte, wait!" But it was too late.

"Hello?" It was Caleb.

Sarah cleared her throat. "Hi Caleb, it's Sarah. I just wanted to say thank you for helping out with the kids."

He sounded about as nervous as Sarah was feeling. "Aw, it's nothing. Really, it's my pleasure—they're good kids. I told Charlotte that if you needed a hand for a longer term, I'd be happy to come and stay at yours while you...uh, while you..."

"While I get over my husband's death?" Sarah offered.

"Sorry. That was a dumb thing to say," Caleb said.

"No—don't worry about it. It's exactly what I need to do." She held a breath in. "It's just proving to be very difficult."

"I mean it though," he continued. "I'm happy to help. I'm not doing anything at the moment. I'm great with kids. And I've never been to Carlton Bay, believe it or not."

His voice put a smile on her face. "Do you mind if I think about it first?"

"Absolutely," he said. "Feel free to Google me or Facebook stalk me. I know I would if I was looking to bring some stranger into my house to hang out with my kids. Sounds a bit dodgy, doesn't it? Anyway, it's Caleb Myers. I'm the one with the red cap—not the hunter with a boar."

Sarah laughed. "So, I take it you're not a hunter?"

"Not even if you paid me to do it," he said quickly. "I just couldn't bring myself to do it."

"Fair enough," she said. "Speaking of paying you...I can't. I mean, not yet. I haven't—"

"You'll be giving me a room, food—I assume—and a chance to help someone out. You don't need to pay me."

"But I will though, as soon as I get a handle on the finances," Sarah promised.

"Think about it first," he said. "I'll pass the phone back to Charlotte. Take all the time you need; I'm not going anywhere."

"Thanks, Caleb."

"Good talking to you, Sarah," he said. "Here's Charlotte..."

"See?" Charlotte came back on. "What did I tell you? Totally a mid-life crisis, right?"

"Again—not a mid-life crisis," Caleb said once more from the background.

After Sarah talked to the kids and told them how much she missed them, she took a sip of her tea and wrinkled her face. The tea had gone cold. She tipped the drink in to the sink and went to the living room instead. She sat on her yellow armchair and covered her legs with a blanket. Sarah toyed with the thought of having Caleb over as a *manny* and how it might actually do them all some good. "Goodness knows I'm a mess right now," she mumbled.

Her phone beeped. It was a message from Kate.

Chapter 12

Kate Morgan

After spending some of the day with Abby, Kate decided that she too wanted to take charge of her life. It seemed funny that she was inspired by the words of a teenager who had run away from home. But in many respects, Kate felt like she was in the same situation. She picked up her mobile phone and sent a group text message to Sarah and Louise. *Hi ladies! Shall we get together for tea tomorrow at 2.00pm? I'd love to see you both.*

Sarah was the first to respond. *Yes, yes, and yes!*

Louise quickly followed with; *I'll be at the bookstore. Can we meet there? Looking forward to seeing you both.*

Kate was glad that both women were eager to see her—or at least to get together. Despite the circumstances, she had really enjoyed being with them.

The following day, Kate cleaned the house and took some beef out from the freezer to defrost. She was going to make a beef and barley soup for dinner and wanted the meat ready to cook when she got back.

At ten minutes to two, she'd found a parking space and made her way towards Chapter Five.

There was still a lot of exploring Kate needed to do of Carlton Bay. In the last six months since she'd moved here, she hadn't yet had the chance to get to know her new town. Evan was always away at the farm and didn't like her going out on her own. So, Kate's routine had consisted of cleaning, cooking, and doing the grocery shopping. But she was determined to change all that. It was time to gain her independence back.

Kate locked the car and walked along the dockside, acknowledging the sun as it tried desperately to push past the gray winter clouds. She pulled her bright yellow scarf higher around her neck. She still couldn't get over the incredible views of the bay. She crossed the footbridge to get to the other side of the street, passing by the Bay Market & Deli, which was normally busy with fishermen getting their bait and tackle. It was just as well that the same bait shop also doubled as a coffee and gift shop.

Her thoughts traveled to the *wet markets* in the Philippines. As opposed to the *dry* grocery stores one might normally shop in, wet markets offered farmers and fishermen alike a place to sell their catch and harvest. Common though as they were—and possibly good for the market sellers—Kate hated them. Having been once, Kate was left disgusted by the putrid air and the floors wet with mixed mystery liquids which seeped from the concrete counters laden with fresh slaughter and ocean catches of the day.

Kate put a hand to her mouth to keep from retching. The thought made her sick. It was one of the things she'd openly refused to do when she was in the Philippines. She'd happily run errands for her parents to go to the grocery store, but never to the wet markets.

Relief came to Kate when she'd spotted Chapter Five from where she was. It was right next to the arts and crafts store that Kate had made a mental note to visit one day. She liked the array of old-fashioned hand towels, knitted mermaid dolls, and handmade jewelry that sat on the display window.

A pair of bells jingled from above when Kate opened the door to the bookstore. She let out a soft gasp at the sight of all the Christmas decorations. Soft festive music played in the background. Almost immediately, Kate felt warm and fuzzy.

"Kate,"—Louise smiled and waved at her from the counter— "how are you, darling?"

"I'm so glad you had the time to catch up," Kate said as Louise came out from the behind the counter.

"Of course—such a great idea," Louise said, wrapping Kate in an embrace as if they'd known each other all their lives.

"I love what you've done with the store," Kate motioned to all the Christmas trimmings. "It's absolutely heart warming."

"Oh, thank you. I'll be sure to let Olivia know. She loves decorating for all types of seasons and holidays."

"She's done a really great job." Kate looked around. "Is Sarah here?"

Just as Louise replied to the contrary, the bells sounded once again. They'd both turned around. "Speak of the lady devil!"

"I hope it's all good things," Sarah said with a smile. "Because that's all I can deal with today."

"Let's make sure that today is a day of good thoughts and good vibes." Kate was excited to be with her new friends. "Where's a good place for some tea?"

Sarah looked at Louise, who wrinkled her nose.

"Good question," Louise said. "How about the Dockside Cafe?"

"Dockside sounds good to me," Sarah said.

Being the newbie to town, Kate asked, "That's not the one that I just passed that sells fish and bait, is it?"

"Oh no, that's the Market Bay and Deli." Louise said. "Dockside Cafe is just a couple of stores up from here. They make nice little cakes, pies, and sandwiches. I'm sure we can get a decent enough pot of tea for us there."

"Sounds good." Kate was glad it wasn't that place she'd seen. It made her positively sick just walking past it.

"Who's going to look after the bookstore?" Sarah asked.

"Olivia's here," Louise said. She turned around. "Olivia? We're heading out now, darling. Can I get you anything while I'm out?"

Olivia popped her head out from the back office. "I'm fine—nothing for me, thanks. You ladies have a good time!"

Chapter 13

Louise Delaney

There were few tables vacant when they got to the cafe. "I had no idea it would be so busy at this time," Louise said.

"And aren't we the lucky ones to get a table by the fire?" Sarah added.

"Yes, I'm freezing," Kate said as she rubbed her hands together.

"Oh, darling," Louise touched Kate's arm. "Are you dressed warmly? You are wearing thermals underneath all that, aren't you?"

Covered from head to toe, Kate shook her head. "What are thermals?"

"Thermals are a must in the winter here," Sarah said. "I'm sure I have some you can use. We're about the same size, I think."

"You're way taller than me though," Kate said rather seriously.

Louise laughed. Kate was in fact a lot shorter than most. Petite might be the proper word to use. It was nice that they were all able to get together like this. "How about we order something?"

After looking through the menu, they'd each gotten a slice of cake. Louise went with lemon and poppy seed. "And we'll have tea for three, please," Louise smiled up at the waitress who she knew as the daughter of a woman from church.

"This is such a nice place," Kate said, looking around.

"Haven't you been here before?" Louise asked.

"I'm surprised Evan hadn't taken you here sooner," Sarah said when Kate shook her head. "There really aren't too many cafes here."

Kate smiled, her mustard beanie covering most of her forehead. "He's really busy." She pulled her jacket around her. "Gosh, it's freezing. I'm having trouble keeping warm."

"Oh, you poor thing," Sarah reached out and rubbed her hand over Kate's. "It must be difficult adjusting to new weather."

"It's so different here," Kate said. "But also similar in many ways."

"Do you like living in the Bay?" Louise asked, remembering that Kate had seemed a bit hesitant to talk about Evan the last time they were all together.

Kate nodded slowly. "I do like it here. It's very nice. But it's also a bit hard to fit in."

"How do you mean?" Sarah asked.

"Okay, ladies"—the waitress was back with their order—"I've got a lemon and poppy seed slice for Ms. Louise, Olive for Ms. Sarah, red velvet for your friend, and tea for three."

"Thank you, darling," Louise smiled.

"I don't think I've seen you here before." The waitress addressed Kate as she stood with her hands on her hips. "Are you visiting from out of town?"

"I moved here six months ago," Kate said softly.

"This is Kate Morgan," Louise said. "She's married to Evan Morgan."

"Oh, I see." A hint of realization swept across the young waitress' face. "Where are you from? Your English is very good."

"Thank you," Kate said. "I live in Mulberry Lane."

"No," she said, "I mean, where are you *really* from? Like, I'm really from California, but I moved to Carlton Bay fifteen years ago. So, where you *really* from?" she asked again.

"Oh, I'm from the Philippines."

Louise looked at the waitress' name tag. "Jacqui, is it?" And when she nodded, "Darling, I know your mother from church—lovely lady. Now, we both know you're *really* from South Africa," Louise said.

"Yes, but my parents immigrated here when I was a baby," Jacqui said.

Louise poured some tea into the three cups. "Well, I'm sure that your parents will happily entertain the discussion of genealogy and ancestry. We may even discover that your lineage can be traced back to the Khoisan people. Where then will you say you're *really* from?"

Jacqui's mouth hung open. "I was just asking where she's from," she said with a pout.

"Perhaps next time,"—Louise added a splash of milk to her tea—"you can find another, less insulting way of asking someone where they're *really* from."

Jacqui glanced at Kate. "I'm sorry."

"No, it's okay—" But before Kate could finish, Jacqui had turned around in a hurry and went back inside the cafe.

"Oh my goodness, that was an incredible show." Sarah laughed. "How do you even know about the Khoisan?"

Louise waved a hand. "I like to read."

"Well, it's a good thing you own a bookstore then!" More seriously this time, Sarah turned to Kate and asked, "is that what you mean by it being hard to fit in?"

Kate nodded. "There aren't many non-Americans in Carlton Bay. Sometimes, the questions are a lot more intrusive."

"I think you mean a lot more insulting. It's human nature," Louise sighed. "People are either curious or afraid of what they don't know. They just need to learn—it will take time. But mostly, I think I can confidently say that they're not being malicious. I can guarantee you that many of us here have not been outside of the United States. Some might never have even had the opportunity to go outside of Oregon, much less the Bay."

"I feel bad for Jacqui," Kate said.

"Don't." Louise shrugged. "Jacqui's young and curious; that's all. You'll see—she'll come around and realize what she's done. She's a good girl. I know her parents and they've raised her well."

"That's true," Sarah said. "Jacqui is actually a sweet girl. But I can also appreciate how questions like that can come across as being insensitive—especially if you're always on the receiving end of it."

"Louise," Kate began, "I wanted to tell you something."

"Oh?" Louise took a sip of her tea. "What's that, dear?"

"Well, yesterday, I dropped by your house to see if you were home. And your stepdaughter, Abby, answered the door."

"Ah, yes."

Kate nodded. "She invited me in and so we had a cup of tea. Well, I had a cup of tea and she had a hot chocolate. I hope you don't mind—I didn't mean to—"

"Darling, it's fine. She told me when I got home. I'm glad she was able to talk to someone closer to her in age." Louise was actually glad when Abby had told her about Kate's visit. She herself hadn't been able to sit down and spend any time with the girl. And it wasn't so much that she didn't have the time to. Louise just wasn't sure how to approach the whole thing.

"She's a lovely girl. Bless her young heart," Kate sighed. "She must be feeling all ugly right now."

Louise wrinkled her nose. "Ugly? Why? Because she looks like Warren?"

Sarah laughed aloud. "I'm sorry—I shouldn't be laughing."

"Laughing is good for you, Sarah—it's very healing," Louise said approvingly.

"Oh, you guys!" Kate said with a smile. "What I mean is, I think she's lonely and maybe confused. Like, I know if I told someone that *I* was their husband's daughter, I'd feel really ugly about myself."

Louise cut her fork into the slice of lemon cake. She hadn't thought about that. She'd been so consumed harboring feelings of betrayal that she hadn't once thought about what all this must feel like for Abby. Her thoughts went to her stepdaughter. Louise didn't even say goodbye that morning.

Kate leaned in. "I hope you don't think I'm overstepping—"

"No, no...I'm glad you said that. I hadn't thought of it that way." Louise paused for a moment. "You're right."

"I mean, she didn't ask to be born to a daddy who couldn't keep his pants up." Kate's face was both sweet and stone-cold serious.

Sarah snorted with laughter. She laughed so hard that Louise couldn't keep it in as well.

"You know I'm right," Kate waved her fork in the air. "And if my grandmother was here, she would say we should dig him up and knock some sense into him until he falls right back into his grave and pays for his sins."

Louise wiped the tears from her eyes and followed Kate, who made the sign of the cross with her hands. Whether they were tears of sadness or tears of laughter was no longer important. "Sarah and I went to Portland yesterday. That's why I wasn't home. We went to see Abby's mother."

"Oh my gosh, really?" Kate's eyes widened like a frightened child. "What did she say? Abby's worried that you're going to send her back to her mother."

"Is she?" The truth was, Louise had tossed and turned all night. She'd been battling with her thoughts—some positive and possibly helpful. For the most part, however, her thoughts were driven by anger and regret. "If there's anything that life has taught me in my old age—"

"Please, Louise! You're not old," Sarah laughed.

"Really? Because it certainly feels like I've aged considerably in the last two days!" Louise laughed along. "If there's anything I've learned in this life, it's that one should never make any important decisions when angry or upset."

"So you're angry?" Kate took a sip of her tea.

"We could use another place that sells tea though. Maybe you can open up a tea shop or something. Tea,"—Louise said theatrically, moving her hand up and across like a sign board—"and scones." She paused and smiled. "And yes, I am angry! There's no point in denying that. My anger is so strong right now, I'm afraid it will come out as hemorrhoids!"

Sarah was the first to laugh out loud, covering her mouth as she threw her head back.

"How can you laugh and make jokes at a time like this?" Kate asked after the laughing had settled.

"Darling, without laughter, no amount of face yoga will smooth fifty-nine years' worth of wrinkles." Louise patted her face. "And Sarah, darling, I am truly happy that you are laughing. That's wonderful. As the saying goes, laughter is the best medicine."

"I'll drink to that," Sarah said, as she raised her cup of tea. "To laughter," she said. "And good friends."

"To laughter and good friends," Louise and Kate echoed as they clinked their cups together.

Chapter 14

Sarah Gardner

Sarah genuinely enjoyed being with the girls. Her laughter was real and her soul was relieved for the chance to let go, even if only for a moment. For the first time in a long time, Sarah found she was able to inhale a full breath—and release it.

"What about you?" Louise asked her. "Have you thought about bringing the *manny* to help you out?"

"What's a manny?" Kate asked.

"A manny is a male nanny," Sarah answered Kate. Looking at Louise, she said, "I'm not sure. What do you think?"

"Well, having someone to help you at home is definitely a good thing," Louise said. "Can you think of any reason that you shouldn't take him in?"

"I've never heard of a manny before. In the Philippines, all nannies are women." Kate leaned in. "But if it's someone you know then it might be okay. Like sometimes, back home, families that are less than well off, family members stick together and pay each other in kind."

"What do you mean?" Sarah asked.

"Well, for example, if someone moves to the city for a job, right? Childcare is very expensive so they might ask extended family for help," Kate said. "And if someone in their wider family is without a job, that person might move in with that family. They will then work for them—like look after the children or the house chores—and then they get paid in the way of accommodation and food, and maybe an allowance. But because they are family, everyone looks after everyone."

"Interesting," Louise said thoughtfully.

"Yeah, so my cousins...they had this man living with their family. I think he was the cousin of my aunt; I can't remember. But he would do chores around the house like cooking, doing the laundry, and stuff."

"Well, isn't that basically what Caleb would be doing?" Louise asked Sarah.

"Do you remember Charlotte?" Sarah asked Kate, knowing that Louise already knew her. "She was the one that did the catering at Adam's funeral."

Kate nodded. "I remember."

"Well, she's Adam's cousin, and she knows this guy, Caleb, who is the brother of Charlotte's best friend." Sarah paused.

"So, Caleb is the brother of..." Kate processed the relationship and connections. "Okay, got it," she said with a laugh.

"Charlotte basically grew up around Caleb and his family. Now, Caleb is back in Willow Oaks and he's unsure of what to do with his life right now." Explaining the situation to Kate and Louise gave Sarah another chance to sort through her own thinking. While she was worried about bringing a stranger into the house to help look after the children, there was some comfort in knowing that Caleb wasn't a complete and total stranger. Charlotte trusted him, and Sarah also knew his sister.

"That sounds like an arrangement that could work out well for everyone," Louise said.

"Charlotte says that he's really good with the children—especially Liam." She told them about how angry Liam had been acting since Adam passed away.

"I can understand how confusing it must be for Liam," Kate said thoughtfully. "It took me a while to coax him out of the little hideaway he had in your garden."

"Tsk,"—Louise clicked her tongue—"the poor darling. Well, you know that whatever happens, we're here for you." Louise placed her hand over Sarah's. "Whatever you decide to do."

Louise's hand over hers felt like an unspoken promise. A promise that she was not alone. "I know," Sarah nodded and smiled.

"Let's give him a chance," Louise encouraged.

"Yes," Kate said. "And we'll be your backup."

THAT NIGHT, AND AFTER a lot of thought, Sarah called Charlotte and spoke to Caleb. She asked if he was still interested in moving to Carlton Bay for a while.

"Absolutely," Caleb said.

Sarah twisted the edge of her t-shirt around her finger. "And you know that I can't pay you—at least not until I figure the finances out." It felt wrong to have someone helping her out around the house and not being able to give them anything in return for it.

"I'm not worried about that. It's a chance for me to explore other places as well. Trust me—you're helping me just as much as I'm helping you."

"Mid-life crisis, huh?" Sarah tried to joke.

Caleb laughed. "Not a mid-life crisis!"

"Thank you, Caleb." She sighed with relief.

"So the kids and I will see you on the weekend, then?"

"Yes, Charlotte and Ben are bringing the children back. I'll have your room ready by then." Sarah was looking forward to seeing her babies again. One week had felt like one year. But she had to stop beating herself up about it. Had it not been for Charlotte and Ben—and Louise, of course—she might not have reached out to Dr. Butler. Who knows what else may have happened, had she not gotten some help? The antidepressant and antihistamines seemed to be doing the job. Although she hadn't had any profound moments that made her think she was on the way to being okay...she also hadn't had any experiences that made her feel like she couldn't move forward.

"Sounds great," Caleb said.

And that was that. It was done. She officially had a manny coming over to stay.

Sarah decided to turn in for an early night. She breathed in and sighed. It had been a good day. She'd managed to clean and keep the house tidy. She'd been out to see the girls. Given how she was feeling, Sarah considered it was a successful day. Tomorrow, she hoped to be able to cook some meals to freeze for when the children returned home. But—that was for tomorrow. Tonight, she would try to sleep in her bedroom again. *One step at a time. One day at a time*, she reminded herself. That was her new mantra. One step at a time, one day at a time.

IT WAS DARK WHEN SARAH woke up; save for the faint glow from the moon. Feeling a chill in the air, she tried to pull the blanket up to her chin, but it wouldn't budge. A heavy weight wrapped itself around her waist and kept her from turning freely.

It wasn't the first time that Sarah had woken in the middle of the night, unable to breathe.

Breathe, Sarah, she told herself.

Inhale. Sarah closed her eyes and took a deep breath. But that time, unlike all the other previous nights, Sarah breathed in a familiar scent. It was Adam's cologne.

Sarah turned on her side and felt the weight of his arms around her. "Adam?" Sarah opened her eyes.

And there he was. It was Adam. In bed, next to her.

A sense of relief washed over her. It had all been a bad dream. The last three months were all just a bad dream.

Her husband was lying next to her, his eyes closed. The rise and fall of his chest were soft and even.

Sarah put her hand on his cheek and Adam's eyes flickered open.

"Hi, beautiful," he whispered.

Sarah's lips quivered. She blinked back her tears. "I had a bad dream."

"Come here." Adam pulled her close to him and put an arm underneath her neck.

Sarah buried her face in the nook of his neck. "I had a dream that you'd died." Sarah's voice broke and tears filled her eyes. "I thought you'd left me."

Adam combed the hair off her face. "I'm always with you."

Sarah closed her eyes as she felt Adam's kiss on her forehead. "I was so scared." Her tears flowed freely. No longer did she have to hold her fear in. No longer did she need to pretend to be strong. It was all just a bad dream.

"I'm always with you," he said again, stroking her arm until she fell back asleep.

The next morning, Sarah woke to the sun pushing its piercing rays through the bedroom curtains as if eager to tell her a secret. She closed her eyes to avoid the glare and turned to face the other side of the bed.

She reached for Adam.

But he was gone.

Once again, her chest tightened, and she struggled to breathe. Her breath felt stuck, unable to flow.

"Adam!" Her eyes stung and tears pushed against her eyelids.

Sarah opened her mouth. "*No,*" she tried to scream. "*No!*" But all that came out were the sounds of her trapped breath; gasping, choking.

No, she thought again. *No!* And then, without warning, a loud, harrowing wail escaped from her throat like a newborn crying its first few breaths into life. Sarah was suffocating.

Chapter 15

Abby Delaney

Apart from the afternoon she'd spent talking to Kate, Abby had spent the last few days on her own. But she was used to it. Abby's mom was never home, and if she was, there was always a boyfriend with her.

School was not too different either. Abby didn't have many friends and spent most of her time in the library. The school librarian always asked her why she wasn't at the school cafeteria like the rest of the kids at lunch. Abby's response was always the same—a shrug here, a nod, or 'I don't know'.

"Do you have a boyfriend?" Mrs. Wisler had asked her one day.

Abby scowled before saying that she didn't have time for boyfriends. Poor Mrs. Wisler must have wondered what she'd ever done wrong to have Abby Delaney in her library every single day.

Despite appearances though, Abby recalled Mrs. Wisler with fondness. She was probably the only adult that Abby didn't mind. She often imagined the doting old librarian as her grandmother.

Mrs. Wisler was a small woman. Aside from her size however, nothing else about her was small. To Abby, she had a big heart. Her short, white hair was always tidy. Sometimes, she parted it to one side and braided it. And she always wore big statement jewelry—but not so in-your-face. The necklaces Mrs. Wisler wore around her neck were either handmade or vintage pieces. The last time Abby had seen her, Mrs. Wisler was wearing a long necklace with turquoise beads of varying sizes. She'd told Abby that she had made it while at a craft group with some lady friends. Abby had secretly wished that Mrs. Wisler would invite her along to do crafts one day.

Thinking about Mrs. Wisler hit Abby with a pang of sadness. She wondered if leaving home was the right thing to do.

"What did you think would happen?" Abby mumbled under her breath as she looked inside the fridge for something to cook. She thought that maybe, if she pulled her weight around the house, Louise would finally talk to her. Apart from the first day when Abby turned up in Mulberry Lane, no other words were exchanged. Louise either left her notes under her door or on the fridge. *Did you really think you were going to play happy family?*

Abby rummaged through the fridge. Although she'd spent a lot of time cooking or preparing food for herself, she'd never really cooked anything substantial or remotely fancy. After some consideration and looking for recipes on *Pinterest,* Abby decided to make some grilled cheese sandwiches and a creamy tomato soup.

She'd never had tomato soup before—unless you counted those canned Campbell's soups her mother used to empty into a bowl and pop in the microwave. She grabbed a notepad and jotted down a list of the ingredients she needed:

- *1 can roasted tomatoes*
- *1 cup of chicken broth*
- *3 cloves of garlic, minced*
- *1/2 onion (chopped)*
- *1 teaspoon salt*
- *1/2 teaspoon black pepper*
- *1/2 cup heavy cream*
- *1 cup of Parmesan cheese*
- *2 tbsp olive oil*
- *Fresh basil for garnish*

She'd never made soup before, not counting two-minute microwave noodles, of course. Everyone's had those. She read and reread the recipe and decided it was simple enough to follow. Louise had most of the ingredients in the fridge and pantry, except for the fresh basil.

What was meant to be a thirty-minute cook had turned in to an hour and fifteen minutes for Abby. Amazingly, she'd managed to cut herself and it stung like a mother bee. Who knew chopping onions could make you cry like that? She'd made the stupid mistake of rubbing her stinging eyes with her unwashed hand. She was never going to make that mistake again. In spite of all the pain and tears, she was happy with how the soup had turned out. She sliced the grilled cheese sandwiches in triangles like she'd seen fancy people do on TV and set the table, ready for when Louise arrived, which was normally around 6:00pm.

Abby quickly got to her feet when she heard Louise's car drive up. She opened the front door, eager to greet her. "Hi, Louise," she said with a smile. "How was your day?"

Louise looked a little tired. Her shaggy dark brown hair fell loosely around her face, and her eyes featured dark rings that weren't there before. "Good, thank you, Abby."

Abby stood aside to let Louise through. "Can I help you take anything in? Your coat?"

"No, thank you, darling."

Though Louise called her 'darling', Abby felt far from being one. It was the same story as everywhere she'd ever been. Abby was always the *unwanted one*. "I made us some dinner," she beamed. "Grilled cheese and tomato soup."

Louise stopped to hang her coat and purse on the coat rack, and looked at Abby. "Did you?" Her mouth hung slightly open, but shut back into a line all too quickly. "I'm not hungry. Why don't you go ahead and enjoy your dinner? I might have something later on."

"I can wait for you," Abby said, almost pleadingly.

"No," Louise said quickly. "I'll—I'm not hungry." And with that, Louise went straight up to her bedroom.

Abby watched as she disappeared up the stairs. When she heard the door shut, Abby went to the kitchen and looked at the food she had prepared. She blinked back the tears that threatened to fall. She didn't like crying.

"I'm such an idiot," Abby said to herself as she pulled out a chair and sat down. All the effort she had put into making dinner was for nothing. She bit her fingernails and stared at the red-orange soup that mocked her.

Abby picked up the bowls of soup she'd plated and tipped it into the sink, and did the same with the rest of the soup in the pot. Grabbing one of the triangles of grilled cheese, she put on a jacket and walked out the front door. The winter wind brushed her cheeks.

As she stepped out of the house, Abby saw Kate pull into her driveway across the street.

Kate got out of her car and called out to Abby. "How are you?" she asked with a wave

"Fine, thanks," Abby said, wiping any crumbs off her mouth.

"Where are you off to? It's getting pretty cold out here."

Abby shrugged. What did it matter where she was going? Nobody cared. It wasn't as if Abby could tell her stepmother's friend that she was '*not fine*'.

"Get on over here," Kate urged. "Is something wrong?"

Another shrug was all Abby gave.

"Okay—well you don't have to tell me." Kate put her arm around Abby's shoulders. "But you're not going out tonight in that flimsy jacket. You're coming inside with me."

Much to her own surprise, Abby didn't fight Kate on her suggestion. Instead, she allowed Kate to lead her inside 604 Mulberry Lane.

The house was spotless, but everything was big, dark, and chunky. It didn't *feel* like Kate. Big tree trunks fashioned into side tables stood next to a dark leather sofa. On the floor was some kind of animal skin rug. The house seemed nothing like Kate. She saw some glimpses of Kate, though—small feminine touches dotted the living room. A vase of some red flowers, a pink throw over the couch—but that was it. Even the Christmas tree looked sad. Abby followed her through to the kitchen.

Kate pressed some buttons on the oven and then opened a bag of bread. "I had to do a last-minute shop. I forgot to get some bread this afternoon and Evan likes his spaghetti with garlic bread."

Abby chewed on the last of her sandwich.

"That wasn't dinner that you'd just polished off, was it? You need more than that. Why don't you stay for dinner? There's plenty of food."

Abby shook her head. "I don't wanna be a bother. I was just going to go out for a walk. Don't mind me."

"Nonsense." Kate popped the garlic bread into the oven. "Does Louise know you've gone out?"

"She doesn't need to know." Abby avoided Kate's eyes.

"Come and sit down." Kate pulled out a chair for the girl. "What would you like to drink?"

"I'm fine, thanks." That seemed to be her go-to response now.

"Let's get you some iced tea." Kate got three glasses from the cupboard and set them on the table. "Actually, could you help me set the table?" she asked Abby. "The plates are in the top cupboard and the cutlery is in the drawer."

She hesitated at first, but went ahead and did what she was told. It's not as if she had anything better to do.

"There's a jug of iced tea in the fridge. Would you mind bringing it out and topping the glasses off?"

Abby nodded and poured the iced tea.

"How's everything going over at Louise's place?" Kate asked casually.

Horrible, Abby thought. "I made dinner tonight."

"Did you? Abby, that's lovely."

"Louise didn't want any of it, so I threw it down the sink."

Kate stopped and turned around. "You what?"

There was no mistaking Kate's surprise. She must have thought Abby was an ungrateful and impolite teenager. That's what everyone thought of her anyway. Abby pulled her hood over her head and sat back down. "She didn't want any, so I threw it out."

"Oh, Abby." Kate pulled Abby's hood off and sat down facing her. "Look, I know it's not my business, but I do know what you're going through is hard. I can't imagine what you must be feeling right now." She sighed. "From what I've come to know about Louise—she's a lovely person with not a single bone of nasty in her. I'm sure she has a good reason for not having any of the lovely dinner you'd prepared."

Abby rolled her eyes. "It's because I'm Dad's bastard."

Kate's eyes widened, probably horrified at the rude word Abby had used. "Don't say that!"

"It's true." Abby looked away, blinking back tears. She didn't want to cry. Only losers cried. "She doesn't want me. I mean, of course she wouldn't. I don't know what I was thinking coming here. But Dad said that if I ever had any problems, I should go and see Louise. He said she would understand."

"Understand what?" Kate's brows furrowed with concern.

"Louise didn't know about me. Dad never told her about me—about us, me and Mom."

Kate listened.

"There wasn't anything to tell anyway. It's not like we were important to him or anything like that. I think he only came to visit me because he felt responsible for me." That was the first time that Abby had ever spoken to anyone about her family before. No one had ever really asked. "I was a mistake. Like, I mean...Mom and Dad, they weren't really anything. They weren't, like, a couple or anything special. I think Dad met Mom one night, and then that was it. It was supposed to be a one-night stand. But when Mom found out she was pregnant, she told Dad. I guess she wanted him to pay for child support" It was difficult to keep her tears from falling, but she tried.

"Oh, Abby..."

"But he was a good dad. He tried. Like, he'd come to see me once or twice a year. Mostly on my birthdays and sometimes, if he could manage it, Christmas." Abby told Kate everything she'd been keeping inside her. She couldn't help it. The words just kept coming out. "You know, that time—when he died—he was on his way to see me. It was my birthday." Abby scoffed. "When he didn't show up, I thought he'd forgotten 'cuz that's happened before, you know. I tried to call him but I couldn't get through to his cellphone. And I couldn't call him at his house, because he said never to call him there. Anyway, it was a few days before we found out that he'd died in a car accident. If it wasn't for me, he'd still be alive." Abby shrugged.

"Honey, that was not your fault." Kate had tears in her eyes.

"You know what? On my thirteenth birthday, he gave me some letters."

"What did they say?" Kate asked.

"I don't know—they were sealed and there were instructions for when to open them. On the front of one of the envelopes, it said I should open it if I needed help. So I did. It said that if I had no place to go or was scared or needed help or something, that I should go see Louise and give her the sealed envelope that had her name on it. Another envelope said to open it when I turn twenty-one."

"What about the others? How many were there?"

"There were thirteen letters. I guess because it was my thirteenth birthday. I don't know."

"And you haven't opened any of them?"

"I have—like the ones that said to open if I was bored. Another one was for when I was sad." Abby smiled as she remembered them. "There was this one that said to open it if I needed a laugh."

Kate smiled. "Yeah?"

"Yeah, and it was a dumb knock-knock joke."

"He sounds like he was a funny guy."

"He had a lot of dad-jokes. They were like the most non-funny jokes in the world."

"That's really sweet that you were able to enjoy those moments with him. What about the other letters?"

Abby shook her head. "I only opened the ones that I could. He's never asked anything else of me. So it was the least I could do."

"Do you ever get curious?" Kate asked.

"When I think about it—yes, I do." She'd been curious many times—mostly when she was home alone or bored. But she'd always managed to stop herself.

"Have you given Louise's one to her?"

"I meant to give it to her the first night I arrived, but when she took me to my room, she closed the door and left. And since then, we haven't really talked." Abby wrung her fingers together. "I wanted to give it to her tonight."

The oven bell went off, indicating that the garlic bread was done. Kate stood up and took it out using a pair of oven mitts. "Maybe you can just leave it under her door? Or on the kitchen table?"

"I guess. I was kinda hoping we could read it together or... well, I don't know what I was thinking."

The front door opened, and a man's voice filled the house. "Kate?"

"In the kitchen," Kate called out. "That's Evan," she whispered.

A tall man dressed in a plaid shirt, and tan pants walked in to the kitchen. He took his dark navy-blue baseball cap off and gave a single nod to Abby. "Who's this?" he asked, rubbing the black and white beard that ran along the side of his face and around his mouth.

"Evan," Kate stood to greet him, "this is Abby Delaney. She's Louise Delaney's stepdaughter. Abby will be joining us for dinner."

Another nod was sent to Abby. "Your mom not home?"

"She is," Abby said.

Evan grunted and grabbed a beer from the fridge. "What's for dinner?"

Chapter 16

Louise Delaney

Back in her bedroom, Louise collapsed in bed. She knew she was being hard on Abby, but she couldn't help it. Every time she saw the girl, it was Warren's face she saw. It didn't help that Abby also looked like Madison. They could have easily been sisters. Louise groaned. *They are sisters.*

She covered her face with a pillow to muffle her screams. *How can I possibly take care of a walking, living, breathing reminder of Warren's infidelity?* It was all too much and her thoughts were of no help.

Louise had seen the pained look on Abby's face when she declined dinner. She must have spent a lot of time preparing and cooking it. Abby looked so excited to see her and yet, Louise couldn't bring herself to even feign interest or some kind of appreciation.

She swept the fringe off her forehead and stared at the ceiling. "Why me, God?" she mumbled. "What have I ever done to deserve this?" *I thought we were happy.* Louise wiped the tears as they cascaded down her face. "Please—give me a sign. What am I supposed to do? I'm not strong enough for this. Tell me what I should do!"

Since Abby turned up at her doorstep, her conversations with God had become few and far between. Doubt had crept through her like a noxious weed, and no amount of *Our Fathers, Hail Marys*, and *Glory Bes* could fix what she was feeling now.

Louise reached for her phone and hit the Facebook icon. She searched for Madison's profile and clicked on it. It had been a while since she'd checked her daughter's profile; what with everything going on.

The first thing she saw was a photo of Madison and her husband, Scott. They looked happy, and she was glad for her daughter. It was all that a parent can ever wish for their child—happiness.

She studied their photo. "Is that"—Louise sat up—"is that a baby bump?" Louise pinched her fingers over the image and zoomed in. Scott was standing behind her, arms around her stomach. The caption read: *Soon to be three. He's no longer Scott-free.* It was followed by a number of emojis. Louise read through the comments—*congratulations, well wishes, hooray, you're going to be great parents, Scott-free - LOL*. It went on and on.

Louise looked up from her phone. "Madison's pregnant?" Her baby was having a baby.

It had been years since Louise had seen her daughter. Years.

It seemed that no amount of love and apologies that could fix the ever-growing crater that stood between them. Whatever love Madison had left for her was borne out of obligation.

The truth was—or so Madison has always liked to say—Louise had never really *seen* her.

When Louise first found out that Madison was dating a New Zealander, the first thought she had was that they made a good couple. Facebook always made happy couples look happy. Nobody ever posted updates on the bad stuff. The arguments, the hidden resentments, the ugly.

It was Warren that had told her about it. He was always much closer to Madison than Louise was. Madison had let him in—but not her.

From what she could see, Scott was sweet and doting—any mother would have loved to have someone like him with their daughter. She hadn't thought about Scott taking her daughter away to another country on the opposite side of the world. Although, if she was being honest, it wouldn't surprise her if Madison had chosen to move to New Zealand—if only to finally get away from Louise.

When Warren died, Madison did what any daughter would do for their mother. She stayed by Louise's side. She'd even moved back home for a few weeks, though not more than a month.

The atmosphere was strained, but Louise couldn't be bothered pointing it out. Her husband had died and her daughter was finally at her side—a perverted wheel of fortune.

The day that Louise had finally emerged from her bedroom and was able to make a cup of tea for herself, Madison began packing her bags. It was never going to last.

But still...she was grateful that Madison was happy. That was all that a mother could really hope for—that the child she had carried, raised, and loved more than life itself, would be happy. There was nothing quite like the pain of seeing your child hurting. She was glad that Madison was no longer hurting.

Louise clicked her phone to lock when she heard the doorbell. She listened and waited to see if Abby would get the door. When it rang a second time, she wiped her face and went downstairs.

"Abby?" Louise called out as she walked to the front door. Met with silence, she opened the door.

"Hi, Louise," the man said.

Louise froze. He looked exactly the same as he did when she last saw him. A couple of grays, no more than the average older man. She was sure it was him.

His smile caught her—as it did all those years ago.

With a hand on her chest, Louise released the breath she'd unconsciously held in. "As I live and breathe...what are...?" The words escaped her.

"How are you?"

Louise placed her hand over her forehead, another on her hip. "The last time we saw each other was—"

"When I officiated your wedding," he said with a nod. He always knew what she was thinking; finishing her sentences for her.

"Philip..." His name came out as a sigh. Louise held her arms open. She'd asked God for a sign. This had to be it. Standing before her was the first man God had ever taken from her. "It's really you," she said as she let herself be taken in by the warmth of his embrace. "What are you doing here? Are you home? For good? Why didn't you tell me you were coming?" The questions spilled out, one after the other.

"Can I come in?" Philip asked with a grin.

Louise took his arm and pulled him inside—and into an embrace. When she felt him hug her back, she melted into his arms and burst into tears.

"Hey,"—Philip cupped her face in his hands and wiped her tears with his thumbs—"what's this? Why the tears? I thought you'd be happy to see me," he joked.

"I'm sorry." Embarrassed, Louise wiped her tears and stepped aside. "Please, come in."

Philip followed her inside.

She led him to the kitchen and turned the kettle on to make some tea. "Do you still like the same tea? Earl—"

"Grey," he said, once again completing her sentence.

Louise smiled. It was like he'd never even left.

"And you still like peppermint?" he asked with a twinkle in his eyes.

Louise nodded. "And everything else."

Philip sighed. "You haven't changed one bit, Lou."

Lou. No one else had ever been able to call her Lou. That was Philip's nickname for her. When Warren tried to use it, she swiftly asked him not to. No one else could call her Lou. It felt good to hear Philip say it. "I've aged plenty, but thank you," she said, this time, laughing.

"Well, you're as beautiful as I remember."

Louise felt her cheeks get hot. It had been a long time since a man had complimented her. “When did you get back?”

“An hour ago,” he said.

He had been Louise’s first love. Philip was the one that got away, so to speak. After meeting for the first time at a church youth group, they became as close as two coats of paint. Both active in the church, they did everything together.

Louise had always hoped that Philip would one day tell her that he loved her—maybe as much as she loved him. But when the Lord called and Philip answered, Louise knew she had lost him.

They’d remained close even after Philip went to complete his residential degree program at a seminary in Portland. But the three years apart had weakened Louise’s hope that anything would ever happen between them. Instead...Warren happened. And when Philip returned to Carlton Bay, it was he—the man she had lost to God—who had officiated their wedding ceremony. Six months later, Philip told her he was moving overseas to serve in the Philippines.

Louise prepared the tea and joined Philip at the table. “So you flew across the world and I’m the first person you’ve seen?”

“Well, yes—apart from the taxi driver.”

Philip was still as handsome as she recalled. It broke her heart when he’d left. “What are you doing here? Are you back home for good?”

Philip took a sip of his tea and nodded. “I’ve been trying to get a transfer for a while now. Been putting some feelers out. I told the diocese that it was time for me to come home. I had hoped to return sooner," he said seriously. "I was sorry to learn of Warren's passing."

She ignored the last comment with a wave of her hand. "Philip, that's wonderful news. And will you be working with the vicar?" she asked. "Or is he going to be moving?"

"I'll be in the background. Paul is the priest-in-charge. I'll be working in a part-time capacity. Think of it as pre-retirement."

The talk of retirement brought with it the realization that they were no longer the young ones they'd used to be. "It's incredible how much time has passed. Here we are...turning the corner on to gray hairs and walking sticks."

"We're nowhere near that corner, Lou." Philip laughed—just as he did when they were young and restless. "I might be... but you're certainly not."

Louise blushed like a schoolgirl. She couldn't believe he was back. Her Philip was finally home.

Chapter 17

Kate Morgan

The atmosphere at dinner was the same as it was every night in the Morgan home. Evan ate his food just as quickly as he'd sat down. He grabbed a second bottle of beer and took it to the living room, where he watched the news. "Can I get you anything else?" Kate asked Abby.

"No, thanks." Abby smiled. "That was really good."

Kate beamed a little too much at Abby's compliment. "Sorry about Evan. He's harmless—just a bit rough around the edges."

Abby shrugged. "At least he comes home to you."

Although there was truth in what Abby had said—about Evan coming home to her; Kate knew that there was something missing in their marriage. Something big. Gone were the days when they would cuddle by the fire and talk about their hopes and dreams for the future; the days when they would sneak kisses around every corner. Kate tried to remember the last time she'd felt Evan's arms around her. It was as if they'd become roommates. Or worse, she'd become what everyone in town thought she was—the mail-order-bride who cleaned the house, cooked dinner, and did everything that Evan so desired. A shudder ran down her spine.

"My mom goes with any man that'll have her," Abby scoffed.

"Abby, that's not a nice thing to say about your mother. I'm sure that's not the case."

Abby shifted in her seat. "It's true—she's like an ice cream factory with a new flavor every month."

"It's difficult to know what people are going through. And sometimes, it's hard to understand why they do the things they do. Maybe she's lonely," Kate offered.

"It doesn't mean you should jump into bed with every man with dingle between his legs." She rolled her eyes when she spoke.

"Abby!" Kate covered her mouth in surprise.

"What about you? If you're not happy with Evan—why do you stay?" Abby with the blatant apathy of a teenager.

Kate gasped. "Ssh!" Kate looked around to make sure that Evan hadn't heard what Abby had said. "That's not a nice thing to say, Abby," she hissed. "You're being rude."

"Doesn't make it untrue." Abby was relentless.

"You don't know anything about my life." Kate gathered the plates and began to rinse them. She felt her defenses go up like a wall.

"I don't have to." Abby took a sip of what was left of her iced tea. "It doesn't take a genius."

For such a young girl, Abby was incredibly perceptive. Rude, but perceptive. Kate thought about her life. It shamed her to know that even a sixteen-year-old could tell that her marriage was not a happy one.

"Why do you stay with him?" Abby whispered next to her. "He's gross and rude. And he doesn't appreciate you."

"You don't know that." Kate didn't look at her.

"I'm just saying—I've watched my mom bring home man after man since I was a little girl. I've seen how men treat her. I can tell that he doesn't deserve you—I know that much." Abby leaned against the counter next to Kate.

"Why are you doing this?" Kate blinked back her tears.

"You're helping me—or at least you're trying to. I can tell." Abby ran her fingers through her long, curly black hair. She glanced towards the doorway to the living room. "I want to help you too."

"I think I've made my bed. Now I've got to lie in it." Kate was embarrassed. She couldn't believe she was talking to a teenager about her life.

"Then get out of bed!" Abby said. "You know...that's why I'm never going to get married or have kids."

"Probably a wise decision," Kate conceded. She wiped her hands. Leaning on the counter next to Abby, she sighed, "I'm doomed."

Chapter 18

Sarah Gardner

The weekend came around quickly. Before she knew it, Sarah was standing in the driveway helping Charlotte and Ben get the children out of their minivan. "Thank you so much for taking the kids," she said to Charlotte, taking her into an embrace.

Charlotte hugged her back. "They were no trouble at all."

Sarah turned to Ben. "I don't know what I would have done without you guys." It was Ben's turn to get a hug.

"Any time, Sarah," he said. "You just let us know if there's anything at all that you need."

Sarah picked up Zoe and hoisted her on to her hip. "Did you kids have fun?"

Zoe wriggled and reached her little arms out. "I want go to Auntie *Shallot*!"

Charlotte laughed. "You'll come and visit very soon, okay princess?"

"What about you, big guy?" Sarah turned to Liam, who shrugged and pushed past her. He headed straight for the house. "Liam," she called after him. "Please say thank you to your aunt and—" But Liam slammed the front door shut.

"He's tired—and I'm Caleb."

"Hi." Sarah was taken aback. Caleb was not at all what she'd expected. Her eyes traced the length of his tattooed arm as he picked Noah up.

"What about you, buddy? Are you tired too?" Caleb asked.

"No!" Noah squealed with excitement as Caleb lifted him around his neck and over his shoulders.

"You're never tired!" Caleb teased.

When Sarah spoke to Caleb over the phone, she had no idea he would be so good-looking. Sarah felt her stomach flip. His hair was cut perfectly close to his head. His beard was perfectly trimmed. His face was perfectly shaped. There was too much perfection—it was ridiculous. "It's nice to meet you, Caleb. Thank you so much for all your help." Sarah tried to keep her voice formal, usually reserved for special events like funerals.

"He's been amazing with the kids," Charlotte said. "Isn't Caleb amazing?" she asked Noah, who nodded his head excitedly—unable to stop the drool that fell on Caleb's head. Charlotte laughed. "Someone's got spit on his head," she teased Caleb.

"What?" Caleb's face was of shock and horror. "Did you spit on my head, buddy?"

"Uh-oh...not the hair!" Charlotte teased.

Noah laughed some more. "No!"

Caleb put him down and pretended to chase him around the front yard. "I'm gonna get you!"

Sarah's chest tightened at the sight of Caleb running after Noah. It hurt knowing that Adam would never see his children grow up.

"I guess we should get going," Ben said. "We left the twins with my sister."

"Oh, yes, how is Amy? And her husband—is it Sam?" Sarah had met them at Charlotte's cafe in Willow Oaks. "How's their Bed & Breakfast doing?"

Ben towered over her. "They're doing really well. The B&B is a hot spot for tourists, so they've been busy."

"You'll give them my love, won't you? I should visit you guys more often." Although she said it, Sarah knew that making a trip to Willow Oaks—even if it was just twenty minutes away—wasn't something she was ready to do just yet. She needed to get her life in order first.

"Oh my gosh, yes, you should! And you're welcome to stay at ours any time!" Charlotte beamed.

"I'm so lucky to have you guys," Sarah said. And she meant it. "Are you sure you won't stay for a cup of tea?"

Both responsible parents, they shook their heads and said they needed to get back to the twins.

As Sarah watched Charlotte and Ben drive off, she kissed Zoe's head as she nuzzled into her neck. "I want auntie Shallot," she whimpered.

"I want Auntie Charlotte, too," she said. "We'll go and visit them soon." Even at two-years-old, Zoe still had the baby smell that Sarah loved.

The next few days took some getting used to. As much as Sarah looked forward to having some help around the house, having another man that wasn't Adam proved to be more difficult than she'd anticipated. The small talk was awkward in the same way that first dates were; so Sarah tried her best to keep her attention focused on the kids instead.

She observed how Caleb interacted with the children. It was as if the kids had known him all their lives—and he, them. He had an effortless way with them, particularly with Liam.

They'd spent the rest of the week preparing for Christmas. It was going to be the family's first Christmas without Adam and the thought made Sarah sick to her stomach.

On Thursday morning, they drove to a Christmas tree farm just outside of Carlton Bay. While Sarah didn't want to, Caleb had put up a good case. *"It would be good for the kids to do something fun with you. Make Christmas something they can look forward to,"* he'd said. So they went Christmas tree hunting.

The boys enjoyed running around and choosing their favorite trees.

"This one!" Liam shouted as he pointed at the tallest tree he could find, eager to gain Caleb's approval. "How about this one, Caleb?"

"No, I want this one," Noah followed suit, making sure that his preferences were heard too.

Poor Zoe tried her best to keep up with her brothers, but her little legs just weren't fast enough. Sarah watched how, sensing Zoe's frustration, Caleb swooped in making helicopter sounds and lifted her on to his shoulders. Zoe, of course, squealed with delight. "Let's look around and we can all vote for our favorite one," Caleb said.

The sight of them brought a smile to Sarah's face. But still, she was torn. A part of her was anguished by Adam's absence. It was the part that was painfully aware that he would never again get to share any special moments with the children. The other part of her though was grateful for Caleb and, dared she say it, the presence of a male figure. The thought washed guilt over her and made her shudder.

THE NEXT DAY SARAH went to Dockside Cafe to meet Louise and Kate. They'd all agreed to meet once a week over tea—they'd called it their *Tea for Three* dates. It was something that Sarah had begun to look forward to.

As she walked along Lighthouse Road, Sarah couldn't help but smile. The storefronts were all adorned with festive decorations and the air was filled with the hope and cheer that only Christmas could bring.

From a short distance, Sarah saw three young girls. They were no more than ten, maybe eleven or twelve-years-old. As she neared them, Sarah could see one girl holding a pair of maracas. Another shook a tambourine. And the one in the middle—the one in a yellow coat two sizes too big—proudly held up a triangle and swayed her little hips as they sang Rudolph the Red-Nosed Reindeer.

Sarah stopped to watch them for a moment. And when they'd finished their song, Sarah showed her appreciation by clapping excitedly for the trio. She pulled out a dollar from her purse and placed it inside the Santa Claus tin can that she could see had several coins and a few bills already in it.

"Thank you!"

"Merry Christmas!" Sarah said, with a bit of spirit peeping from within her soul.

When Sarah arrived at the cafe, Kate and Louise were already there. "Were you guys waiting long?"

"I just arrived myself," Kate said. "I did a bit of shopping before coming."

"I came early and to have some lunch," Louise said. "I didn't get the chance to sit down earlier. The bookstore has been incredibly busy—not that I'm complaining, mind you."

Sarah took her coat off and hung it on the back of her seat. "I saw the cutest girls singing Christmas carols at the dockside," she said. "I couldn't help it—I had to stop and watch them."

"I saw them too," Kate said. "They were so cute!"

As Sarah sat down, unwrapping her scarf from around her neck the waitress turned up. "Hello, ladies," she said brightly. "How are we today?"

"Good, thanks, Jacqui," Sarah replied. "How are you?"

"I am so good," she said giddily. "I love Christmas—don't you? I wish it could be Christmas every day."

"It's definitely my favorite time of year," Louise said.

"Kate?" Jacqui walked around to where Kate sat.

"Hi!" Kate smiled. "What's up?"

"I was hoping I'd see you when you came in last week, but I wasn't working last Friday." Jacqui bent down beside her. "I'm really sorry about what I said when we first met."

Kate appeared shocked but quickly waved a hand in front of her. "Oh, no...don't be."

"No, I am and I should be," Jacqui said. "I thought about it and there were better ways for me to ask where you come—I mean—" Jacqui's cheeks turned a soft shade of rose.

Kate smiled. "Really, it's fine."

"You must get so sick of having people ask you all the time."

Kate laughed. "You weren't the first. Let's put it that way."

"I'd like to"—Jacqui stammered—"what I mean is, I'd like to—"

"Darling, she's fine," Louise placed a hand over Jacqui's. "You're fine. We're all fine. It's a lesson we all learned from."

"I've heard people talk about you," Jacqui said.

"Oh?" Louise titled her head.

"About Kate, I mean. They say you're a...but I know that you're not and I—uh...," Jacqui stammered again.

"Jacqui," Kate said. "I'm fine. I really am. I know that people think I'm a mail-order bride. Or a website bride. That's what you're trying to say, right? I've heard it a few times myself."

"I'm sorry, I shouldn't have said anything." Jacqui brought a hand to her forehead. "I feel so stupid."

"We all know she's not," Sarah said. "And that's what's important. What anybody else thinks is their business."

But Jacqui persisted. The poor girl. "Yes, of course, and—"

"How about you take our orders, darling?" Louise suggested. She was so good at moving things along.

"Yes, please!" Jacqui sighed with relief. "Can I?" she asked, taking a pen and notepad out.

"What shall we have ladies?" Louise asked.

"You know," Jacqui said, "since you guys have been coming more regularly, the manager started keeping more tea in stock for you."

"Has she?" Sarah smiled. "That's kind of her."

"Yup—she ordered a variety box. It was my idea. I told her that you ladies enjoy your tea," Jacqui said proudly.

"That's really lovely," Sarah said. "Do you know what kind of teas are in the box?"

"Oh, yes! That was why I came by in the first place—sorry, I forgot." Jacqui pulled out a folded piece of paper from the pocket of her apron.

"Jacqui," Sarah said, trying to be like Louise, "relax."

She laughed and shook her head. "Okay,"—she read from the piece of paper—"there's peppermint, Earl Grey, pomegranate and raspberry, and blood orange and cinnamon spice."

"Ooh, I don't think I've ever tried blood orange tea before." Sarah glanced at Kate and Louise. "Should we try that?"

They both nodded. "And bring us a slice of the pie of the day, will you, dear?" Louise asked.

"Pie of the day...and a blood orange and cinnamon spice tea for three. I wonder what blood orange is?" Jacqui mumbled as she scribbled on her notepad.

"It's just a different variety of orange—a bit sweet, and a little tangy," Louise answered. With that, the young waitress turned on her heels and walked away, her ponytail bouncing at the back of her head.

Kate leaned in. "I feel bad that she feels bad," she said with a sigh. "She seems like such a nice girl."

"She's actually a lovely girl," Sarah said about Jacqui. "And don't feel bad. You did nothing wrong." In an ironic kind of way, Sarah felt good being the *comforter,* not the *comforted.* "There aren't many people from outside of town in Carlton Bay, much less from overseas. So it can be a bit of a learning experience for some."

"Enough about that," Louise said, changing the subject. "What are you all doing for Christmas?"

The last few Christmases were fairly quiet for Sarah and Adam. They'd been focused on building traditions for the children. Sarah had grown up with very little stability, much less traditions. Her father had worked for the United Nations and they'd moved around a lot. She and Adam agreed that they wanted the children to grow up in one place—a place they could return to when they were adults; a place to call home after they'd found their places in the world. It scared Sarah to think of how different things would be this Christmas. "I don't know," she sighed. "We don't have any family here, and Adam and I have kept things simple over the last few years."

"Is Caleb staying for the holidays?" Kate asked.

Sarah hadn't actually thought about Caleb, and whether he was going home over the Christmas period or not. "I'm not sure, actually. Maybe. I'll ask him tonight."

Kate nodded. "If he has to go home and you need some help with the kids, just let me know. I'll be happy to give you a hand."

Sarah smiled. Kate was so sweet. "Thanks, Kate—you've already done so much for me. I can't possibly take you away from Evan at Christmastime."

"Ladies,"—Jacqui came with their order—"I've got your tea for three and the pie of day, pecan."

Louise thanked her and proceeded to cut the pie in three.

"I don't think Evan will mind."

"You mentioned you did some shopping," Louise said. "Show us what you bought."

"Oh, yes! What did you buy?" Sarah used to always love Christmas shopping. Buying things for the children always made her happy.

Kate shook her head. "Oh, it's nothing. Just some stuff I came across."

"Did you bring your own bags to put the shopping in?" Louise glanced at Kate's shopping. "That's very good of you—very environmentally friendly. I've always admired people who brought their own canvas shopping bags to the grocery store. It was something I had wanted to get used to doing myself. Maybe I should make it a goal this year." Louise poured the tea into three cups.

Kate took the cup of tea Louise handed to her. "Evan kicked me out," she said, her voice a soft whisper.

"Come again?" Sarah could not hide her surprise.

"He what?" Louise hissed.

“He told me to leave the house.” Kate rubbed her face, clearly frustrated.

“I don’t understand. What happened?” That was the last thing Kate needed. The poor girl was alone in the new country, a new town. How could Evan ever do such a thing?

Chapter 19

Kate Morgan

Despite still being in shock herself, Kate told them about what had happened the night before, after Abby left.

SHE'D MADE A CUP OF tea and went to the living room to sit with Evan. He was in his TV chair, reclined like the classic *Lazy Boy*.

"She gone?" Evan looked up from the TV.

Kate nodded. "I told her to go back home. It's too cold for her to be out at this time. And it's not safe—she's only sixteen."

"So, I guess old man Warren couldn't keep his belt buckled, huh?" Evan snickered.

"Evan! That's not nice."

"You got some other bright idea of how Louise ended up with a sixteen-year-old girl in her house?" Evan was crude in his manner. "I can guarantee she wouldn't be housing no kid now if everyone's pants had stayed on."

"Look, it's hard enough for everyone." Kate shook her head. She couldn't believe how unsympathetic Evan was.

"Only one person was hard, I tell ya—and that was old man Warren." Evan laughed at his own joke. "Everyone makes their own bed, Kate."

Kate swallowed and took a deep breath. Just like she'd made her own bed, she thought. And now she needed to lay in it. She hoped that one day, her bed could once again be warm and inviting. "Evan, I'm pregnant."

Evan stared at the TV with his hand on the remote. He said nothing.

"Did you hear me?" Kate shifted in her seat. "Evan, I said—"

"I heard what you said." Evan's voice was low and without emotion.

Kate waited for him, secretly willing him to speak.

"I told you I didn't want babies, Kate." His eyes remained fixed on the TV.

She held her cup tighter. She could tell something was coming. "I know that. It's not like I—"

Evan pushed himself up from the chair and threw the TV remote across the room. "Haven't you been taking your birth control pills? Is this some kind of joke?" he growled.

Kate flinched at the rise in his voice. "I've been consistent with my pills," she said.

"Then how in God's name did you get pregnant?" He kicked the heavy recliner which fell on its side.

"I don't know—I—Evan, please don't take the Lord's name in vain!"

"Don't you dare tell me what I can and cannot say!" Evan came up to her and towered over her. "Did you think I would just change my mind?"

Kate felt his bubbles of his spit on her face.

"You're getting rid of that—that thing!"

Kate's eyes widened—in fear, in horror, in shock. "Evan, no! What are you saying?" Abortion was a sin. There was no way she could terminate her pregnancy. "We can't do that!"

"I told you, Kate, no babies! I didn't marry you just for you to become some stay-at-home boar!"

"A boar?" Kate couldn't believe what she was hearing. "Is that what this is about? You're afraid that I'd get fat? Like a pig?"

"You're getting rid of that thing—whether you want to or not."

"Evan,"—Kate drew in a deep breath—"No. I won't do it."

Evan glared at her. His eyes were dark. "Don't test me, Kate."

Kate could feel the rage emanating from his pores. "I'm not testing you. This isn't some game. You can't just get rid of a baby!" Kate could feel herself shaking, but she stood her ground.

"Then get out of my house and go back to where you came from," Evan hissed. He grabbed his jacket and turned to face her.

"Where are you going?"

"I'm staying at the farmhouse tonight." He held the door open. "You better not be here when I get back tomorrow. So help me—you don't want to see how serious I am."

"Evan, please. Let's talk about this."

"There's nothing to talk about." With that, he walked out the front door and slammed it shut.

SARAH HELD A HAND OVER her mouth the whole time that Kate spoke. "Oh, Kate, I'm so sorry—I can't believe he—"

"What a nasty piece of work!" Louise was unimpressed. "Is that what's in all your bags? Your personal stuff?"

Kate nodded, embarrassed about how her life had turned out. "It's my fault, really. I knew he didn't want to have children and—"

"Kate,"—Louise stopped her—"do *not* even go there."

"I agree with Louise," Sarah said, her brows furrowed. "You cannot blame yourself for how Evan reacts."

"But I knew he didn't want children," Kate said. "I should have been more careful."

"Are you kidding me?" Louise shook her head. "Uh-uh, no. You do not put this on yourself. It takes two to tango, young lady."

"It doesn't matter. He asked me to choose—him or the baby." Kate couldn't hold her tears back any longer. She'd tried to be strong, but nothing could have ever prepared her for this. "There's no way I could ever abort this baby."

"And no one should ever ask you to—especially not Evan." Sarah placed a hand on Kate's shoulder and handed her a napkin. "Where are you staying tonight? Do you have anywhere to go?"

Kate shook her head.

"Then you should stay with me," Sarah said.

"No," Louise said. "You've got your hands full, Sarah. Kate, you're staying with me."

Kate looked up at her friends. "I can't ask you to do that. You've already got Abby to worry about."

Louise shook her head. "It's settled," Louise continued. "You're staying with me."

"But, what about Abby?"

"Maybe you can help me figure out what to do," Louise said, dabbing a napkin over her lips. "To be perfectly honest, I have no idea what I'm doing when it comes to that child."

"Is everything okay?" Sarah asked.

"No," Louise said.

Chapter 20

Louise Delaney

To Louise, life had become—for lack of a better term—a bit messed up. She'd gone from thinking she'd enjoyed a blessed thirty-seven years of marriage, to meeting her dead husband's sixteen-year-old daughter, and learning he had been unfaithful for sixteen years, at the very least. To further complicate matters, Philip Burns was back in Carlton Bay. Philip was the first real love of her life; the one she had lost to God.

As wonderful as it was to see Philip again, it was as if an old chest wound had been ripped open—its stitches snapping to a coordinated dance of tragedy. Her heart had once again been gouged.

Despite the years that had passed between them, Philip still made her heart beat erratically—a bit faster, then a little slower. Softly at first, and then somewhat stronger.

When she'd told Philip about Abby and being confronted by Warren's infidelity, all bets were off. Her pain was raw. And every day that she saw Abby was another sprinkling of rock salt over it.

"Where is she now?" Philip asked.

And just like that, the front door opened and in walked Abby. Although she wore a hood over her head, tight curls peeped out from underneath. "That's her," Louise said softly. "Abby? Can you please come into the kitchen? I'd like you to meet an old friend of mine and your father's."

Abby walked into the kitchen. "Hi."

"Abby, this is my old friend, Philip. He also knew your dad."

"Pleased to meet you, Abby. Your dad was my best friend." Ever the gentleman, Philip stood and shook the teenager's hand. "Won't you join us?"

Abby glanced at Louise as if asking for permission.

"You can join us if you want to." A myriad of emotions overcame Louise. "Shall we have some of that soup you made?" Louise asked.

Abby bit her bottom lip. "I—uh—I threw it out."

"You what? Why?"

"I'm sorry." Abby's face turned a bright shade of pink. "I thought you didn't want it. I mean, when you didn't want any, I got upset and I, I...what I mean is—"

"It's alright, Abby." Louise felt terrible knowing that she was pushing the girl away. But what could she do? How could she possibly be expected to look after the product of Warren's infidelity? Not only was it unfathomable; it was cruel and unfair to ask it of her. "Do you want me to make you something for dinner?"

Abby shook her head. "I saw your friend Kate from across the street. She invited me in for dinner."

"Oh, did she?" Although it surprised Louise, she was glad that someone was looking out for the girl. "That was nice of her."

Abby nodded. "Maybe I should leave you guys." She looked at Philip. "It was nice to meet a friend of my dad. Oh, and Louise,"—Abby wrestled with her backpack and unzipped it. She took out a crumbled white envelope that had seen better days and handed it to Louise—"I was supposed to give this to you."

"Oh? Is it from Kate?" Louise took the envelope and proceeded to open it up until she saw the handwriting on the front.

"It's from Dad," Abby said nervously before she turned around and left the kitchen.

Louise stared at the envelope in her hand and glanced at Philip. "I don't understand," Her voice quivered.

"Are you going to open it?" Philip asked.

"I can't." Louise could not stop the tears from falling. Not even if she tried. She slid the envelope to Philip. "Would you do it for me?"

"I don't think—"

"Please." That was all that she could muster.

LOUISE TOLD HER FRIENDS about that night. The pain, the humiliation, and worry that she'd felt. Inside the cafe, the three of them cried tears—tears for themselves and tears for each other.

"What did the letter say?" Sarah asked.

Louise told them of how she had asked Philip to read it.

"READY?" PHILIP ASKED.

Louise closed her eyes and nodded. She took a deep breath and held it in.

Philip sighed and began, "My dearest Louise..."

My Dearest Louise,

If you are reading this, then it means that I am gone and no longer able to care for the people that I love most in the world - you, Madison, and my daughter, Abby.

I'm sorry that you had to find out this way. There were so many times that I wanted to tell you. So many times that I could no longer hold it in.

Please forgive me. Please forgive my daughter. None of this was her fault.

I suppose you'd like to know how it happened. Why it happened. I know I owe you that much.

I didn't have an affair. I know that's what you must be thinking. If I could take my actions back, I would. My lack of judgement has caused me great pain and I am sorry for the pain I know that it will bring you.

First, let me say, I am sorry. I never meant to hurt you or Madison.

Abby's mother is a troubled woman. I met her one night, many years ago. It was after we'd lost Amari. I was distraught. And you had begun to pull away from me.

It happened once, when I was away at a business conference in Portland. I'd had too much to drink - more than I could handle. The night got out of hand, and my senses went out the window.

It was only one night. That was all it was. But two years later, I was back at that same bar with some work colleagues. I saw her. I didn't recognize her, but she recognized me. She was drunk and slurring her words, yelling obscenities at me.

At first, I couldn't understand what she was saying, but then I noticed that she had a young kid with her. The kid was no more than a year old. But I knew. I knew it right away, Louise. That baby was mine. She looked just like Amari.

Nothing ever happened with Abby's mother after that. I'd promised her that I would pay child support, and so I did. But I couldn't leave Abby. She was my daughter. I couldn't leave her to live with a woman like her mother. So, every year on her birthday and sometimes at Christmas, I'd visit her. I'd promised to look after her.

When Abby turned thirteen, her mother started dating a new man. He was a vile and abusive man. Abby was terrified of him. I knew that I wouldn't always be there for her. I was getting older and who knew how long I would have left in this world? So I wrote this letter and gave it to Abby. I made her promise that if she was ever alone or needed help, that she should come and find you and give you this letter.

You are a kind and generous woman, Louise, and I have never deserved you. You were always a better person than I ever could be.

I know that in doing this; I am asking a lot of you. I don't deserve your forgiveness. And I certainly don't deserve to ask you any favors. But as for Abby - Louise, if you are reading this now, it means that she needs help.

I hope that you can find it in your heart to please take her in and share your love with her.

Until we meet again,

Warren

By the time Philip finished reading the letter, her face was drenched. Her nose was clogged and her anger was fierce. But above all, her heart ached for Abby. Louise wondered what could have caused her to run away from home. Had the man done anything to her?

"Are you okay?" Philip asked. He stood to get a glass of water and handed it to Louise.

She nodded, drained and defenseless. "Thank you."

They sat in companionable silence for some time. Louise's mind raced with thoughts of Warren—thoughts of Abby, her mother. Thoughts of Madison. Thoughts of Amari. "What should I do?" Her voice was a hoarse whisper.

Philip took her hands in his and gently squeezed them.

"Philip, what do I do?" she cried again. Louise doubled over and leaned against Philip's chest.

Philip embraced her and held her close. "It is in times like these that our faith is tested."

Louise hadn't cried this hard since Warren had died. Or that time she'd found out that Philip was leaving for the Philippines. The pain took her breath away.

"Jesus opened his arms to anyone and everyone—tax collectors, criminals, prostitutes. Despite all the difficult times in his life, he acted with grace and forgiveness."

Louise listened. Her heart slowed, and she listened.

"So, I ask you, what would Jesus do?" Philip stroked her hair.

"I can't Philip," Louise sobbed, "I can't."

"Because Jesus forgives us, we must also forgive others." Philip's voice was calm and clear. "Are you willing to extend love, grace, and forgiveness to this child who has done nothing wrong, but whose parents have caused you great pain?"

Louise didn't know if she could. But then she thought of her own daughter. When Louise was ensconced deep in mourning the loss of her daughter, Amari, who was there for Madison?

After years of trying to give Madison a sister, Louise and Warren had resigned themselves to the fact that it just wasn't meant to be. But fourteen years later, at the age of forty, they'd welcomed a baby girl into the world.

It was her miracle baby. They'd named her Amari, which meant miracle of God. Because she was exactly that—a miracle of God.

But on the thirtieth day, their miracle was taken away.

Before then, Louise had never heard of SIDS. Sudden Infant Death Syndrome.

"*I'm sorry,*" the paramedics told her.

"*I'm afraid it is more common than one might think,*" the doctor said. "Such deaths are unexplained."

"It's also known as crib death."

People tried to comfort her. They cooked food. The church had led prayers for the '*Delaney Family and their miracle, taken too soon*'.

That was the moment that Madison lost her mother. Following the death of Amari, Louise fell into deep depression. She'd pushed everyone away—including her husband and their living daughter.

Their relationship had never been able to grow after that. Madison had to find her own way in life. And when she did, she no longer needed her mother.

Louise sighed. She asked God to give her his love. His love for this young girl—for Abby, who now walks alone.

"Only you know the path that you can walk. Only you know if there is ample room in your heart for one more." Philip's voice soothed her. "Whatever you decide, I will be with you."

Louise looked up at Philip to find him gazing at her. "Why did you go?" she asked, tears falling down her face. "Why did you leave me?"

Philip smoothed the hair off her face. "I couldn't stand to watch you with someone else."

"But you became a priest," Louise wept.

"That never meant that I didn't love you," Philip said. "My love for Jesus has never diminished my love for you."

AFTER LOUISE TOLD THEM what has happened, Sarah dabbed at the tears in her eyes. "Louise, I had no idea," Sarah said. "I'm so sorry about Amari."

"It happened a long time ago," Louise said.

"But it never really goes away, does it?" Kate asked. "It must have taken a great deal of courage and strength."

She shook her head. "No. And that's how I lost Madison. Now, she about to become a mother herself."

"That's wonderful! Congratulations," Kate beamed.

"I won't get to know my grandchild," Louise said softly. "When Warren died, it seemed that anything that tied Madison and I together had ended."

Louise told them about her estrangement with her only daughter, now fully acknowledging that she had never been there for Madison.

"I've failed both my daughters." Louise wiped her tears. "I can't fail another one."

Chapter 21

Sarah Gardner

Christmas had come and gone without any surprises. They'd all decided to have dinner together. Louise, Abby, and Kate had gone over to Sarah's house, so that the children could remain in their element. Caleb was there, of course. And Louise had invited Philip.

Together, they cooked their favorite dishes, forgoing the traditional Christmas menu of roast and side dishes. Louise made some spaghetti and meatballs. Kate cooked pork *adobo*—apparently a Filipino classic—and steamy jasmine rice, which went down well with the children. Sarah made her favorite of beef burritos. For dessert, Philip had brought a trifle, and Caleb prepared an impressive baked cheesecake. It was a mismatch of food, but to Sarah, it symbolized new beginnings. It had been the most that she'd had in a very long time.

As they sat down to dinner, Philip led them in prayer.

"Heavenly Father," he began.

Feeling every word that was spoken, Sarah closed her eyes. Her heart pressed against itself. Exhaling slowly, she felt a hand press into hers. Sarah opened her eyes to Caleb, who was sat next to her. His gaze asked if she was okay.

Sarah nodded and gave him a smile.

Caleb took her hand and brought it to his lips.

It was a small peck, but just the same, Sarah's heart skipped a beat. It wasn't the kind of skip that hurt. It wasn't the beating that she had grown accustomed to in the last few months. No. It was a skip that she didn't understand.

Sarah looked at Caleb, but his eyes were closed.

"We thank you for your graciousness; for the blessings you have bestowed upon each one of us at this table; and for the friendship that binds us," Philip continued.

"Mommy, I want chicken," Zoe said loudly during the prayer.

"Ssh..." Sarah smiled and stroked Zoe's head. There was no denying it. She was happy, and the feeling was spreading through her.

"May the good Lord, who has carried us out of darkness and into his astonishing light, bless us and fill us with peace."

"Mommy?" Zoe spoke up once more. "Mommy, why you cry? Don't cry, Mommy, okay?"

"Amen," Philip said.

"Amen," Sarah said under her breath. She could still feel Caleb's lips on the back of her hand. *Why did he kiss me?* she wondered. Zoe climbed on to Sarah's lap and took her face in her small hands. "I love you, Mommy."

At that very moment, Sarah's heart filled with hope. "I love you too, sweet girl," she said.

"Merry Christmas, everyone," Louise said, raising a glass.

A flurry of greetings passed across the table. Philip's prayer was perfect and embodied what they were all feeling that night.

"I'd like to make an announcement," Louise said as she stood up. "Abby,"—Louise gestured for her to stand up—"as you all know, Abby, my stepdaughter, will be staying full time with me."

"That's wonderful!" Sarah brought a hand to her chest. It felt almost impossible to feel any happier than she did that night.

"After an honest and wonderful talk, Abby and I have decided that she will return to school after the Christmas break and will continue her junior year at Carlton Bay High." Louise smiled proudly. "Would you like to say anything, Abby?"

"No thanks," Abby said shyly. But she smiled beautifully, her happiness glowing from within.

"Congratulations, Abby," Kate said, raising a glass of cranberry juice.

"I couldn't have done it without your help," Abby said. "You're like a big sister to me."

"Okay, okay," Sarah said, "no need to remind us of how young you and Kate are—and how much older the rest of us are getting." It felt good to share jokes and laugh with friends.

"Speak for yourself," Louise said. "You are only as old as you feel. I feel fantastic." Louise patted her hair.

"Forever twenty-one, huh?" Caleb joked.

"Oh, goodness forbid! Who would want that? Twenty-one is a dreadful age." Louise wrinkled her nose. "Forever fifty-nine."

"Hear, hear," Philip agreed.

The children were on a high. The Christmas tree was beautifully decorated—thanks to Caleb. And the house was filled with a warmth that Sarah had missed. Her heart ached for Adam...but as hope slowly crept in, she longed for a year of blessings and new beginnings.

Spring

"The Lord is near to the brokenhearted and saves the crushed in spirit."

~Psalm 34:18

Chapter 22

Sarah Gardner

Any feelings of hope and optimism that Sarah had were short-lived. Guilt quickly overcame her.

In the months that passed, she grew fonder and more attached to Caleb. His presence was like a warm blanket on a cold winter's night. But despite the calm she felt within, her heart was wracked with guilt. Was she falling for him? How could she possibly be falling for someone else? Adam had just died, for goodness' sake! The questions kept piling up and guilt consumed her from the inside, out.

Sarah walked down the hall, peering at the family photos that lined the walls. She stopped just outside the boys' bedroom when she heard Liam talking to Caleb. His voice was soft but serious. "So where is my daddy now?"

Sarah leaned against the wall. It broke her heart over and over again to know that nothing could ever bring his daddy back.

"He's in heaven," Caleb said. His tone was matter-of-fact.

"Can I see him?" Liam was his daddy's boy. Adam was overjoyed when the ultrasound showed their first-born would be a boy.

Sarah blinked back the tears that had threatened to fall once more.

"Buddy..." Caleb paused briefly. "Heaven is a pretty special place. It's not somewhere we can just visit."

"Why not?" Disappointment lined Liam's voice.

"Well, not everyone gets to go to heaven. There's a certain time for all of us."

Sarah knew it couldn't have been an easy discussion for Caleb.

"But I saw my daddy—I know where he is!"

"You do?" Caleb asked.

"Yes, because I saw them put him in a big hole in the grass," Liam said. "He's in the *smet*—the *semeet*—the *semastory* inside the ground." Liam was adamant. "And they put lots of soil to cover him. Why can't we go there?"

"Ah, I see," Caleb said. "That's called the cemetery. Good job remembering the name, Liam. That's where people's bodies are laid to rest when their souls go up to heaven."

"My daddy is resting?"

Sarah stopped herself from going inside the room. As unfair as it was for Caleb to have to manage the conversation, she couldn't—she just couldn't.

"Well, his body is resting," Caleb said. "You see, when someone dies, their body gets left behind to sleep for a very, very long time. But their soul flies up to heaven to be with God."

"My daddy's with God?" Liam sounded disappointed, but hopeful.

"Yup—and you know what? I'll bet he's with my dad."

"Your daddy is in heaven too?" Curiosity filled his voice.

"He sure is," Caleb said. "He went to heaven a long time ago. So when your daddy went up there, I think my dad was waiting to greet him so that they could be good friends and your daddy wouldn't be lonely."

"Is Daddy sad?"

Sarah's heart broke once more. It was another crack that would never ever be whole again.

"Well, I think I would be sad too if I had to leave you," Caleb said.

"And Noah and Zoe too?"

"And Noah and Zoe, too."

Caleb was so good with Liam.

"And your mom," Caleb said.

"Do you know what?" Liam asked. "I think Mommy's sad."

"You think so?"

"Yes, because she doesn't smile and play with us anymore." Liam let out a small cough.

"It will take some time. Mommy lost her best friend, so it's very hard for her right now."

"But I can be her best friend," Liam mumbled.

"Are you sad, Liam?" Caleb asked.

Sarah didn't hear Liam answer, but from Caleb's response, she knew he'd said, yes. Defeated, she slid to the floor and buried her head in her hands.

"Come here, buddy." From the sound he'd made, Sarah assumed Caleb had picked Liam up. "It's okay to be sad."

"Mommy only smiles when you're here. She doesn't smile for me."

"Do you think so?" Caleb asked.

Liam didn't answer, but again, Sarah assumed that he nodded.

"Did you know that you make me smile?"

"Yeah?"

"Yeah," Caleb said. "I'm here for you, buddy. For your brother and your sister, and your mommy too."

"And your daddy will look after my daddy?" Liam asked.

"I think they're probably best friends by now," Caleb said with a chuckle.

"I'm happy your daddy is there with my daddy. I don't want him to be sad."

"My dad will make sure that he isn't sad."

There was a moment of silence before Liam spoke again. "Caleb, will you be my new daddy?"

Sarah held her breath and listened.

"You know, buddy...your daddy will *always* be your daddy. *I* can be your best friend."

"And mommy's too—so she won't be sad?"

"I love your mommy very much," Caleb said. "I'll do everything I can to make her happy."

"You have to tell her, so she can be happy, and then she can play with me again."

"I will. But not right now, okay? Your mommy needs some space right now. But I'll be right here."

"But—"

"Hey, how about we build something with your legos?" Caleb quickly changed the subject.

"Can we go see the boats?" Liam perked up. "My daddy always bringed me to see the boats."

"He brought you to the boats, huh? Yeah, we can do that. Let's go get you guys ready."

"I can get ready by myself—I'm a big boy."

"You sure are!" Caleb said. "You get ready and I'll help Zoe and Noah."

"Yeah, because they're not big like me."

Before Sarah could get up and slip out of the hall, Caleb came out of the room. She looked up at him. Her face was a mess and her eyes, puffy. Sarah reached up for the hand Caleb held out for her and let him pull her up against his chest. Sarah cast her eyes downwards. She couldn't look at him. "I'm sorry—I didn't mean to—"

"It's okay," Caleb said.

Sarah wasn't sure what she was apologizing for—for eavesdropping? For saddling Caleb with her kids? For being a mess? She felt she had lots to apologize for. She looked up at him. "I don't know what to say," she whispered.

"You don't have to say anything."

Sarah closed her eyes as Caleb gently kissed her forehead. It was a simple gesture that weakened her knees and caused another dam of tears to break. Sarah wept—and wept some more. And Caleb? He held her close and whispered words that eventually brought her calm.

IT WAS THE FIRST FRIDAY of spring and Sarah was on her way to meet Louise and Kate at Chapter Five. It was a beautiful day and fishing had once again perked up with anglers, each hopeful to catch the rumored thirty-pound spring Chinooks.

Sarah pushed the door open and was greeted by Kate, who popped out from behind a children's bookshelf. Louise had given her a part-time job at the bookstore after her assistant left for a once-in-a-lifetime scholarship in Europe. "Hi Sarah!"

"How's the new job going?" Sarah walked over to where Kate was busy stacking shelves and was surprised to find a courier guy helping her with the books. "Oh, sorry! I didn't realize you were—"

"No, Sarah, it's okay," Kate beamed. She smiled as she organized a small display of Jacqueline Wilson books. "This is Mark," Kate said. "He's just helping me unload the boxes."

"Hi," Mark said as he looked up at Sarah. "I was just helping. The boxes are really heavy."

There were two boxes between them and neither one was any bigger than a standard office box. Sarah smiled. "It's nice to meet you, Mark."

"Anyway," Kate piped up, "I love the job so much! I've met so many new people and everyone's been so nice."

"I can see that Mark's *really nice* too." Sarah winked at Kate.

"Oh, I don't mind," Mark said. "I've got some time to spare."

"Thanks, Mark. I really appreciate it." Kate placed a hand on his shoulder.

Sarah's heart fluttered for Kate. She was happy for Kate. It was obvious that working at the store was doing her plenty of good. "I'm really glad to hear you've settled nicely into the job, Kate." Things hadn't been easy for Kate and she needed some good things happening in her life. "How's the little one coming along?"

Kate stood up and rubbed her belly. "Can you see it?" she asked excitedly, hyper-extending her back. "I mean, I know it's still small, but I can definitely feel my clothes getting tighter."

"I think you're blooming. Pregnancy suits you." Sarah smiled." What do you think, Mark? She's really blooming, isn't she?" Sarah teased.

"Uhm—Kate's very—yeah, she's really..." Mark's face turned beet red.

"Don't mind, Sarah," Kate placed a hand on Mark's back as he stood up. "She's just teasing."

"There you are," Louise sang as she came out of the back office. "I made us some tea. It's brewing in the office. Oh, and I also picked up those little Danish pastries we enjoyed—do you remember those?"

"Perfect!" Sarah said with a nod.

"Come,"—Louise motioned for them to follow her—"I've set up a little table for us to sit and chat. I'm sorry we couldn't go to Dockside as we normally do."

Mark got up. "I guess I should get going."

"Oh! Would you like a cup of tea, Mark?" Louise asked once she realized he was there.

"Oh, no thank you, Mrs. Delaney. I've got to get going anyway." He glanced at Kate. "I'll see you tomorrow?"

Kate nodded. It the happiest Sarah had seen her since they'd first met. "Thanks again for your help, Mark. I'll walk you out."

Sarah joined Louise. Together, they watched as Kate walked with Mark to the front door. "I didn't know you escorted couriers out the door now," Sarah whispered.

"What bothers me more is that he calls me *Mrs. Delaney*; and yet, he calls her Kate," Louise whispered back. She gave Sarah a soft nudge. "Am I really that old?"

Sarah laughed. "I think they make a cute couple."

Kate turned from the door and walked towards them. "I told Louise I could stay and look after the shop, but she—" Kate stopped. She looked at Sarah first and then at Louise. "Okay, what's going on?"

"Nothing," Sarah said with a sly grin. "Right, Louise?"

"Oh, nothing at all," Louise said. She was good at picking up the cues. "I was just saying that you need to tell that boy to stop calling me Mrs. Delaney. If he's going to keep calling you Kate, then I insist he call me Louise."

Sarah laughed. "I think he called me Sarah. Didn't he call me Sarah, Kate?"

"Why yes, Sarah, I do think he did," Kate said, teasing Louise.

Louise rolled her eyes. "Very funny, ladies."

Kate giggled sweetly. "Anyway, as I was saying, I told Louise that I could stay and look after the shop, but—"

"Nonsense," Louise said. "Then we wouldn't be able to enjoy our tea for three."

"I agree with Louise," Sarah said. "I'm just happy to be with you guys. It's been a long week."

Chapter 23

Kate Morgan

Kate was grateful for the part-time job she had at the bookstore. Not only did she get to meet new people...she met Mark.

Getting to see Mark was the highlight of Kate's week. He was the new courier assigned their location, and they'd instantly hit it off. Talking to Mark was easy, and Kate enjoyed the attention he gave her. It wasn't like there would ever be anything between them—she was going to be a new mom soon and she wouldn't have time for relationships.

"So, what's he like?" Sarah asked of Mark.

Kate blushed. She wasn't used to talking about men. "He's really nice."

"I gathered that—I was surprised to see him behind the bookshelves," Sarah laughed. "But...what makes him nice? Like, how did you know you liked him?"

"Who said I like him?"

"Oh, darling, trust me. Everyone that sees the two of you in action would know it straight away." Louise poured the pot of hot tea into three cups. "This is raspberry leaf tea, by the way. They say it's good for women, especially during pregnancy."

"Does Mark know you're expecting?" Sarah leaned in.

Kate wrinkled her nose and shrugged. "I think so. I mean, I haven't kept it a secret or anything. And besides, it's not like anything can ever happen between us."

"And why not?" Louise took a sip of her tea. "Oh, that's beautiful tea!" She pointed at her cup. "You're a single woman and you can do whatever you please."

Kate tried the tea. "Well, technically, I'm still married."

"Have you heard from Evan lately?" Sarah asked.

Kate shook her head. "He called me last week. Apart from that, no."

"I didn't know he called you." Louise's frowned with concern. "What did he say?"

"He asked if I've come to my senses yet about—his words, not mine—the thing in my stomach."

"Oh, he's a terrible person." Sarah frowned. "That baby you're carrying is a miracle. If he doesn't know it, then he doesn't deserve either of you."

"Mark looks like he'd make a good father," Louise smiled.

Kate blushed once more. "I don't think he's looking for that kind of relationship. No one wants a single mom. Too much baggage."

"It looks to me that our young Mark doesn't see anything wrong with lifting excess baggage." Louise winked.

"He looked mighty comfortable picking those boxes up," Sarah said with a laugh.

"What about you and Philip?" Kate asked. "How are things going between the two of you? He's been to the house every day since he got back."

Louise smiled and sighed.

Chapter 24

Louise Delaney

It was true. Philip visited Louise every day since he returned from service in the Philippines. As it turned out, he was the vicar at the parish in Kate's hometown. But because she had moved to Manila for work, they didn't know each other. It was quite a spectacle to watch when they'd realized the degree of separation. Life sure was funny like that.

So when Kate asked how things were progressing between her and Philip, it was hard not to smile. Myriads of wonderful things have happened since his return. It was as if he'd never left Carlton Bay—or her side. "He truly is a wonderful man and I am so grateful to have someone so dear back in my life."

"Do you think you guys are..." Kate paused.

"What?" Louise raised her eyebrows.

Kate smiled. "You know...dot, dot, dot."

"Do you mean sex, Kate? You're a grown woman with a baby on the way. You can say sex," Louise said with a laugh.

"I can't!" Kate covered her face. It was amusing how she was so shy about certain things.

"You're funny, Kate," Sarah said. And then, turning to Louise, she asked, "Is there a chance you guys would?"

"Oh my goodness," Louise threw her head back. "Don't tell me you can't say the word either."

Sarah laughed out loud.

"We're not there yet."

"Yet," Sarah repeated. "I like that."

"I'm not too clear on why Philip has returned," Louise continued.

"What did he say was the reason?" Sarah reached for a pastry.

"Well, he did say that I was the reason he'd come home; but truly, it seems too far-fetched that he would wait thirty years just to be with me. Retirement seems like more realistic."

"Does it matter?" Sarah asked.

Louise twisted her mouth. It mattered to her. Philip had left her. He answered a calling; and although it took a long time, Louise had later come to terms with it. The thought that he'd come back to her simply because it was time for Philip to retire did not bode well with her.

"Well, he did say that he had left because you'd married Warren, didn't he?" Kate asked.

"Did he?" Sarah leaned in. "Oh my gosh, that's heart-breaking."

"I know, right?" Kate beamed. "It's like a romantic movie! I swear, seeing them together almost every day gives me hope that maybe one day, I'll get it right."

"It ain't over till it's over, darling." Louise patted Kate's hand. "You're young and there are plenty of fish in the sea."

"I don't want a fish—I want a man who will love me and treat me right," Kate said.

"That could be Mark," Sarah offered.

"I doubt it." Kate sighed. "Hey, speaking of fish in the sea...do you know why they say, 'it's not over until the fat lady sings?"

Louise laughed. "It's an old saying—it really only means that you shouldn't make any conclusions until the show is done, so to speak. The show being the opera; and the fat lady would be the soprano at the final scene. Sopranos were traditionally overweight, you see. The theory was, the larger the lady, the bigger the lung capacity—hence the fat lady."

"Hmm, interesting. It's such a funny saying."

Louise noticed that there were many things Kate seemed unaware of. It could be her age, or perhaps some kind of naivety. Whatever it was though, she was glad that Kate felt comfortable enough to be able to ask them.

"Anyway," Louise said, moving on. "What about you, darling?" She asked Sarah. "How are things at home?"

Chapter 25

Sarah Gardner

Sarah told the girls about her growing feelings for Caleb. She couldn't hold it in anymore. The guilt was driving her crazy. And after hearing how he'd spoken to Liam about Adam made him all the more attractive in her eyes.

"He said that to Liam? That his dad was probably best friends with his own father?" Louise asked with a hand over her chest. "That's such a lovely way of putting it."

"I know." Sarah shook her head and sighed. "Maybe it was a mistake to bring a man in to the house. I mean, even if he is a *manny*—he's still very much a man."

"And you're still very much a woman, my dear," Louise said. "Widow or not."

"I think the children are very lucky to have someone like Caleb in their lives," Kate said. "Like, the fact that he is able to talk to them about their father is just so amazing. Take it as a blessing."

"Adam would roll in his grave if he knew I was having these feelings." Sarah took a sip of tea. "Maybe I should tell him to go back to Willow Oaks."

"Why? Because you're attracted to him?" Louise leaned back in her chair. "Sarah, it's not a crime to fall for another man."

"But so soon after Adam?" Sarah couldn't believe she was even entertaining the idea. "I can't. It—it's just wrong. It's too complicated."

"Who gets to say what's wrong and what's right?" Louise said with a confidence that gave her hope, even if only a little.

"What would people say?" Sarah asked, horrified.

"Let him who is without sin cast the first stone," Louise used her finger to drive a point. "Isn't that what the bible says?"

"Well, if I cared about what everyone here thought of me, I might need to go to the post office"—Kate laughed—"and mail myself off to be someone else's bride."

They all laughed together.

"I hear there's a big demand for good wives." Louise joked. "We can get your handsome courier to drive you to your next husband."

Kate laughed the loudest that time. "But seriously, Sarah, who cares what people think?"

Sarah could see where they were coming from. But a big part of her felt that by even thinking of another man, she was betraying Adam. Cheating on him. "Sometimes, I wish I lived somewhere else...a place where people didn't know everything about everyone."

"Then you wouldn't have us. What fun would that be?" Louise asked with a chuckle. "Darling,"—she put a hand on my arm—"take it from an old woman. Life is too short to worry about what other people think. Take the reins and ride that bull."

"She means figuratively," Kate added. "Like, don't ride Caleb straight away. Maybe on the third date."

Sarah laughed so hard, she had to cover her mouth with a napkin.

"Did you just make a sex joke, young Kate?" Louise asked in amusement.

"I think I may be spending too much time with you girls." Kate laughed. "You should never sleep with a man on the first date."

"Okay, so what should I do?" Sarah asked. "I've been out of the dating scene for so long. I mean, Adam was my last boyfriend! I don't think I've even looked at another man since Adam and I started dating."

"Surely you've looked at other men," Louise said. "You were married—not blind."

Sarah laughed. "You know what I mean."

"Why don't you just tell him?" Kate asked.

"Tell him what? That I like him?" Sarah was horrified. "I could never do that. Oh my gosh, what would he think? What if he doesn't even like me that way?"

"Oh, pish-tosh! Life is too short for *what-ifs*. I say, just do it!"

"You know—Louise is right," Kate said. "I've decided that I want to take control of my life. I want to take my life back."

"That's the way!" Louise cheered.

"I'm going to grab the bull by its horns and ride it!"

"Very good," Louise said, nodding approvingly. "You go, girl!"

Kate pretended to take a bow. "I mean, I hadn't realized how much I depended on others until I married Evan and moved here. Everything revolved around him."

"It's good that you'd like to take control of your life, Kate," Sarah said. "It really is. Have you told Mark that you like him?" she teased.

Poor Kate blushed again for the hundredth time. "Well, no. I mean, I don't know if I *like* him."

"Of course you do." Louise laughed. "Everyone can see that."

"This time, I want to take it slow," Kate said. "Evan and I—what we had; it was just so fast. In hindsight, my mom was right."

Sarah nodded thoughtfully. "Hindsight is always 20/20 isn't it?"

"You know, I never really understood that saying until now. I feel that having all this time to think about the things I've done—you know, how I've made my bed and everything. Looking back, I would have done things differently. I may even have listened to my mom." Kate rested her chin on her hand. "But don't tell her that," she laughed.

"Well, you've got us," Louise said. "We've got each other."

It felt good and was a relief to Sarah that she'd been able to confide in the girls. After everything that they'd all been through, they were still able to laugh and find comfort in each other.

The thought of telling Caleb that she liked him terrified Sarah. "*My husband has just died and I have no business falling for someone else,*" she thought to herself.

Chapter 26

Louise Delaney

That weekend, Louise had agreed to meet Philip for a picnic at the Village Park next to St. Anthony's Church on Ivy Place. Although Philip had told her not bring anything, she took with her a thermos of hot coffee.

The Village Park was a beautiful place. Rich with a history that Carlton Bay residents took pride in, it boasted of lush, green landscapes. In 1863, a mulberry tree was planted to commemorate the opening of the St. Anthony's Church—with several more planted after that. It was the town's first and, now, oldest church. Through the years, the church and the townspeople had worked together to make the park the living museum that it was today. Fourteen acres of magical gardens had become home to thousands of floras; and over the years, its popularity had grown with both locals and tourists alike. Families took their children to play in the lush green grounds, young lovers walked hand-in-hand among the lanes of beautiful hedges, and the elderly strolled along walking their patient and ever-loyal dogs. It was the pride of the town.

For Louise, however, St. Anthony's was much more than its age and beautiful gardens. It was where she and Philip had first met. They were young teens—both idealistic and impressionable. They'd belonged to the church youth group and happened to meet during a weekend project painting fences along the dockside. The two hit it off instantly and fast became inseparable. When Philip's best friend, Warren, joined the youth group, not a day went by that the three didn't see each other.

From the day that Philip left to join the seminary, Warren stayed by her side. He'd comforted her, made her laugh, and surprised her with little gifts to help ease the pain of Philip's departure. As the days and the years passed, it was Warren that filled the gaping hole in Louise's heart. And slowly, as the wound healed, she learned to breathe again.

Everyone said they would fall in love and, in time, Louise believed it too. Warren had won her heart...just as God had won Philip's.

By the time Philip returned from his religious studies, she and Warren had become the town's *it* couple. It broke her heart yet again when Philip made no mention of their relationship, except to congratulate them.

A year after Philip's return—and continued silence—Louise and Warren got married.

On the day of her wedding, as she walked down the aisle of St. Anthony's church, Louise looked at the two men she loved most in the world; both men waiting.

One stood as her groom, waiting to make her his wife. While the other stood as the priest, waiting to officiate her wedding.

That was the last time that Louise had ever set foot in St. Anthony's church. It bore too many memories, painful and beautiful.

Returning to the place where her heart had been both broken and put back together was overwhelming. When she'd agreed to meet Philip at the park, she hadn't expected just how much it would affect her.

Philip was exactly where he said he would be. "*Meet me at the center of the Village Park, by the Mulberry Picnic Garden,*" he said over the phone. It was there, on one of the Mulberry trees, that they had carved their initials.

As Louise walked towards him, feelings of regret overcame her. She wondered what life would have been like had she not married Warren. She wondered what might have happened if she'd only waited for Philip. Thoughts raced through her mind and it made her anxious.

"I was beginning to think you weren't coming," Philip smiled as he stood from the picnic table to meet her. He greeted her with a light kiss on the cheek.

"I haven't been here in years." Louse looked around. "It's changed since I last saw it."

"Time has a way of doing that—changing things, places, people." Philip stood with his hands on his waist. "When were you last here?" he asked. He placed his hand on her lower back and led her to the table.

Louise set her bag and the thermos of coffee on the table. "My wedding day," she said.

"That long ago?" Surprise colored Philip's face. He was never very good at hiding his emotions—except when it came to her. "All this beauty at your doorstep—it's surprising to know you hadn't been here in over thirty years."

Louise sat down. "I don't know. I guess it was too painful."

"Well, that's a first for me," Philip laughed. "I don't think I've ever heard anyone describe their wedding as a painful memory." He emptied the contents of a picnic basket he'd brought with him. Two sandwiches, crackers, some cheeses, and something covered in icing sugar. "Would you like a drink? I brought us some juice and Coca-Cola. I didn't know which one you'd prefer."

Louise shook her head and reached for the thermos. "I brought us some hot coffee."

"Good idea," Philip said. "It's chillier than I thought it would be."

Her emotions built up—one on the top of the other. It overwhelmed her and she could no longer hold it in. "Why did you leave?" Louise blurted. Feelings of betrayal swept through her, just as they did when she had learned Philip was leaving for seminary school.

"What?"

"You know what I mean!" Her voice came out louder than she'd anticipated. "Why did you leave me?" Tears filled her eyes.

"Lou," Philip sighed and sat down. He rubbed his face. "I didn't leave you." His voice shook. "You chose—"

"You left me!" she cried, losing all calm within her. It was as if she was eighteen again, crying as he told her he was leaving.

"Lou...you got married." His face crumpled as he spoke, turning his normally happy eyes, downward.

"You left me—for God!" Her choice of words surprised her, but it was not the time to weave her feelings into poetry. There were no two ways about it. He chose God.

"I went to seminary school, Louise." Philip reached for her hands.

"Exactly! You chose him over me, and—" she stammered and pulled her hands away.

"What do you mean? Lou, I love you. I have always loved you. I thought you knew that?"

"There was never a chance for us." She wiped her tears. "How could I have ever competed with God?"

"You were never meant to." Philip shook his head. "You never had to."

"Then how? We couldn't have ever been together."

"Lou, priests can marry," he said.

Louise looked up at him.

"It was always my intention to propose to you—after I completed my studies." Philip looked down and clasped his hands together. "That's why I wrote to you—every day. I told you I loved you."

Louise rolled her eyes. "You'd stopped writing! Clearly your intentions had changed."

"That's not true—" Philip reached for hands again. "I wrote to you every single day, Lou, even when you stopped writing me back."

Tears that cascaded down her cheeks. "I never got anything from you."

Philip's eyes widened. His face, bewildered. "But...I wrote to you, Lou. I loved you—so much. And when I came home from seminary school, you were the first person I went to see."

"That's not true," she sniffled. "I didn't hear from you until a week after you'd arrived."

Philip shook his head and sighed. "I'd come to see you. When I got to your house, your mother let me in. She showed me out to the garden where she'd said you were, but then—" He stopped.

"But then, what?"

"What I saw shocked me," he continued. "So I left."

Louise looked at him, her eyes pleading for an explanation.

"You were there—with Warren... you were with my best friend."

It was Louise's turn to look down at her hands.

"You were gardening," Philip said. "Warren must have said something funny, because you laughed and he pulled you close to him and kissed you."

"Philip," Louise looked up at him.

"It looked as if it was the most natural thing to you both," Philip continued. "I figured that was why you'd stopped writing me back. I didn't want to cause any problems for you. You looked happy. I thought it would be best if I just left. So I did."

"I didn't know," Louise said softly, her voice raspy from crying. "My mom didn't tell me you were there. I didn't know..."

"Would it have changed anything if you'd known I was there?" Philip asked. His lips formed into a soft smile.

Louise looked up into Philip's dark brown eyes. They had always reminded her of a strong cup of hot coffee—warm and inviting. His hairline had receded and his facial hair was speckled with gray. Apart from some lines around his eyes, he hadn't changed. "But the letters...you stopped—"

"I wrote to you every day."

Louise pulled a tissue from her purse.

Philip stood up. "Lou, I think this was a mistake."

Louise wiped her tears and watched as Philip packed the picnic away.

"The last thing I'd hoped for today was to cause you pain."

"You shouldn't have come back," Louise said under her breath.

Philip stopped and looked at her. "You don't mean that, Lou."

Confusion was rife in her heart. As far as Louise knew, he'd stopped writing her. That was why she'd agreed to marry Warren. Until then, she'd clung on to every bit of hope that they would one day be together. And now Philip dared tell her that he'd written her every day. If he did, then where were those letters? And if he truly loved her, why did he only come back for her now? Between Warren's infidelity and Philip's confession, it was all too much for Louise. "I don't know what

I mean anymore." Louise stood up and without looking at Philip, she walked away.

"Lou, wait," Philip called out.

She stopped and turned around. "What is it?"

"You forgot your thermos."

Louise huffed and quickened her pace. The thermos was the last thing on her mind.

Chapter 27

Kate Morgan

Kate had just locked up behind her, when she heard someone call her name. Her lips formed a smile when she turned to find Mark running towards her.

Mark took his baseball cap off. "I'm glad I caught you," he said.

"It's a bit late for a delivery isn't it?" Kate had volunteered to do the weekend afternoon shifts, so that Louise could get home early and spend some time with Abby. It was the least she could do after everything Louise had done for her. "Where's your van?"

"Just around the corner," he said. "I was just at the Inn Keeper—do you know the one?"

Kate nodded. "I've walked past it a few times."

"My friend owns it so I drop in sometimes." Mark had a handsome smile. It was a friendly one. His eyes were kind and welcoming. "They do some nice Irish meals."

Kate looked up at him and wondered what her life might have been like had she met Mark, instead of Evan. "Do they? That sounds nice." She wasn't sure that she'd ever had an Irish meal before. There was an Irish pub back in the Philippines, but the Irish menu was small, and the rest were either Italian or Filipino.

Mark ran a hand through his hair. "So—uh, I guess I'll see you again soon."

Kate smiled and wrinkled her nose. "Is that what you ran here to tell me?"

"I know—I'm not—I was actually hoping to ask if you might want to have dinner with me." Mark shoved his hands in his pockets. "I mean, if you don't have any other plans, of course. If you're free. Tonight. Or, or, maybe tomorrow. Or next week—"

"Mark,"—Kate laughed—"I'd love to have dinner with you."

He beamed. "Tonight? Or, you know, whenever you can." And then feigned nonchalance.

"I'd love to have dinner with you tonight," she said with a smile. Were they on a date? Kate felt like she was in high school again and her crush had just asked her out.

When they got to the pub, Mark led Kate to a booth. He already had a drink for himself.

"That's a very dark looking beer," Kate said as she slid into the booth.

Mark remained standing as he waited for her to get comfortable. "It's called a Stout beer. Have you tried it? I mean, before—not now, of course."

So he knows I'm pregnant, she thought. As she'd told the girls when they'd met last Friday, although she hadn't told him outright that she was pregnant, she hadn't kept anything secret either. It just never came up. "I'm not a big drinker."

Kate shook her head. "I never really got in to alcohol. I guess you could say I'm a cheap date," she said with a grin. That was what Evan used to say when they first started dating.

"So, are we on a date?"

Kate felt the warmth rise in her cheeks and looked around the pub.

"I'm just kidding," Mark said.

"This must be the famous, Kate!" A man with a strong Irish accent approached their booth. "I've heard so much about you," he said with a grin.

"Kate, this is my buddy, Connor," Mark said. "Connor, this is Kate."

Kate smiled up at Connor, whose dark curly hair hung loosely over his forehead. "It's nice to meet you, Connor."

"I guarantee you, Miss—the pleasure is all mine." Connor crossed his arms over his chest. "Since this one here"—he motioned at Mark with his thumb—"met you, you're all he's talked about. Kate this, Kate that—"

"Okay, Connor, don't you have some work to do?" Mark joked, eager not to be embarrassed by his friend.

"Oh no, it's okay. Keep going," Kate teased.

"Alright then," Connor grinned. "It was very nice to meet you, Kate. I'll leave my lad to look after you. You're in good hands, my dear."

Kate enjoyed talking to Mark throughout dinner. She'd ordered a plate of *bangers and mash*, which made her giggle, not having heard of it before. Mark was easy to talk to, and they laughed all through dinner. They'd talked about anything and everything, and it felt good not having to walk on eggshells like she did with Evan.

"Do you mind me asking,"—Mark paused—"and you don't have to tell me, if you don't want to..."

"Why I'm no longer with Evan?" Kate decided to finish his question for him. She didn't want to risk things getting awkward between them. "I guess, to make a long story short, you could say that we didn't want the same things anymore." There was more to just that, of course; but Kate didn't feel like she needed to explain more than was necessary.

"I'm sorry to hear that," Mark said.

Kate shrugged. "It is what it is."

"If you don't mind me saying, you look like you're coping well without him."

Kate laughed. "You mean without a man?"

"Well, no—sorry, that's not what I meant." Mark stammered. "It's just...I know it can be hard. Breaking up, losing someone you love and all that."

It was true. She couldn't deny that. It was difficult. She thought she'd found forever with Evan—that was until things changed. Until he'd changed. "It is," she said in a soft voice. "But the least I can do is try."

"Kate,"—Mark reached out for her hands and cupped them in his—"I, I like you. I like you a lot," he said.

Kate enjoyed the feeling of his hands over hers, but she wasn't ready to be in a relationship. Not yet. Not now. Not when she had a baby on the way.

"Hey!" A woman approached them, her voice hoarse and aggressive. The deep lines on her face spoke of a hard life. "Aren't you Evan Morgan's wife?"

"Norma," Mark said, "I think you should get going."

"Says who?" she blurted. "She's damaged goods, boy," she said, using her thumb to point at Kate. "You shouldn't waste your time on no foreign cow—her milk's already been tasted."

Mark stood up. "Norma, you're drunk." He waved over to the bar at Connor, who came over quickly.

"I'm sorry, Kate," Connor said. Turning to Norma, he said, "Let's get you home, Norma. It's late."

"I'm not ready to go home," Norma said.

"I'm cutting you off and we'll call your son to come and pick you up." Connor put his arm around Norma and led her away as if it was an occurrence he was used to. "And when you're good and sober tomorrow, you're gonna apologize to Kate."

"I don't wanna apologize to no one!" she hissed.

"You will—once you realize what you've done. Come on, let's go."

After Connor took Norma away, another woman came by to talk to them. "Kate," she said, "I'm Linda. I'm sorry about that. Not everyone is like Norma and we're glad to see you here with our boy, Mark." Linda's smile was soft and her eyes, kind.

"I'll second that," another man stood over Linda. "Norma's a good one—except when she's had too much to drink. Don't let her put you off from coming back."

"Thank you," Kate smiled shyly at them. While she didn't like being the center of attention, she welcomed their kinds words.

"Are you okay?" Mark reached for her hands again.

While some of things Norma said were not new to Kate, she had never had anyone scream in her face like that and it shook her.

"Hey, Kate!" a heavily built man called from the bar. "Don't you worry about Norma. She's harmless. Her words will be back to bite her in the morning, and then you won't be able to get rid of her. She'll be your best friend after that."

"I guess you want to go home now, huh?" Mark asked.

Kate nodded. "I'll walk home."

"No, I'm sorry about what just happened. Let me drive you home." Mark stood up and put his jacket on. He helped Kate out of the booth and called out to Connor. "I'll see you in the morning, brother." Connor waved at them as they walked out the door.

Darkness covered them like a blanket as soon as they stepped out of the pub. Mark stopped and turned Kate to face him. "Are you okay? I'm really sorry you had to experience that."

"It's not your fault, Mark," Kate said. "And besides, I'm used to it." How had she become desensitized to such hateful words? Kate wondered if she would ever be accepted in the small town.

"No one should ever have to get used to anything like that." Mark shook his head. "Kate"—Mark took her hands—"I promise you that I will never ever let anyone talk to you like that again. You hear me?" Mark looked deep in her eyes and brought her hands to his lips. He kissed them and asked, "Is that okay?"

Kate smiled. *What are you doing, Kate? Don't even think about it,* she scolded herself. Was it okay? Yes, it was okay. It was more than okay! She wanted to wrap her arms around him—but at the moment, all she did was smile.

On the short drive home, they talked about the people around town, the holidays, and her baby. The baby she was carrying—Evan's baby.

"He doesn't want anything to do with the baby?" Mark asked, keeping his eyes on the road.

"He never wanted a baby, and I was fully aware of that." Kate sighed. "It was unexpected. So when he found out, he asked me to get rid of it." She placed a protective hand over her growing bump. "But I could never do that."

Mark's gripped tightened around the steering wheel. He shook his head.

Kate could see his jaw tighten. "Babies are not for everyone."

"Yeah, I get that. But they're not something you just get rid of either." Mark cursed under his breath. "He doesn't deserve you, Kate." He glanced at her. "He doesn't deserve the two of you."

A part of her felt a warm glow from being with Mark. The other part of her was afraid she was playing with fire. The idea of going from one relationship into another—so soon—seemed wrong. The last thing she needed right now was to get involved with someone. Her divorce was yet to be finalized, and she had a baby on the way for crying out loud. She needed to be honest with Mark. She didn't want him to get the wrong idea.

Mark got out of the van and helped Kate down. He walked her to the front door and gazed into her eyes. "I had a really nice time tonight," he said.

Kate smiled. She'd forgotten how good it felt to be the focus of someone's affection that she felt like a giddy teenager. "I had a really nice time, too."

Mark leaned in to kiss her on the cheek.

She closed her eyes for a second. Now—*do it now,* she told herself. "Mark, there's something I need to tell you."

"Kate!" Out of nowhere, Evan marched across the road shouting at the top of his lungs. "Is this how you want to do it now? I turn my back for a few seconds and you're kissing some chump."

"Evan—what are you doing here?"

"You're my *wife,*" he said. "I have every right to be here." He glared at Mark, who raised his hands as if to say, keep calm.

"I don't want any trouble, man. I was just dropping Kate home." Mark put his hand on Kate's elbow.

"*Just* dropping her home, huh?" Evan growled. "Because it looked to me like you two needed to get a room!"

"Evan! Please—stop it this instant."

Evan turned to face Kate. His face was red. "This instant?" he spat. "So you're all tough now because of this delivery schmuck?"

"Evan, you've been drinking. Please, just go home!" Kate hoped he would listen to her plea.

Evan stepped up to Kate, towering over her. "You think you've got it made now, huh?"

"Look, man, I think you should go." Mark stepped in between them in a bid to protect Kate.

Kate's anxiety rose within her. Evan was considerably bigger than Mark. She didn't want either of them to get hurt. "Evan, please."

Evan's face had grown redder. "Evan, please? Evan, please?"

"What's going on here?" Louise opened the door and stood with her hands on her hips.

"Louise,"—Kate walked up to her—"I'm so sorry. It's nothing. I'll take care of it."

"Evan Morgan! You should be ashamed of yourself," Louise snapped at Kate's drunken ex-husband. "How dare you come to my house and harass my friends! I suggest you turn around the way you came, or I will have the Sheriff here sooner than you can say you're sorry."

And just as quickly as he'd charged at them, Evan turned into a blubbering mess. "Come home with me, Kate. Please. Please, Kate. I'm sorry." He reached for Kate, and once again, Mark stepped in to block Evan. "Who do you think you are?" Evan yelled in Mark's face. His saliva gathered around his mouth and around his beard.

"You heard the ladies, man—it's time to head on home." Evan stood his ground.

"I'm talking to my wife," Evan said through gritted teeth.

"You lost your wife the moment you asked her to kill the baby," Louise said, stone-faced.

Evan cursed loudly and spat off a series of obscenities. "This is none of your business, lady."

Mark put a hand on Evan's arm. "Come on, man."

Without warning, Evan swung his arm up.

"Evan, no!" Kate screamed. It was almost like telling a misbehaving dog off. "No! Stop it!" One by one, Kate could see the sleepy houses on Mulberry Lane light up.

Mark stepped back, avoiding Evan's shaky fist.

Evan clumsily stumbled forward and spat on the ground. He straightened himself up and hurled expletives at Mark. Enraged, Evan darted for Mark like a bull to a matador, once again missing. Evan fell to the ground.

Kate gasped in shock.

Without warning, Evan buried his hands in his head and blubbered amidst tears. "Kate—just give me another chance, please."

"Let it go, Evan," Mark said. "Go home, get sober—you can check in on her in the morning." Mark extended a hand out to him. "Kate, you should go inside with Louise."

Evan glared up at Mark. "Who the heck do you think you are, huh? You think you're some knight in shining armor?" Evan tried to push himself off the ground, but his elbows buckled beneath him. He let out a loud moan as his face rubbed against the cold, rough asphalt.

Kate ran to Evan and kneeled by his side to help him up. "What are you doing?" Her voice was soft as she pulled him upright.

Evan grabbed Kate by the arm and effortlessly dragged her tiny frame across the street; to the house that had once held her hopes and dreams for a happily ever-after with Evan.

"Evan—no!" Kate struggled to free herself from Evan's grasp.

Mark charged at Evan and the two men got into yet another scuffle.

"That's enough!" Louise shouted. "I'm calling the Sheriff!"

"No, Louise," Kate pleaded. "Please don't. I'll take care of it."

"What? No!" Louise demanded. "Get inside, Kate."

"Evan," Kate called his name. "Evan!" she said again, this time, louder. "Please, that's enough. I'll come home with you."

"Kate, no, you mustn't," Louise objected.

Kate saw Sarah come up from her house and stood next to Louise. "What's going on?"

"Evan, did you hear me? Please, that's enough," Kate said again, only louder, "I'm coming home with you."

Evan shoved Mark to the side and looked at Kate.

"I'm coming with you," Kate said once more.

"Is she serious?" Kate heard Sarah ask. "Kate, you can't!"

"Mark,"—Kate pulled him by the arm—"go home. I'm sorry you got dragged into this."

"Kate," Mark said.

"Just go!" Kate cried. A tear slipped from her eyes as she looked up into his worried eyes. It was too much for her. Evan was the father of her baby. She needed to give him a chance.

"Kate, you don't have to do this," Louise said.

"Evan is my husband," she said softly. It hurt her to say it, but Evan was her husband. It was her job as his wife to do everything she could to appreciate, respect, and value her husband; just as her mother had done all these years, and her mother before her.

Kate walked towards Evan and took his extended hand. She looked back at Sarah, Louise, and Mark—and just as quickly looked away.

"Kate, please!" Sarah's voice cut through Kate like a hot knife to butter.

"Mind your own business, woman," Evan growled.

"It's okay," Kate mouthed to her friends. And with that, she let Evan lead her back to the house they shared; their house on Mulberry Lane.

Chapter 28

Sarah Gardner

The weekend had gone by like a blur. Sarah's thoughts went to Kate. She couldn't, for the life of her, understand why Kate had chosen to go home with Evan.

Before that night, it had been months since Evan had made any attempt at a reconciliation. According to Louise, Evan was an alcoholic; and it worried Sarah. And yet, as much as she disagreed with Kate's decision, she had to respect it. After all, Kate was a grown woman—naïve perhaps, but nonetheless, an adult capable of making her own decisions.

But still, Sarah could not rid herself of the niggling worry for Kate. She was their friend and Sarah felt a sense of responsibility for her. What if something terrible happened to Kate? Sarah couldn't bear the thought of it and made a promise to herself that she would be there the moment Kate needed them.

"Sarah?" Caleb popped his head in the kitchen, startling her. "I'll be heading out soon," he said.

Sarah turned around and wiped her hands on the apron she wore. "Thanks for letting me know," she said. She still hadn't gotten used to having Caleb move around so freely at home. Although he was a lot of help with the children, she struggled with his presence and how he made her feel—like that time she accidentally walked in on Caleb shaving his face, wearing just a towel around his waist.

But there was no way she could bring herself to tell Caleb how she felt. No, absolutely not.

Every thought and every feeling she had about Caleb felt like a betrayal to Adam and the happiness they'd shared. It frightened Sarah to think that Adam might be able to hear her thoughts, so she tried her best to shut them down as quickly as they popped up in her mind.

Sarah reminded herself, every night as she lay in bed and allowed her tears to flow, that falling for someone else was an impossibility. She couldn't give in. She *shouldn't* give in. Giving in was a sign of weakness—her heart was merely looking for someone to patch up the gaping hole that Adam had caused when he died.

"Are you going to be okay here?" Caleb asked, breaking through her thoughts. Earlier in the week, Caleb had found a new job as the new soccer coach of the new youth program at St. Anthony's Church, as well as the Carlton Bay school's soccer team.

Sarah nodded. "I will, thanks." She'd expected that things would change—particularly when it came to his involvement with the kids. The *mannying* gig wasn't to last forever. So it surprised her when Caleb insisted on taking the children with him to the training sessions. "Are you sure having the boys with you isn't too much of a nuisance?" Sarah asked.

"Yeah, absolutely—they love it," Caleb said. "You should see Liam in action. Sarah, he's a natural." His excitement was catching.

When Sarah had first learned of his new job, she feared for the children and what it would do to them if they lost their relationship with Caleb. But the truth was, little had changed. Caleb insisted on taking the children with him and that eased her worries. Had Caleb just disappeared, it would have been as if they'd lost another father-figure. "I should probably come around some time to watch them."

"We'd love to have you there—I mean, the kids. They'd love to see their mom there." Caleb grinned. "Why don't you join us today?"

Sarah thought about it. "I would—except, it's *Tea for Three* Friday. Louise and Kate will be expecting us." With the boys at soccer, Zoe had been an honorary member of the Tea for Three group.

"Oh, yeah, I forgot about that." Caleb ran a hand through his hair. "Why doesn't Zoe come with us to practice then? She'll love it."

"Oh, no, no—that's too much to ask of you." Sarah shook her head. "That's very kind of you, but I couldn't ask you to do that." Despite practically living together, there was still a sense of formality between them.

"Come on...you know she'd love it." Caleb raised an eyebrow at her.

Sarah found it almost impossible to resist him. She smiled back at him. "I know she would. But I doubt you'll love having to chase after her."

"She'll be running after the ball, just like all the other kids," he pressed. "It'll be great. Tell you what—Zoe can come with us, and then when you finish, you can come join us at the Village Park. You can see them all at play."

Sarah hesitated. "Are you sure?" It sounded like a good idea.

"Yeah—one hundred percent!"

"Okay," Sarah said with a smile. "I'll head on straight to the park after I see the girls."

"Awesome! I'll get the kids ready," Caleb said as he disappeared into the living room.

"Caleb?" Sarah hurried after him through the kitchen doorway and peeked out.

Caleb stood waiting. The shirt he wore hugged him in all the right places, making his chest look all toned and muscled. It was enough to make any woman swoon.

Sarah shook her head—and along with it—her thoughts. "Thanks," she said. "I really appreciate all your help with the children." She reminded herself that Caleb was there for the children, not for her. It was likely that he held no feelings for Sarah in return.

"You got it," Caleb winked and bounded up the stairs. "Kids!"

AFTER MEETING THE GIRLS, Sarah headed straight for the Village Park. She was looking forward to seeing the children...but another part of her was also excited to see Caleb. Sarah bit her lips as she wondered if Caleb had invited her along to see him in action too. Thoughts of Caleb trying to impress her on the field with some fancy soccer footwork thew her off. *Stop it*, she thought to herself and rolled her eyes.

As Sarah walked past the church and through to the soccer field, she saw Philip and smiled.

He waved and called out to her. "Sarah," Philip smiled as he jogged towards her. "How are you?"

"Fine, thanks," Sarah said rather frostily that she'd surprised herself. She knew from Louise that things weren't quite so good between them and feelings of protectiveness came over her.

Philip smiled. "I guess you've heard then," he said.

"I don't know what you mean." Even if Philip was a priest; at the end of the day, her loyalties were to Louise.

"Look," Philip said. "I love Louise—always have, always will. I'm not going anywhere this time. And you can tell her that."

"I'm sure you can tell her that yourself."

"In time."

While Sarah was certain that Philip had no ill intentions towards Louise, something inside her snapped. "What is it with you men? You think you can just take your time—string us along until you're well and ready? And what if you never reach that point? Should we still wait?"

Poor Philip didn't know what had hit him. "Sarah, I would never—"

"I'm sorry, Philip." Sarah shook her head, embarrassed. "I don't know...I'm sorry, I crossed the line."

Philip waved a hand of forgiveness like only a priest could. "Is there anything you'd like to talk about?" he asked.

"I have to..."—Sarah pointed towards the sound of laughing and screaming children—"the kids are playing.

"I don't mind a bit of a walk. I was heading over to see them myself." Philip fell into step with her. "Do you mind?"

Sarah shook her head.

"How have you been?"

It was a question Sarah dreaded every time she saw someone. It was a question she'd come to hate, never knowing how to answer it. "Fine."

"And the children? They must enjoy having Caleb around. He's a fine young man."

It had come as no surprise to Sarah that Caleb's arrival in Carlton Bay had set the town tongues wagging—*lonely widow takes in hot soccer coach, plays happy family*. It was such a cliché and too juicy to ignore. "I'm sure you've heard the stories going around."

"Stories are simply stories."

And then a dam broke. Before she knew it, Sarah was confessing all her thoughts and worries to Philip. "I feel like it's wrong. I shouldn't be entertaining such silly ideas," she said of Caleb.

Philip smiled. "Why not?"

Sarah's eyes widened. "Because Adam just died!"

"*The Lord is near to the brokenhearted and saves the crushed in spirit,*" Philip said. "It's perfectly natural to feel tenderness for someone who loves your children as you do. There is nothing wrong with that. But if I may, Sarah, it seems to me that if you have feelings of doubt, then perhaps it may not be the right time."

Sarah recognized the truth in Philip's words, but it did not lessen her feelings of guilt.

"Perhaps, at this time, it would be a good idea to give yourself some time to process what you are feeling. Time could help you determine if your feelings for Caleb are in fact real."

"Mommy!"

Sarah cleared her throat at the sound of Liam's voice. It had been a long time since he'd called for her. She smoothed her skirt and turned to Philip. "Thank you, Philip" she said. "For everything."

Philip nodded. "You're welcome," he said. "Looks like someone's excited to see you."

"Hi there, my big boy!" Sarah got down on her knees to give Liam a hug, and paid no mind to the cold that seeped through her stockings. Try as she might, Sarah could not remember the last time she'd seen Liam laugh. Adam's death had made him angry and withdrawn, choosing only to talk to Caleb and no one else. Liam had pushed her away, and it made her heart leap to have him hugging her at that moment. Sarah pushed her tears back. "Are you having a good time?"

Liam nodded his sweaty head. "Look at me kick the ball, Mommy—watch me, okay? Watch me!"

Sarah watched as Liam ran towards Caleb and picked up one of the balls off the ground. Her stomach turned when Caleb waved at her, but she managed a smile in return.

Liam set the ball down before running towards it and giving it a kick so strong that it surprised Sarah. He turned back to look if Sarah was watching.

"Sweetheart, that's incredible!" Sarah clapped eagerly.

"Did you see me?" Liam asked as he ran towards her. "Caleb told me that I'm really good at soccer!"

"I saw how you kicked that ball," Sarah said. "Caleb's right, you are very good. I'm so proud of you."

"It's called a soccer ball, Mommy." Liam took Sarah's face with both his hands to make sure she was looking at him. "It's called a soccer ball."

"Do you like soccer?"

Liam nodded. "Uh-huh. Watch me again!" Liam picked the ball up and ran to the center of the field to do it all over again.

Sarah walked over to Caleb, who was flocked by children and their parents saying goodbye. He really was very good with children.

"The kids seem to really enjoy playing," Sarah said after everyone had gone. She looked around for Zoe, who was trying to run after the ball with Noah.

"They're such good sports," Caleb said with a grin. He ran a hand through his hair. "How was your date with the girls?"

"It was nice to see them." It made Sarah feel good to have someone asking after her. It reminded her of how Adam used to ask how her day had gone. "I always have a good time when I see them."

"How's Kate doing?" Caleb asked. "All good with Evan now?"

Sarah twisted her lips. She liked how Caleb knew who her friends were. It was like they shared a secret. "I don't really know yet. Honestly, I'm kinda worried about her."

"I can understand why you'd be worried about her. She's got a good friend in you." Caleb said. "Wanna get out of here?"

Sarah felt a rush run through her body. Yes, she did want to get out of there. She wanted to get out of there with *him*—as if they'd arrived together and were leaving together; as if they were a couple.

"Kids!" Caleb called out. "Liam! Get your brother and sister. It's time to go home."

Sarah watched in awe how Liam quickly leaped into action and knew exactly what he needed to do. "Well, I'll be...what have you done to my children?" she teased.

"They're good kids." Caleb picked up his sports bag while the kids gathered the balls and brought them to him.

BACK AT HOME, SARAH turned the kettle on. "Liam, why don't you go on upstairs and wash your face and your hands?"

Liam ignored her and instead opened the pantry. "I'm hungry."

"Honey, Liam—I asked you to go and wash up before you eat."

Liam shut the pantry door and went to open the fridge.

"Liam," Sarah said firmly. She placed a hand on the fridge and shut the door. "I told you to go—"

"No!"

Sarah stood frozen in surprise as her four-year-old stood with a scowl on his face. Just like that, her happy child had once again switched off. "Liam—"

"No!" Liam covered his ears with his hands before sputtering a series of more "no's".

Caleb came into the kitchen and squatted in front of Liam. "Hey, buddy,"—he took Liam's hands off his ears—"how about you go and wash up like your mom said, while I make us something to eat? Do you want some cheese pockets?"

Liam nodded and ran off upstairs to his room.

Caleb turned to face her. "He's probably just over-tired." He took a box of cheese pockets from the freezer.

"I'd appreciate it if you don't get between me and my son. I'm perfectly capable of getting him to do what needs to be done." Sarah's heart pounded. Flustered, it embarrassed her—angered her—Liam refused her.

Caleb emptied the box of pockets. "He'll come around," he said. "Want one?"

"I'm serious, Caleb! You don't get to come in here and act like you're in charge." Sarah shook with anger.

"Hey, hey, hey." Caleb put the snacks down and put his arms on her shoulders. "What's all this? I'm sorry. I didn't mean to—"

"Caleb, I'm sorry. I—I don't know what came over me." Sarah's tears betrayed her as they flowed down her face. She wiped her face with the back of her hand.

"There's no need for apologies. He'll come around," Caleb pulled her into an embrace. "You'll see."

Sarah weakened in Caleb's arms and allowed herself to melt into him. She rested her cheek on his chest and inhaled his scent, just as she did whenever she hugged Adam.

"Are you okay?" he asked.

Sarah nodded. In his arms—yes, she was okay. In his arms, everything was good. Sarah reached up and around his neck. Sarah's heart lurched into her stomach. *What are you doing?* she asked herself, but she didn't wait for an answer. She tiptoed and brought her lips to his, sealing the small distance that separated them. In that brief moment, Sarah was pacified. She stayed lost in the kiss—not realizing that she was alone in the experience.

Caleb slowly stepped back. "Sarah," he said, "I'm sorry if I've given you the wrong impression."

"What?" Hot blood pumped inside her and rushed to her cheeks. She was burning; she could feel it. "Oh my gosh." Sarah took a step back. "You didn't want that—you didn't want that kiss," she stammered. Sarah covered her face.

"Sarah,"—Caleb took a step forward—"look, it's fine."

What have I done? Her breathing increased. Humiliation filled her. "No, actually, it's not fine!" Her embarrassment turned to rage. "I'm sorry—I can't do this. You need to get out."

"Sarah—"

"Caleb, you need to go. Just go!" Like an angry teenager, Sarah ran to her room and slammed the door shut. *I've never felt so humiliated in my life. What was I thinking? What a disaster.*

Chapter 29

Louise Delaney

It had been a week since Louise saw Philip at the park. He had tried to see her a few times—once at the bookstore and twice at home—and for the most part, Louise had been successful in avoiding him. But every time that she watched him walk away, a familiar hurt ran through her. It was the same pain she'd felt when he left for the seminary and again, the same pain she'd felt when he'd left for overseas service.

They say that time heals all wounds. Age and experience have certainly blessed her with maturity and a good head on her shoulders. Yet there she was...agonizing over a love lost—a love returned.

"I'm leaving," Abby said.

Louise looked up from her cup of coffee to see the teenager standing at the kitchen doorway. As time went by, and without any notice, their relationship had deteriorated and turned in to a stepmother and stepdaughter cliché. It was the first time she'd ever been a stepmother, so Louise was feeling her way through the dark. "Don't you want any breakfast?"

"I'm not hungry," Abby said with her lips in a small pout.

"You can't think on an empty stomach, Abby."

"Then I won't think," she snapped.

Louise looked at her with shock, quickly followed by irritation. "I'm just thinking about you, Abby."

"Oh my gosh! Can you just please stop?"

Louise cradled her coffee. "Stop what?" She wasn't cut out for the riddles and drama of teenagers.

"Just stop nagging me!" Abby huffed and turned on her heels. As one might expect, what followed was the sound of a door slammed shut.

Louise closed her eyes and gritted her teeth, prompting herself to take deep breaths in...and then out. It had become a daily performance in their household, with unwelcome encores two or three times a day. It would be a lie if Louise said she was enjoying having Abby at home. The truth was, she had a mind to send the girl back to her mother.

"I don't think it should be my problem," Louise voiced her concerns to Kate that afternoon at the bookstore. "She's Warren's child—not mine. I don't see why I have to be the one to deal with her teenage tantrums. I've been there, done that, and I don't want any more of it." Her frustration was rife.

"I have noticed that the air's a bit heavy at home right now. Have you spoken to Abby about the way she's been acting?" Kate asked.

Louise leaned her elbow on the counter and rested her chin on her hand. "Of course, I have. You don't think I'd let her just carry on being rude like that."

"What did she say?"

Louise scoffed in an attempt to mimic Abby. "Nothing."

Kate sighed. "I'm sorry you guys are going through this. I'm sure it's just a phase."

"I know it's a phase. But I'm tired. I hardly think I deserve this."

"Would it help if I talk to her?" Kate rubbed her growing belly.

"Be my guest." Louise shrugged. "Right now, I'll take any help I can get. It won't be long before I lose it with her."

Kate smiled sympathetically. "What about Philip? How are things going? Any updates?"

Louise rolled her eyes. She reached her hands behind her waist and stretched her back out. "That's another thing I'm too old for. Now I remember why I never dated after Warren died."

"You're not old!"

"Tell that to my back," Louise groaned. "I need a massage."

"Okay—who are you and what have you done to my best friend?"

Although Louise knew that Kate was joking, what she'd just said had struck a chord. Things were changing so fast. It seemed as if she was losing control of her life and she didn't like it. Not one bit. Louise liked to be in control. She liked knowing who, what, why, and when. Her life at that point was just too full of unanswered questions.

Louise felt her phone vibrate in her pocket at the same time that Kate's phone went off. They looked at each other before checking their respective phones.

The message was from Sarah. *I need tea - or something stronger. Can we all meet tonight?*

Chapter 30

Abby Delaney

Abby hadn't meant to slam the door that morning—or to yell at Louise. She hadn't meant for lots of things to happen, and yet they continued to taunt her at every turn.

It didn't help that school sucked either. She shut her locker door and headed down the hall past the cafeteria. Abby never ate in the cafeteria. Instead, she took her packed lunch to the track field and sat on the bleachers.

During her first week in school, Abby quickly realized she was a sore thumb that stuck out. Everywhere she went, whispers followed. She'd heard so many different versions of her own story, even she was now confused—she was the love child of Mr. Delaney and a prostitute; her mother had sent her away because she was a drug addict; and her favorite yet which deserved an award for creativity...Abby was a runaway who had been saved by the priests of St. Anthony's and given to the lonely and childless owner of the bookstore.

Abby had come to hate Carlton Bay. Sure, it was fancier than where she'd come from, but at the end of the day, everyone was just a sheep in wolves' clothing.

She picked a spot not far from the top bleachers and sat down.

"Haven't you got some other place to be?"

Abby looked up at the top row where a skinny guy with bright purple hair sat about ten feet away from her. "Who? Me?"

The purple-haired guy rolled his eyes. "You see anyone else I could be talking to?"

"I'm just here to have lunch—I'm Abby."

"Don't think I'm going to be your friend just 'cuz you're on your own, newbie," he said.

It was her turn to roll her eyes. "And you think I'm sitting here 'cuz I want you to be my friend? Please—don't flatter yourself." Abby sat down and put her earphones on as she listened to Joni Mitchell's *Both Sides Now*.

The guy nudged Abby from behind.

Abby turned around and took one earphone out. "What?" she asked, annoyed.

"What are you listening to?" he asked.

"Why do you care?" Abby plugged her ear again.

He pulled her earphone off. "Are you always so catty?"

"What's your problem?" Abby yelled.

"I hate my parents. I hate this town. I hate my life," he said. "Take your pick."

Abby scoffed. "Well, someone's a bit *emo*."

"I'm Tobias—but you can call me Shelby."

Abby studied the boy sitting next to her. His skinny face was smooth, almost porcelain like. His purple hair flopped effortlessly to the left of his face. "So, your name is Tobias but I can call you Shelby," Abby repeated what he said.

"Correction—I *want* you to call me Shelby."

"Shelby, huh?" Abby twisted her lips and nodded slowly. "So you want to be a girl?"

"I am a girl—thank you very much," Shelby said. "I'm a *she*, a *her*. I'm a gal and a lady. I'm a Miss and one day in the future, I'll be a Missus," she said theatrically and flipped her hair with a flick of her hand.

Abby enjoyed Shelby's little performance. "Cool," Abby extended a hand. "I'm Abby."

"Oh, I know," Shelby said with a laugh. "So what is it? I'd like it straight from the mare's mouth! Are you the daughter of a prostitute or a runaway saved by Anglican priests? I kinda like the story about you being a runaway. It's got a better spin to it."

Abby grinned. "That's my favorite one too," she said. "So why aren't you at the *caf* with all the plebs?"

Shelby leaned back on her arms and raised her face towards the sun. "Because they're boring and don't deserve my awesome company."

"Or is it because they don't want you there?" Abby chuckled.

"That too," Shelby giggled.

Abby enjoyed talking to Shelby. They'd hit it off instantly—like two peas in a pod. The two girls spent the rest of the lunch period just talking about anything and everything. Conversation came easily between them, and it made Abby feel good to finally have a connection with someone. "I wish I'd met you sooner," Abby said.

"All good things take time, my dear," Shelby said with a smile. "Hey, do you wanna hang out after school?" She stood up as they got ready to head back to class.

"Yeah, for sure." Though Abby tried to downplay her excitement, she was pretty stoked to have found a new friend—never mind that they were both the outcasts of Carlton Bay High.

"I've got Art History for my last period. I'll meet you at the art lab. Do you know where it is?"

Abby knew where it was. It was her favorite subject—one of the few that interested her. "Sounds good. I'll see you there," she said. "I gotta run."

"Hey, Abby," Shelby called after her.

Abby turned around. "Yeah?"

"You never told me what you were listening to."

Abby grinned. "Joni Mitchell."

"Classy," Shelby said with an approving wave as they parted ways.

Chapter 31

Kate Morgan

Seeing Sarah's text message worried Kate. Sarah had done so well moving forward after her husband's death and she was making good progress riding the waves of her depression. But as much as she wanted to be there for her dear friend, Kate knew that Evan wouldn't approve of her going out after work. They'd already argued about Kate keeping her part-time job working for Louise at the bookstore. Going out was bound to cause another big disagreement between them and she didn't want that. But Kate decided she would cross that *Evan-bridge* when she got to it. In the meantime, her friend needed her. Sarah was there for Kate when she had problems—not that the problems had gone away, but she was not going to let anything stop her from being there for Sarah.

They'd all agreed to meet at Louise's place that night. Kate went straight home with Louise. In the car, she typed out a text message for Evan: *I'll be at Louise's place for a bit and will come home after.* And after rereading her message, she hit send and tucked the phone back in her purse.

Back at Louise's house, Sarah opened the front door and let herself in. "I'm so glad you guys are here," Sarah said as she leaned on the door behind her.

"We just got home." Louise said. "Come in—I'll turn the kettle on for us."

"Is everything okay?" Kate asked. She heard her phone ring, but chose to ignore it.

Sarah looked a mess—tired. The bags under her eyes told of tears and lack of sleep. Sarah shook her head. "No," she said, straight to the point.

Kate took Sarah's hand and led her into the kitchen where Louise had taken out three mugs.

"What's going on?" Louise asked.

Sarah sat down and buried her head in her hands. "I kissed Caleb."

Kate sat down next to her. "You kissed Caleb?"

"And?" Louise asked.

"And then h—" Sarah groaned and buried her face in her hands. "I can't. I'm too embarrassed!"

"You know you can tell us anything," Kate said softly, stroking Sarah's hair.

Sarah lifted her head. "He backed away from me," Sarah murmured.

"He backed away from you?" Louise looked up from what she was doing. "Caleb backed away when you kissed him?

"Oh, Sarah," Kate comforted. "Maybe he was just taken by surprise."

"He was." Sarah looked up at them. "He said he was sorry if he'd given me the wrong impression."

"The wrong impression—as in he *doesn't* actually like you?" Louise poured hot water into the mugs.

"I'm sure that's not the reason." Kate heard her phone go off again. "What happened after that?"

"I told him to go away." Sarah covered her face again. "I'm so embarrassed! I thought he liked me. I thought we had a mutual thing. How could I have gotten this so wrong?"

"Look," Louise said, "I'm sure it's all a misunderstanding—"

"On my part, yes!" Sarah cried. "*He* didn't misunderstand anything. It was all me!"

Kate began to speak but was interrupted by a loud banging on the door.

"What on earth..." Louise stood up.

A shiver ran through Kate. Following Louise to the door, a part of her just knew it would be Evan banging at the door.

"For goodness' sake, what's gotten into you?" Louise said when she opened the front door.

"Where is she?" It was Evan's voice.

Kate grabbed her belongings and quickly went to Louise's side. "I'm so sorry Louise. I should go."

"Kate," Louise placed a hand on her arm.

"No,"—Kate stopped her—"this is my fault. I'm sorry."

"Damn right, it's your fault!" Evan shouted. "What the hell were you thinking?"

"Evan, please—not in front of my friends." Kate took his arm. "Let's go."

Evan glared at Louise. "This is all your fault!" he pointed at her. "You've been living alone for too long, you ain't got no respect for men!"

"I beg your pardon!" Louise's voice shook.

"That's right! You should be begging for pardon!" Evan spat. He pulled Kate by the arm and dragged her across the street.

"Evan!" Louise called out. "Evan if you so much as hurt her, I swear to you, I will—"

That was all that Kate had heard of what Louise was saying. Evan pulled her into the house and slammed the door shut.

He grabbed her by the shoulders and yelled at her, his face just inches away from hers. "What have I told you about going out after work?"

"Sarah needed to talk. And I was just across the road, Evan. What's the big deal?" Kate tried to reason with him. "You could have just asked me to come home."

"I called your phone several times, and you didn't answer."

"I'm sorry—like I said, Sarah needed us."

Evan pushed her against the wall and wrapped his large fingers around her neck. "I need you, Kate. It's me you should be thinking of!"

Kate grasped at his hands around her neck. She felt Evan's spit on her face as he yelled at her. The smell of alcohol was strong in his breath. His bulging eyes frightened her. "Stop it, Evan. You've been drinking again. You're scaring me."

"You should be scared! I have told you time and time again. You forget where your place is." And without any warning, Evan slapped her across the face.

Kate instinctively raised her arm up to defend herself and used the other hand to cover her baby bump. She leaned against the wall and shrunk, cowering to protect herself from the blows that followed. She didn't know how long it lasted. It could have been one minute. It could have been ten. It could have been one hour. All she could think about was how to protect her baby.

"Evan Morgan!" Kate heard a yell at the door followed by loud knocks. "Evan Morgan, it's Sheriff Jones, open the door!"

Evan released his grip on Kate and spat on the floor as he took a step back from her.

Kate remained on the floor, and before she knew it, Sheriff Jones and his men had pushed their way in through the front door. Kate looked up and cried with relief when she saw Louise and Sarah.

Summer

"Do what you feel in your heart to be right – for you'll be criticized anyway."

~Eleanor Roosevelt

Chapter 32

Sarah Gardner

Sarah couldn't bring herself to send Caleb away. The kids loved him and she couldn't let them lose another person who bore such influence on them—particularly, Liam. It would have devastated him. Instead, she took Louise and Kate's suggestion of seeing a therapist. *"There's more that you need to work through,"* they had said. *"It's not just about having feelings for Caleb."*

So there she sat, on a beautiful Wednesday morning, waiting for her therapist, Megan Rice, LPC. Together, they'd agreed that Sarah was on a journey—a journey to heal and grow through her grief by taking positive steps. In her eagerness to find her way back to her old self, Sarah memorized that line and hung on to every hope it gave. *"I need to heal and grow through my grief,"* she repeated to herself every morning.

"Sarah?"

Sarah looked up from the magazine she'd been browsing through in the waiting room. She acknowledged Megan and stood up following her into the room where she'd shared all her secrets—at first, with great hesitation; but as the weeks progressed, Sarah learned to trust Megan.

There was something about the way the room never changed that eased Sarah. It was clean and crisp. Everything was organized—a place for everything and everything in its place. The flowers on the coffee table never seemed to wilt; and if they did, Sarah was grateful that Megan could always get the exact same arrangement, week after week. To Sarah, it made things seem stable...dependable. A part of her took comfort in knowing that no matter what might happen during the week, when she'd return to Megan's office, everything would still be the same.

"How are you feeling today, Sarah?" Megan smiled when she spoke. She always smiled. It wasn't a big in-your-face smile. It was sweet. A small smile that said, *go ahead, Sarah, speak, and I will listen.*

So that's what Sarah did. She poured her heart out. "I'm fine—no, I think I'm better than fine."

"That's good. Tell me more."

Sarah leaned back into the sofa and stared at the flowers for a moment. "Father's Day is in two days," she said.

"It is." Megan nodded. "How does that make you feel?"

"Well..." Sarah glanced around the room, thankful that everything was where it should be. "This is going to be the first one without Adam."

Megan sat with her knees together and her ankles crossed. "There will be a lot of firsts to come for both you and the children."

"True. There was our first Christmas. Then the first New Year's, the first Valentine's day. Even Mother's Day was a first—and that didn't go by without my anxieties rising. When does it stop?"

"Do you want it to stop?"

Did she? Sarah panicked, suddenly unsure. If it all stopped, did it mean that Adam no longer mattered to her?

"It's okay to be anxious. You've been through a lot. And these things take time," Megan said.

Sarah grabbed the edge of her skirt and twisted it around her finger. "What if it comes to the point where I no longer get anxious?"

"What's wrong with that?"

"I don't want to stop caring."

"Do you think being less anxious means you care less?" Megan tilted her head ever so slightly. "And what about your feelings for Caleb?"

Sarah bit her bottom lip. She did have feelings for Caleb, but she just couldn't understand them. Sarah shook her head. "I try to act as normally as possible around him."

"So you still have feelings for him?"

Is she judging me? Sarah thought. "Are you judging me?" Sarah quickly caught herself. "I'm sorry," she said before Megan could answer. "That was stupid of me. I know you're not judging me."

Megan smiled. *Go ahead, Sarah, talk and I will listen.*

"I think I still have feelings for him." Sarah stressed the word 'think'. Something about it felt wrong to her, but she wanted to be completely honest with Megan—no, with herself. She wanted to be completely honest with herself. "Sometimes, I wonder if I really do have feelings for him...or if I'm romanticizing his presence. I love the way he loves the children." Sarah smiled to herself.

Megan nodded. "It's perfectly normal to develop feelings for someone who cares for those you love."

That was what Philip had told her as well. Sarah opened her mouth to speak, but when a realization came to her. "What if..."—she hesitated— "what if I love him because he loves the children?"

"Do you think that's possible?"

"What? That I might have feelings for him just because he loves my kids?"

Megan nodded.

Sarah looked out the panoramic window behind Megan. Beyond the shine of the glass, the sky was clear. "I don't know."

"Would you be okay with just a friendly relationship with Caleb?"

She shrugged. "I guess—I mean, that's what we are now isn't it?"

"Not if you have feelings for him," Megan said. "And if those feelings are unrequited, the next question is—how healthy is it for you to be sharing a home with someone who doesn't reciprocate your feelings for them?"

"Are you suggesting I kick him out?"

Megan shook her head. "What you do next is your decision, Sarah. I'm merely posing a question."

Sarah placed a hand to her racing heart. Her palms grew cold and clammy.

"Can you see a future without Caleb in it?"

"I'm not sure." Sarah bit her bottom lip.

"You told me earlier that you couldn't bring yourself to ask him to leave because you were afraid of what it might to do the children."

Sarah nodded. "They're very close to him. Losing him would be very hard on them."

"Is it the children that you're afraid for? Or is it yourself?" Megan let the question hang in the air. "Is it possible that it is *you* that is afraid of being without him?"

"Am I afraid of losing—no, of course not! It's the children I'm worried about!" The question confronted Sarah as she stammered for a response.

Megan listened, her elbows on either side of the armchair.

"I just—I don't know—I mean..." Sarah could not find the right words to say.

"There's only one way to find out," Megan said.

"That's easy for you to say." Sarah crossed her legs. "It's easy for people to say things, especially when they're not the ones in the thick of things."

"I know it's hard, Sarah. That's why I'm here to help you—remember, it's a journey towards healing. And it starts by taking those small but positive steps."

Sarah began to resent how calm Megan was. She was always calm—and all-knowing. Sarah could feel it grating her against the grain. She shook her leg anxiously.

"But there's no rush," Megan continued. "This is a safe place. Here, we can examine and question and consider things...without judgement, without fear."

"So this is all about kicking Caleb out?" Her anger was rising. Sarah hated how calm everyone was—everyone except Sarah herself. Louise had tons of surprises thrown at her, and yet she was still a vision of perfection. And Kate...Sarah could not even begin to imagine what Kate was going through, and yet there she was, always there for everyone else.

"Not at all. Only you know what needs to be done—whether it's waiting to see if a relationship with Caleb is really what you want, or you simply move on without him." Megan sat back in her chair.

"It's not that simple!" Sarah surprised herself. She sounded so whiny.

"This is not about Caleb, Sarah. It's about you."

Sarah sighed and covered her face with her hands. "You're right." Megan was always right. She took a deep breath in and sighed a heavy sigh.

They'd ended the session at that point. Megan had given Sarah some homework to think about. *"Next week, I want you to answer this question,"* Megan had said. *"Who is Caleb to you?"*

THE NEXT EVENING, SARAH told Caleb he had to go.

"I don't understand," Caleb said.

It took all of her strength to keep from reaching out and holding him. She had wanted to tell him that she didn't want him to go. But Sarah knew she needed to. She'd been swimming in a giant pool of confusion, and she desperately needed to come up for air. "I need some space, Caleb."

"Was it because of—"

Sarah knew what he was going to say and stopped him before he could. "This is all on me, Caleb." She said. "I need to find myself—to find the mother I know I am. I need to get a job and to learn how to stand on my own two feet."

Caleb nodded.

"Will you be okay?" Of course, she knew he'd be okay. Caleb was an adult. It was her that was acting like a child.

"Yeah," he said. "Yeah, of course."

"Take as much time as you need," she added.

"No, you're right. I should get back out there too," Caleb said with a laugh. "I've gotten so used to staying with you and the kids," he said. "Have you already told the kids?"

She hadn't. Sarah wanted to kick herself. She hadn't even thought about what to tell the children. "I'll tell them tomorrow."

"Okay," Caleb said. "Don't forget—soccer every Friday afternoon at the park. Zoe likes strawberry yogurt now, Noah needs to get a new pair of shoes, and Liam starts preschool in September. You need to get him enrolled."

"What'll I do without you?" Sarah asked with a smile. And she meant it, too.

"I think it might be the other way around." Caleb laughed the laugh that Sarah had grown so fond of. "What would *I* do without you guys?

"We can make a pact," Sarah joked. "If we're both still lost and single in ten years, we should just give up and get together."

Caleb laughed. "I should start writing my vows then."

Sarah was grateful that they were able to laugh about it. But she knew deep down...when darkness falls and the house grows quiet, that was when it would hit her. That was when it would be clear...she was alone.

Chapter 33

Louise Delaney

"So you asked him to leave?" Louise asked Sarah as she poured some hot water into three mugs. It was after 8:00pm. Their *tea for three* sessions had become more spontaneous—as and when needed—hinting at how close the three women had become; each one dropping whatever they might've been doing to be there for a friend in need.

Sarah nodded. Anxiety dotted her face. "Do you think I did the right thing?"

"You do *you*, darling! You do whatever is best for you and the children." Louise sat down at the kitchen table and called out to Kate. "Tea's ready, Kate."

"I'm here," Kate sang as she joined them at the table, supporting her belly with a hand. Kate had moved back in with Louise after the alarming incident with Evan. "What did I miss?"

"She's asked Caleb to leave," Louise said, nodding in Sarah's direction.

"Oh dear..." Kate took a sip of her tea. "What did he say?"

Sarah sighed. "He said he understood and that he'd be okay."

"Understood what? What reason did you give him?" Louise asked when suddenly the front door slammed shut, startling the three women. "Abby?" Louise called out. "Is that you?"

Silence.

"Abby?"

"Yes, it's me," Abby answered, her voice littered with impatience. "Like—are you expecting the Queen of England or something?"

Louise brought a hand to her mouth and shook her head. "Can you please come into the kitchen?"

"I'm not hungry!" Abby yelled.

Louise breathed in deeply. "Abby, please come into the kitchen—it is not a request." Abby's disrespect felt like a slap in the face, and it embarrassed her that her friends had to witness it.

Some heavy footsteps later, Abby stood in the kitchen's doorway. "What?" she asked as if she'd been terribly inconvenienced.

"It's very late," Louise said. "Is everything okay?"

"Yeah, why?" Abby leaned a shoulder against the door frame.

"Well, I was worried about you." Louise tried again.

"Not worried enough to call the sheriff though, were you?"

"Mind your tone with me, Abby," Louise warned. "Can you at least say hi to Sarah and Kate?" Every day with Abby had become a struggle.

"How are you, Abby?" Sarah asked.

"Fine," Abby replied flatly, refusing to give any more than she was asked.

"How'd it go at drama?" The only person that Abby actually got along with was Kate, so Louise was glad to have her around. Without Kate to keep the peace, who knows what Louise might have already done?

Abby shrugged and let her arms hang limply at her sides. "Dumb, as expected."

"It's all gonna be fine," Kate said. "You'll see!"

"Yeah," Abby raised her eyebrows and turned on her heels, leaving without another word.

Weary, Louise massaged her temples and sighed. "I do not know what is wrong with that girl. She's been so disrespectful. There are days when all I want to do is to gouge her rolling eyes out. My patience has well and truly worn thin."

"It's just a phase," Kate said, placing a hand over Louise's.

"You can say that—she's nice to you," Louise gave a weak smile. "I think I'm too old for this." It was unfair that Louise had to deal with another teenager's moods. She's been there and done that. Her relationship with Madison was, at the best of times, rocky. And yet, there she was doing it all over again. "Have you picked up any clues as to why she's been so horrible these last few months?"

Kate drew her eyebrows together and shook her head. "No, sorry. But don't worry. She'll come around."

"Well, she'd better come around before I lose my patience altogether." Louise sat up straight and adjusted her shirt. "Sorry, Sarah—back to Caleb, where are we at with him now?"

Sarah smiled. "No, it's okay. It's my fault. I'm taking up your family time."

"If that's family time, then I'm happy to trade it in for something else," Louise joked. "We're here to talk about this thing with Caleb. Go on," she encouraged Sarah.

Sarah gazed at her tea. "Well, after I told him to go, I also told him to take all the time he needs."

"Hmm...wouldn't that send mixed messages?" Kate asked.

"Maybe, I don't know. I mean...I know it's not easy to find another place to stay. And he's got his new job, so it's not like going back to Willow Oaks is an option for him."

"Everything is an option, my dear," Louise said. "It's up to him to use whatever option is available to him."

"I guess," Sarah sighed heavily. "I think he'll want to stay though—to be near the kids."

"He's quite attached to them, isn't he?" Kate noted.

"Yes, I noticed that too," Louise said. "What's that about?"

"What do you mean?" Sarah asked.

"Well—oh, look, I don't know—this is his first time nannying, isn't it?" Louise ran a hand over her fringe, pushing it to one side.

Sarah nodded. "Yes, I think so. But he's always worked with kids. He used to be a PE teacher and a soccer coach. Pretty much the same as what he's doing now."

"Did he ever tell you why he went back home?" Kate sipped her tea. "To Willow Oaks, I mean."

"No, I don't think so." Sarah paused. "Come to think of it, I'm not sure that I asked him about that."

"Fair enough." Louise leaned back and rubbed her arms absently. The truth was, her mind was still on Abby and the complete turnaround in her behavior. There had to be something on the girl's mind.

"You're still thinking about Abby, aren't you?" Sarah asked.

Louise smiled. "Is it that obvious?"

"It's new to you and it's new to her. There are bound to be a few ripples here and there." Sarah finished off the rest of her tea.

"We've had more than just a few ripples. They've been more strong undercurrents and tidal waves. I'm worried about the tsunami!" Resentment had been churning within Louise. It was hard to love someone who was distant and disrespectful. "Back in my day, if I ever mouthed off like that to my mother—I tell you—I'd be lucky if all I got was the back of a wooden spoon."

"Don't worry," Kate said. "I'll check in with her tomorrow. I'm sure it's nothing—she's just being a teenager."

"Thanks, Kate." Louise's shoulders were slumped, defeated by a teenager. "She listens to you."

"It's probably just because I'm closer to her age," Kate said.

"You are, aren't you?" Louise laughed. "Ah...to be young once more."

"Would you want that?" Sarah asked. "To be young again?"

"Goodness, no," Louise laughed. "But...youth *is* wasted on the young."

Chapter 34

Kate Morgan

Kate felt for Louise. She knew how much Louise was finding it difficult, so she played middleman between the two and somehow was able to bridge the gap between them. It was, after all, an unusual situation that Louise was in. Given the circumstances, caring for Abby and taking her in permanently could not have been an easy decision to make. But as Kate had learned in the last year, Louise had a big heart.

"How are you holding up?" Louise asked, motioning to Kate's belly.

Kate groaned. "I've been so uncomfortable. I honestly don't know how women do it more than once—I mean, like, pregnancies. I keep peeing and just can't get a full night's sleep." She rubbed her sleepy eyes.

Louise smiled. "You're not too far away now."

That was true. Kate wasn't far from her due date. Three weeks to go. She'd been to see her OB-GYN and everything was going well, the doctor had said.

"Are you excited?" Sarah asked, as if knowing all the happy secrets that motherhood had in store for her.

"I think so," Kate bit her bottom lip and smiled. The truth was, things have changed so quickly in the last few months that Kate hadn't really had time to consider how she was feeling. Evan hadn't been in touch since he was charged with domestic violence, and that was probably for the best. She'd heard from the sheriff that he was due to appear in court in just a few weeks' time.

"You think so?" Louise echoed. "Darling, this is going to be a wonderful time. Just you wait and see. You're going to be a great mother."

"What if,"—Kate hesitated—"what if I'm not a good mother? I mean, what if this baby's getting the short end of the stick?"

"Don't start doubting yourself as a mother before you'd even gotten a chance to be one," Sarah said. "You'll be great. You can't mess it up any more than I have this year, I can tell you that much!" Elbow on the table, Sarah rested her chin on the palm of her hand.

"No, you're being too hard on yourself." It was Kate's turn to comfort Sarah. "You've had so much happen—it's a lot for one person."

"Oh, you both are being hard on yourselves," Louise said. "Kate, just look at the way you are with Abby—how you connect with her and understand her. You will be a great mother. And Sarah, you *are* a good mother. You've experienced a great trauma. It's not every day that a wife finds their husband dead in bed—pardon the bluntness. You are allowed to fail. You don't have to be strong all the time. You will find yourself again. In the meantime, you've got us. Caleb or no Caleb, you are not alone."

Among the three of them, Louise was the wise one. Sarah was the maternal one, and Kate was the young one. Without them, Kate didn't know what she would have done—how she would have gotten through the last year.

"How are things with Mark?" Sarah asked.

"I see him at the bookstore," Kate said. "We talk and he brings me little pastries sometimes."

"That's so sweet," Sarah said dreamily.

Kate shook her head. "But we're not going to go further than where we're at now. I told him that the baby is my priority, and I'm not looking for a relationship."

Sarah nodded. "That's probably wise."

"Mm, yes, I agree," Louise said. "What did he say?"

"He said he understood, and that he wasn't rushing me or anything."

"I wish I had the presence of mind to...to focus. Just focus." Sarah poured herself a drink of water.

"You're focusing now," Louise said. "There's no use crying over spilled milk. Do you want more tea?"

Sarah shook her head. "No, thanks."

"I could be wrong," Kate said, "but I believe there's no right or wrong way to grieve. Everyone grieves in their own way.

Louise agreed. "That's right."

"Adam must be rolling in his grave because of all the stupid things I've done lately." Sarah buried her face in her hands. "I'm so embarrassed."

"Why be embarrassed? So you fell for Caleb—so what?" Louise crossed her arms over her chest.

"I should have been focusing on the children—not the manny."

"I may be wrong, but the way I see it—we do whatever we need to do to get by. I have learned that the heart has its own compass and it will point us in the right direction," Kate said.

"Well, there's some wise for words for all of us right there," Louise said.

Kate finished the rest of tea. "While it may not always make sense, it'll all reveal itself in the end."

Kate had spent many nights awake, ruminating over how she'd come to be in a country where she knew no one. How she ended up married to an abusive alcoholic, and how she was now living in a friend's bedroom. It was as if all the events of her life had conspired to push her to the ground—face first. But she believed in love. She believed in the heart. And right now, her heart's compass pointed to the baby in her belly. Right there and then, Kate decided that her baby was going to get every bit of love Kate had in her heart. And she had plenty of love to give for the both of them.

Chapter 35

Abby Delaney

The next morning, Abby woke up and reached for her phone. She sat up against the headboard and typed out a text to Shelby. "*H8 myself. Lyf sux.*" She hit the send button and then tossed her phone on the bed. It was Saturday and she didn't need to be anywhere. Abby climbed out of bed to grab a book out of her schoolbag. She'd borrowed a new book from the school library about a girl who was born to drug addicts in a dystopian future. It didn't seem too farfetched, given how she'd come into the world herself.

Her phone beeped. It was Shelby. "*Can't b worse than mine. Wot r u doing 2day?*"

"*Blobbing.*" Abby typed.

"*Wanna hang?*"

As much as she hated her life, Abby did admit that things have been better since she'd met Shelby. The days didn't drag on as long as they used to. And the two of them really had a lot in common. "*Sure.*"

"*Meet at village park. Same as last.*"

They'd spent the last few weekends walking around town, just doing their own thing. Their favorite place to hang out in was at the Village Park, next to the cemetery. It was quiet and they could chat about whatever they wanted to without anyone hassling them.

Abby showered and dressed, putting on a pair of black jeans, a black singlet, and a black and white plaid boyfriend-shirt. With her hair slightly damp, Abby put on her black Converse Chucks and ran down the stairs.

"Abby?"

Abby stopped and threw her head back. "Yeah?"

"Come and join us for breakfast," Louise said from the kitchen.

"I'm not hungry."

"That's what you keep saying—get your butt in here right now, please."

Abby rolled her eyes and stomped to the kitchen. "What?"

"And good morning to you too," Louise said cheerily.

"Morning, Abs," Kate said. "Where are you off to?"

"Shelby and I are just going to hang out."

"You've grown quite close to this girl, haven't you?" Louise said. "When are we going to meet Shelby?"

"As if," Abby took a glass from the cupboard and filled it with orange juice.

"What do you mean, as if?" Louise asked.

The thing with Louise was that she always tries so hard—like she needs to be everyone's hero. She was always so proper and fancy, but Abby was willing to bet everything that she wasn't all that on the inside. "Why do you care?"

"Abby..." Kate said. "That's not nice. Don't talk to your mother like that."

"She's not my mother," Abby said and swiftly turned on her heels.

"Thank goodness for that!" Louise yelled from the kitchen.

"I'M SICK OF LOUISE always pretending as if she cares about me," Abby complained to Shelby at the cemetery. "Like, honestly, everyone thinks she's so righteous and all that—taking in her husband's bastard child—but really, she's not."

"At least she pretends to even care. My parents don't even bother pretending." Shelby leaned against the headstone of one Frank Underwood. "Dude, check this out," she said. "This guy was totally born in 1927. I wonder what that was like."

"Oh my gosh, and look," Abby said after getting a closer look at the headstone. "He was born on March eighteenth and died on March eighteenth."

"How creepy is that, right?"

"What year would you have wanted to live in?" Abby asked as she leaned against Frank's headstone next to Shelby. "Like, I totally want to wear the clothes from, like, the eighteenth century."

"Yeah, that would so cool. Hey, did you guys learn about Henry the eighth in history yet?" Shelby pulled out a lollipop from her bag and handed one to Abby.

Abby took the lollipop and shook her head. "No, but I watched it on Netflix."

"Oh my gosh, do you have Netflix? I totally wish my parents would get it. They're just so horrible," Shelby complained. "Anyway, so this guy Henry, he gets married like six times."

"Yeah and he just kills them off when he doesn't want to be with them anymore."

"He's so gross!"

Abby unwrapped the lollipop and put it in her mouth. "Hey, Louise asked when she's going to get to meet you. Maybe you can come hang at the house and we can watch some Netflix."

Shelby wrinkled her face. "I don't think parents like me very much."

"Eew, she's *not* my mom."

"But still—she's your stepmom. I mean, even *my* parents hate me."

"So what?" Abby said. "And besides, Louise likes everyone."

"Not when she sees my purple hair or that I'm a *she* in a *he's* body."

Abby sat upright. "I told you life sucks."

Shelby laid down on the grass. "Do you know he beat me one day? He said it would straighten me out."

"Oh my gosh, really? What did your mom do?"

"What she always does," Shelby said. "She turned a blind eye. She pretends she doesn't know what's happening. What a fake!"

"That's so uncool. You should just come and live with us."

"Yeah, right..."

"Louise takes, like, all the strays she can find," Abby said. "I mean—look at me!"

Shelby laughed along with Abby. "We're the strays of Carlton Bay. Hey,"—Shelby held her pinkie out—"stray sisters!"

Abby wrapped her own pinkie around Shelby's. "Stray sisters!"

"Forever?"

Abby liked how she could be herself with Shelby. No pretending, nothing. Abby could just be...Abby. "Forever."

Chapter 36

Sarah Gardner

The next Wednesday came around quickly for Sarah. In the morning, she went to see her therapist and told her that she had asked Caleb to move out. They both agreed that it was for the best. *"It will be a new type of grief all over again,"* Megan warned. *"So I want you to be aware of it."* Megan was right. It was a different kind of grief and it blind-sided Sarah.

When Caleb finally told her that he'd found another place to stay, it hit Sarah like a speeding truck. She'd been pottering around Zoe's room, tidying the closet and drawers while the kids napped, when he came and told her. "That's good news, Caleb," Sarah said. She dared not look at him and kept fixed on filling up Zoe's diaper drawer.

"Yeah, it was perfect timing, really," Caleb whispered, careful not to wake Zoe. "The roommate of one of the teachers at the school had moved out—got a job in Portland."

On one hand, Sarah was glad that Caleb had found a place to stay and wouldn't need to leave town. On the other, she was saddened. Although she was the one that asked him to leave, it felt like the remaining part of her heart had been ripped out from inside her. It almost felt like they were separating—not that they were in any kind of romantic relationship, of course.

Sarah scolded herself for even thinking that way. Her thoughts were all over the place. She hardly recognized herself. She'd always been level-headed...and smart. But Adam's death had taken its toll on her. Not that it was Adam's fault.

"When are you moving?"

"I was thinking tonight. I've finished my class and there's no soccer practice, so I might as well."

Sarah didn't say anything.

"Is that okay with you?"

"Yes, of course. Why wouldn't it be?" Sarah held a breath in. *Because I would be lost without you. Because I'm scared. Because I'm afraid to be alone. Because, Caleb! Because.*

"Oh, good—okay. I thought maybe we should talk to the kids first."

He always put the kids first. He was so good at that. "You'll make a great father someday, Caleb," Sarah said absentmindedly.

He didn't acknowledge what she said. Instead, Caleb excused himself. "I'd better get packing."

"Sure, okay," she said. And when Caleb shut the door behind him, Sarah covered her face with one of Zoe's dresses and cried into it.

And then Zoe cried.

Sarah turned to see her sweet girl sitting up in bed, her hair a mess. She sat down and lifted Zoe on to her lap. "There, there," she soothed. "Mommy's here." And she intended to be. Sarah intended to be present for her children. "Mommy's here."

Fall

"For this child I prayed and the Lord has granted the desires of my heart."

~1 Samuel 1:27

Chapter 37

Kate Morgan

The baby arrived two weeks early. Kate had woken to the sound of her own moans. She clutched her belly as pain gripped her stomach. She must have been groaning loudly because before long, Louise was kneeling by her bedside.

"It's time," Louise said, gently brushing Kate's hair off her face. "I'll call the ambulance."

"Is everything okay?" Abby stood in her pajamas, her brows wrinkled, her face dotted with worry. "Is Kate going to be okay?"

"She's fine, sweetheart. The ambulance will be here shortly. Why don't you go open the front door for them?"

Abby did as she was told.

"Don't leave me," Kate pleaded with Louise.

"I'm right here," Louise said. "I'm not going anywhere."

KATE COULDN'T BELIEVE it. She was convinced she was going to die. But there she was...holding her baby in her arms. *Her* baby! A part of her wished that she could share the moment with Evan, but that was impossible. There was no way she would ever expose her son to such violence. Not now, not ever.

Staring at her sleeping son, it was as if all the pain she'd gone through had magically slipped away. As Kate smoothed his cheek with her finger, she felt an immense and overwhelming love for him.

Kate put a hand over her stomach. She never imagined that she would one day give birth without a husband or even her parents by her side. She was grateful to have Sarah and Louise with her. Kate felt their love. They loved her for nothing else but her friendship.

"You did so well, honey," Sarah said as she squeezed Kate's hand. "He's just gorgeous. May I?"

"Thanks for being here," Kate said softly, handing Sarah the baby. "Where are the kids?"

"Hi, there, buddy," Sarah cooed when the baby was in her arms. "I'm your auntie Sarah."

"Abby's got the little ones. They're in the family waiting room," Louise said. "Is there anything you want? An extra pillow? A drink, maybe?"

Louise...God bless Louise. She really was a true friend. She'd opened her home to Kate and had never once asked for anything in return. "No, thank you," Kate said. "I'm just glad you're both here."

"Have we got a name yet?" Sarah asked.

Kate looked at her friends as they cooed and fussed over her son. She was tired, but her heart was full. Everyone she loved was in one room. "If it's okay with you, Sarah,"—Kate reached for her friend's hand—"I'd like to name him Adam."

"Adam?" Sarah echoed. She looked surprised.

"It was Adam that brought you into my life," Kate said. "You and Louise. And you girls are the best thing that's ever happened to me." Kate's eyes welled up.

"Oh, Kate, that's lovely." Sarah held one hand to her chest.

"Adam," Louise tested the name out as she held the baby close to her. "Hi Adam," she peered at the baby in her arms. "Adam. Yes, he looks like an Adam." Louise said as she looked up at Kate and Sarah and smiled. "I like it."

"I like it too," Sarah beamed.

"Before I forget,"—Kate leaned into her pillow. Tired, she closed her eyes—"I wanted to tell you how much I love you guys. I am so lucky to have you as my best friends."

"We love you too. Now, get some rest, kiddo," Louise said. "You're going to need it."

"Hi Adam," Kate heard Sarah whisper before falling asleep.

Chapter 38

Sarah Gardner

The last few weeks without Caleb had been hard on Sarah. But she was determined to get back on her feet—to remember who she was before and who she'd like to become.

That morning, she woke with the sun on her face. She'd conditioned herself to getting up earlier each day, giving herself time to enjoy a cup of coffee before the kids woke. The new routine had helped her get through the day. The quiet of the morning and the time alone provided her with a sense of peace and control.

As she turned the kettle on, Sarah made a mental note to get more coffee. Instant coffee was all she could muster. The trouble of preparing a filter coffee each morning was still a daunting task. But even so, she considered it good progress that she was even able to enjoy a daily dose of caffeine.

Sarah had also started writing in a journal. Megan, her therapist, suggested she should write her thoughts and feelings down on paper—the things that happened, things she come across, and how she felt about them. She opened the kitchen drawer where she kept the notebook and took it out.

Sarah ran her fingers along its spine as it reminded her of the *Moleskine* journal she'd gotten for Adam...the one he'd written his funeral plans in. Running her fingers over it, she smiled. With each new day that came, Sarah could feel a bit of her old self coming back.

As she sat down with her coffee and journal, she looked out the window. She had managed to spend some time in the garden over the weekend and was surprised at how much she'd missed it.

It all started when she noticed the azaleas in the garden. She couldn't recall what the blooms had looked like over spring and summer; but it looked like they had stopped flowering and it was time to prune them. Then she noticed she had also ignored her precious dahlias. After dead-heading the dahlias in an attempt to resuscitate them, Sarah turned to weeding. Before she knew it, the weekend had gone by—like the wind.

And now, fall was in the air. The leaves on the trees had begun to turn shades of red and orange. It was a beautiful time of year. Another season passed and a new one came along. Sarah smiled as she thought of a second chance.

She opened her journal and click her pen open.

"What jobs can I do?" she wondered aloud and clicked her tongue as she thought of her skills.

She wrote the options down as the thoughts came to her—not that the thoughts flowed freely. Sarah found herself stuck on number three on her list.

1. Receptionist

2. Waitress - ??
3. ~~Bookkeeper~~

She left number three blank because she didn't know what else she could do. Adam was the one who'd worked and had a career. She was the one who stayed home to raise the children, just as they'd planned.

Sarah rubbed the back of her neck. It worried her to think she had no skills; nothing to fall back on. Adam's life insurance was helpful for the family, but she needed to be realistic. They still had their whole lives ahead of them—she and the children—and the money was not going to last forever. She put a hand to her stomach and bent over. *Breathe.*

"Mommy?"

Sarah looked up to find Noah standing in front of her, his hair ruffled by sleep. "Hi honey," she said, lifting him on to her lap. "You're up early." Sarah kissed his head and closed her eyes. At almost four years old, she was grateful that Noah still let her hug and kiss him. She inhaled his scent and smiled.

"Mommy, where's Liam?" Noah asked.

"He's still asleep, darling. It's still quite early." Sarah combed his hair with her fingers and kissed his forehead. "Do you want me to bring you back up to your bedroom?"

Noah nodded.

Sarah smiled when she felt his little arms around her neck. She'd once read somewhere that the most precious jewels a mother could ever have around her neck are the arms of their children. At that very moment, it was her truth.

She carried Noah in her arms and held him close. *Soon,* she thought, *he would be too heavy to carry. In time, he would not want me to carry him. And then, the time will come, when I will not have the strength, and he may have to carry me.*

With Noah in her arms, Sarah walked slowly up the stairs. She placed a hand under his t-shirt and stroked his warm back. They approached his bedroom door and Sarah pushed it open. "Here we are, my love-bug," she whispered sweetly into his ear.

Walking straight towards his bed, she gently laid him down and pulled the sheets over him. "Go back to sleep." Sarah kissed the tip of Noah's nose as he closed his eyes.

Sarah pushed herself up from Noah's bed, and when she turned around to check on Liam, she let out a gasp. "Liam?" His bed was empty.

Sarah felt the blood drain from her face and her heart banged against the walls of her chest.

She ran to the bathroom and opened the door. "Liam!" And when she saw he wasn't there; she ran to Zoe's room. "Liam!"

Zoe, who'd been sleeping, woke to a start and wailed, adding to the panic in the air.

Sarah let out a cry—whispers of panic slipped from her lips.

"See, Mommy?" Sarah turned around, startled to find Noah standing in the hall. "I told you Liam wasn't there."

"No, no, no," Sarah said over and over, as she ran down the stairs. "Liam!" She looked in the living room, the kitchen, the garden. She even looked in the garage which was usually locked. This time, he was really missing. "Liam!"

Sarah ran back inside. She picked up the phone and called the sheriff's office. "It's my son—I can't find my son!"

SARAH CLUTCHED ON TO Noah and Zoe with all of her strength. Zoe wriggled and screamed to free herself, but Sarah refused to let either of them out of her sight.

"What happened?" Louise burst through the door just minutes after Sarah had phoned her.

"Sarah! Are you okay?" Kate followed quickly behind her with the baby and Abby.

"I don't know where he is," Sarah sobbed. "I don't know where he is!"

"Abby?" Louise turned to her stepdaughter.

"Yes?"

"Can you take the children while we make a plan?" Louise took Zoe and handed her to Abby.

Abby nodded. "Come on, Noah," she said, holding her hand out.

"He was right there," Sarah said. "He was in bed—asleep!" Sarah's voice trembled as Louise took her in her arms. Her worst fear had come true. She had lost one of her children. "He was just in his room, Louise. He was supposed to be asleep!" Sarah repeatedly stomped her foot, desperate.

"When did you last see him?" Kate asked.

Sarah wiped her face with the back of her hand. "I woke up in the middle of the night. Zoe cried, and I gave her a bottle. And then I checked on the boys. They were both there! I swear!" Sarah's knees buckled as she fell to the floor.

"Sarah!" Caleb came running through the door. He scanned the room and headed straight for Sarah. He dropped to his knees and took her by the shoulders. "Are you okay?" he asked quickly. "Are you okay?"

"Caleb..." Tears filled Sarah's eyes as he took her into his arms. "He's gone!" she sobbed. "Liam's gone!"

"We'll find him," Caleb said. He turned to face Louise and Kate. "Have you called the sheriff?"

"The sheriff is on his way," Louise said. "I'll make Sarah a cup of tea."

Caleb held on to Sarah. "Thanks for calling me, Louise."

Louise nodded and headed for the kitchen.

"I'll check on the other kids," Kate said.

"Do you know where he might have gone? Did anything happen?" Caleb asked Sarah.

Sarah blew her nose with the edge of her sweater. "I don't know...I—" It dawned on her that she hadn't any idea where Liam might have run away to. "Caleb, what if we don't find him?" Thoughts raced through her mind. "What if something's happened to him?" Sarah began rocking in place.

"Sarah," Caleb said with a steady voice.

"What if someone's taken him?" Her heart raced, and she felt like vomiting. Sarah retched, but nothing came out. "This is all my fault! I've been so selfish! I did this! I was so caught up in myself—"

"Sarah,"—Caleb's voice was calm—"it will be okay. I promise you; we will find him."

The front door opened. "Hello? Mrs. Gardner?" It was the sheriff. "Sarah?"

"In here!" Caleb called out as he helped Sarah to her feet.

"I have someone here who's missing his mama," Sheriff Johnson said as he walked in holding Liam's hand in his.

Sarah fell to her knees once more. "Liam!"

Caleb rushed over to him and picked him up. "Are you okay? Are you hurt?"

"Mommy!" Liam reached for Sarah.

Caleb kneeled beside Sarah.

Liam climbed on to her and hugged Sarah tightly.

The sheriff's voice echoed in the background, but Sarah remained focused on Liam.

"Thank you, Sheriff Johnson," Caleb said. "Where did you find him?"

"We received a call from a lady who lives on Old Oak Drive. She spotted him and stayed with him until I came to get him."

Caleb let out a sigh. He rubbed his face with his hand. "That's a relief."

Sheriff Johnson nodded. "It was early. Not too many people out yet. Liam followed pretty much a straight path, taking the sidewalks. I asked him where he was going and he told me he was going to see you, Caleb." He glanced at Liam. "Didn't you, little man?"

Sarah looked at Caleb. She held Liam's face in her hands and kissed him all over. "Were you going to see Caleb? Liam, why didn't you tell me?"

"There important thing is that he's home and safe. Seems to be alright. No physical injuries. He might be a bit cold—but nothing that a warm bath and a hot breakfast can't fix."

"Thank you, Sheriff." Caleb shook his hand.

"Well, I guess I'll leave you all to it," the Sheriff said. He looked at Liam and slipped his hat off. He crouched down, knees cracking, next to Liam. "Now you make sure you don't go out without a grown-up next time, you hear?"

Liam nodded and, still holding on to Sarah, buried his face in her neck.

"You can't go scaring your mama like that." Sheriff Johnson ruffled Liam's hair and pushed himself up. "Y'all take care now."

Sarah wasn't sure if she thanked Sheriff Johnson. Or maybe she did. She didn't know. A wave of emotions ran through her. They whirled, slammed, slapped, and tumbled inside her, that she could only do one thing—Sarah ran to the kitchen sink and vomited.

Caleb held Sarah's hair back, away from her face, and gently rubbed his warm hand over her back.

Tears welled up in Sarah's eyes as she retched and spewed an empty stomach. Shivering, she wiped her mouth with the back of her hand and sniffled through a blocked nose. She was embarrassed, not because she'd vomited in front of Caleb. She was embarrassed—horrified—that she'd lost her own son.

She was embarrassed that her own son had run away from home. He ran away from *her*.

Sarah felt weak—not physically, but as a person. She had failed at every turn so far.

AS THE SUN SET ON MULBERRY Lane, Noah laid curled up on the beanbag in front of the TV, engrossed in watching *Thomas the Train*. Zoe was still napping and while Sarah knew she would regret letting her sleep so late in the day, she let it go. They all needed a break.

They sat on the sofa—Sarah, Liam, and Caleb. She and Caleb had decided to talk to Liam about what had happened. Caleb needed to be there; after all, Liam had run away to see him.

"Liam, honey," Sarah began. She wrung her hands together while Liam sat on Caleb's lap. She was inexplicably nervous. "About this morning, could you tell us why you ran away?"

Liam shrugged his shoulders, not fully comprehending the panic that ensued when he'd been discovered missing.

"Hey, buddy..." It was Caleb's turn to try. "Where were you going this morning?"

Liam looked so small and vulnerable slumped against Caleb's chest and big arms. "I went to find you," he said, twisting his fingers.

"Why didn't you tell your Mommy?" Caleb asked. "She could have taken you to come find me."

"I'm a big boy." Liam answered. He responded well to Caleb. He always had; from the first day that they'd met.

Sarah watched how Caleb engaged with him—letting him know that everything was okay. Sarah felt like an outsider in her own family. "Liam, you know that you can always go see Caleb any time, right? You just need to tell me," she said, taking his little hand in hers. Sarah's felt a pinch in her heart when he snatched it away.

Liam grunted. "But you don't want me to see Caleb," he said as he sunk deeper into Caleb's arms.

"What?" Sarah was surprised. Is that what he really thought? "Oh, Liam, honey—that's not true at all."

"You got—you sent—you—" Poor Liam could not find his words. Within a matter of seconds, Sarah watched as Liam regressed back to when he was a toddler; as he brought his thumb to his mouth and closed his eyes.

"Hey, buddy, I didn't go away," Caleb said.

"Mommy told you to go away," Liam mumbled, thumb in his mouth.

Caleb sat Liam up straight. "Look at me," he said. "She didn't send me away. Your mommy and I thought it would be best to take some time apart. That's all."

"What time is it?" Liam asked, his big blue eyes hanging on to Caleb's every word.

"Honey, what Caleb means is that—"

"What time is it, Caleb?" He didn't want to hear from Sarah.

"You know, Liam,"—Caleb ran his hand through Liam's hair—"you're very special to me."

"But you left me," Liam mumbled and began to pull away. "Like Daddy."

Caleb pulled him close. "Your Daddy didn't leave you," Caleb said softly. "He's with my Daddy too, remember?"

Liam nodded, but Sarah noticed that it didn't satisfy him.

"Do you remember when you first met me?" Caleb asked. "At your Auntie Charlotte's house?"

Liam nodded.

"And you were angry?"

Liam didn't answer. He leaned against Caleb's chest and let his legs dangle.

Caleb rubbed his face. "Well, I was very angry too."

"With me?" Liam sat upright.

"No, buddy. Not with you." Caleb's voice was gentle.

Sarah listened, unsure of what Caleb was going to say. But she watched as the two connected.

"I was angry, because,"—Caleb paused—"because I lost my son."

Sarah's heart stopped, and she gasped softly.

Liam popped his thumb out of his mouth. "Your son *runned* away like me?" Liam had the face of an angel; pure and so innocent.

Caleb shook his head. "He didn't run away." He hesitated. "No, his mama—she—" Caleb stopped mid-sentence. "He had to go away to Heaven."

"Like where my daddy and your daddy are?"

Caleb nodded. "And when I met you, you became very special to me. You were like the son I didn't get to meet."

Sarah brought a hand to her chest. She had no idea—no idea of what Caleb was going through. She'd been so obsessed with her own circumstances, her own hurt, that she didn't notice that Caleb was hurting too.

"I can, I can,"—Liam brought his hand to Caleb's chin, forcing him to look down into his little eyes—"you can be my daddy." Liam nodded his little head. "And—also for Noah and Zoe. You can be our daddy."

Sarah's heart ached. Her poor little boy. She'd been so selfish—so self-centered. Her tears fell, relentless; Sarah had to turn away.

Chapter 39

Sarah Gardner

"Why didn't you tell me?" Sarah put a cup of coffee in front of Caleb. "Black and strong, just how you like it."

"Thanks," Caleb said. He shifted in his seat and ran a hand through his hair.

She sat across from him and cradled her own mug of tea. Knowing what she now knew, Caleb looked sad, hurt, and tired.

"I didn't know how to," he said.

"I'm so sorry, Caleb." Sarah reached across for his hand. "I was so consumed by my own troubles...I didn't notice you were hurting too."

Without looking at Sarah, Caleb put his hand over hers. "I'm the one that should apologize to you."

Sarah listened.

"I used you and the children to help me get over my grief." Caleb bowed his head. "I thought it would all be okay. I thought that because I was there to help you get over your grief, I would be able to get over mine."

Sarah held her tears back. There was never any real way of knowing for certain what another person might be going through.

"I should have told you," he said. "Charlotte and Ben—they don't know either."

Sarah let out a breath she'd been holding in. "We were both in pain. We each did what we needed to do to get by." She chewed the inside of her lip. Hesitant at first, she asked, "Do you want to talk about it?"

Caleb sighed and clasped his hands together. He shook his leg anxiously. "She didn't want the baby." He let out a sharp breath and shook his head. "We were going to have a family. I was going to be a father."

It hurt Sarah to see him in so much pain. She wanted to hold him and tell him that it was going to be okay; that they would get through this...together. But she held back. She knew it wasn't her place to say those things.

Caleb clicked his tongue. "I was going to take her home with me...to meet the family. We were going to surprise them. But the weekend before we were due to leave, she told me she'd been to the doctor. And that the baby was gone."

"Did she have a miscarriage?" Sarah knew the answer, but she didn't want to assume.

He shook his head and sniffed. "She terminated the pregnancy," Caleb said, his voice cracking.

"Caleb, I'm so, so sorry."

He shrugged. "So I went back home—but not with her. Not like we'd planned."

"Did you break up?"

Caleb nodded. "I couldn't look at her. It was different. She wasn't the same person I loved anymore." Caleb let out a long sigh. "I mean—I know it's her body and all that, but we were going to do it together. We planned it, we talked about. We were gonna be a family." He rubbed his chin. "So I told her it was over."

Sarah remained quiet.

"She didn't seem too bothered." Caleb picked up his mug, but quickly put it back on the table. He leaned in. "The day I met your kids, I was staying with Charlotte and Ben. Liam—he was so angry and refused to talk to anyone." He clasped his hands together and pressed his thumbs together. "I just sat next to him. I was angry too, but I couldn't tell anyone. So we sat together; both us angry. And...I don't know—it just, it just happened. He asked me what my name was." Caleb let out a small laugh. "And then there was no stopping him after that."

"Thank you," Sarah said.

"For what?"

"For being there for him...when I couldn't."

Caleb shrugged. "We were all there for each other."

He was right. They were. Sarah had relied on him even when she had no right to. "And we still are, right?" she asked with a smile.

Caleb reached for her hands. He looked at her from across the table and brought them to his lips.

Sarah felt her chest tighten.

Caleb pulled her up and led her around the table to where he stood.

Sarah tried to fight what she was feeling. She wished she didn't feel anything...but she did. She desperately wanted him to take her in his arms and cover her with his warmth. "Caleb," she whispered.

"Ssh..." He gently placed a finger over her lips and bent his head down, pressing soft kisses along her neck.

"Caleb, I..." Sarah knew she needed to stop; and maybe even push him off. But it felt good—so good to have someone touch her. It was the touch of a man—strong, certain, confident.

Caleb cupped Sarah's cheek with his hand and ran his thumb down the middle of her neck. His hand pulled her in from the small of her back.

Sarah felt shivers trickle down from behind her ears and along her spine as Caleb ran his fingers through her hair. The touch of his fingers on her scalp felt like a sensual massage. She threw her head back and sighed.

But before she lost herself completely to Caleb's touch and her own desires, Sarah felt her eyes sting. She blinked quickly, desperate to push back the tears that threatened to ruin her one moment of pleasure.

With every blink of her eyes, Sarah saw her children.

Blink. Liam.

Blink. Noah.

Blink. Zoe.

They needed her. She could not continue failing them.

And it wasn't just the kids who needed her. *She* needed her.

It was time to sort herself out.

Now!

"Caleb," Sarah whispered, as she gently pushed him away. "We can't do this—not now."

He silenced her once more...with a kiss so soft and so sweet.

Again, Sarah placed her hands against his chest. "It's not our time, Caleb."

Caleb leaned his head against hers.

"It's not our time," she said again.

Sarah didn't know what she meant about it not being their time. Maybe, she hoped that one day, it might be. Caleb was a good guy. He was a good man. He was someone she could see in her future; together with the children.

But not now.

Not yet.

"I need to fix myself," she said. "I need to find...*me*."

Chapter 40

Louise Delaney

Louise woke to the sound of the baby crying in the next room. She peeled her eyes open and willed herself to see in the dark, shuddering at the chill in the air that kissed her skin. Reaching for the bedside lamp, she switched it on and a soft light glowed. Louise got out of bed and put her robe on.

The cries grew louder as she stood outside Kate's bedroom. It was a good thing that Abby was at a sleepover at Shelby's otherwise she would've woken up as well. She knocked and popped her head in. "How's it going?" she asked.

Kate was up and pacing the room, rocking the baby in her arms. "I'm so sorry, Louise." The rings under her eyes grew darker with each night that passed. "Did we wake you? Is Abby up too?"

"It's no trouble. Abby's at Shelby's. Here,"—Louise cinched her robe tighter around her waist and walked over to where Kate stood—"let me."

"I've tried everything." Kate gave the baby to Louise, shaking her head. "He won't stop crying. I don't think he's getting enough milk." Panic filled her voice. Kate had trouble feeding Adam. She couldn't get the baby to latch on properly.

Louise cradled the baby in her arms and cooed. "What's the matter, Adam?" She ran a finger over his soft cheeks. "Are you not sleepy?" Louise swayed slowly, from side to side, like she did when she held her miracle baby in her arms. Adam's cries softened with each step.

Kate sat on the edge of the bed and reached for a pillow. She hugged it tightly and curled up on the bed. "I'm not cut out for this," she whimpered. "My own baby hates me. I can't even feed my own baby!"

"Kate, darling...it's not about whether you feed him by breast or bottle."

"But even the nurses told me that breast is best. How can I give him the best if he won't latch on?"

"You know what's best, Kate?"

Kate looked exhausted.

"What's best is a well-rested mama. A mama who feeds her baby when he's hungry, changes him when he's soiled, and keeps him safe and loved." Louise turned to talk to Adam. "You know who needs some rest?" she asked singing the words. "Your mama needs rest. Now, why don't you and I spend some time together so she can get some sleep?"

"No, Louise, I can't ask you to do that," Kate said.

"Go on." Louise nodded towards the top of the bed. "Get in to bed and we'll see you in the morning."

"What if he gets hungry? He's always hungry."

"So, then I'll feed him," Louise smiled. "You've got milk in the freezer, haven't you? You've been pumping?"

Kate nodded.

"Then, we'll be fine," she said with a smile. "You, my dear, need to get some sleep."

Louise grabbed some diapers and a change of clothes for Adam, before turning the lights out. She gently shut the door behind her. "Mama's going to get some much-needed rest," she whispered to Adam.

As she walked back to her bedroom, Louise remembered the days when Madison was a baby. The sleepless nights and overwhelming exhaustion. Amari had been an easier baby. From the moment they took her home from the hospital, she slept through the night. Louise felt a pang of longing for the baby she'd lost.

Peering into Adam's small face, his lips puckered, Louise smiled. She recalled marveling every time that Madison reached a milestone when she was still a baby. Despite the estrangement between them, Louise clung on to those memories. They were the ones that no one could ever take away from her.

Things were much simpler back then—before the deaths and cheating. These days, all she had were questions. Questions about Warren; about Madison, Amari, Abby, and now...Philip.

There was no way to describe the year that had been.

Thirty-seven years...was any of it real?

Louise laid Adam on the bed and checked his diapers. "Ah, is this why you were crying?" she asked softly. "Looks like it's time for a change."

Adam frowned as he moved his little arms and legs sharply.

"Did you just snort?" Louise teased, smiling with each whistle and gurgle the baby made.

She swaddled Adam and picked him up in her arms, humming as she tried to rock him to sleep.

Louise thought about Abby and how she might be able to mend their relationship. When Abby first came to her, she was a polite enough girl. But as the months passed, Abby had grown distant and rude.

Louise wished she knew what troubled Abby. It all happened very slowly. The moods, the swings—they crept in. What was Louise doing? How did she not notice it?

It was just like it was with Madison. It had been a slow withdrawal, too. She hadn't noticed it because she'd been grieving the death of Amari. Louise had failed to see the daughter that stood before her, hurting. And before long, it was too late. She'd lost another daughter—the living one.

Despite her own feelings of hurt and betrayal, Louise tried hard to fight the demons within herself. *Enough*, she told herself.

From that moment, Louise decided to go down a path of love and forgiveness. Once again, there was a young girl, standing before her—asking to be seen and to be loved. She'd be darned if she was going to lose another daughter.

Chapter 41

Kate Morgan

The next morning, Kate woke with a start. Her first thought was of Adam. "No, no, no," she sat up and look around her—beside her, behind her. She'd read many articles about parents accidentally suffocating babies in their sleep. "Adam!"

Then it came to her. Adam was with Louise. *Thank God.*

Kate covered her face with her hands and groaned. *I'm such a terrible mom*, she thought. *I can't even look after my own baby through the night.*

She pushed the blanket off and sat up. It was 6:00am and there was a giant blood stain on her bed. "Great," she mumbled under her breath. She went to the bathroom and pulled her undies down. The sight of her full *thunder-pads* grossed her out. It was lucky that the hospital had given her a lot, otherwise all she'd have were tampons and liners from before her pregnancy. She had no idea she would be bleeding after giving birth. "Ugh,"—she mumbled as she peeled her pad off—"where is all this blood coming from? Might as well wear a diaper!" Kate winced as she cleaned herself, afraid to tear off any stitches down there.

She quickly changed and made the bed. Glancing at the mirror, she caught a glimpse of herself. The accidental messy bun on her head was neither sexy nor cool; not like it was in her pre-pregnancy days. The dark rings around her eyes made her look she'd slept in without removing her mascara. And the baby-less bump in her belly—it was depressing.

Kate walked quietly to Louise's room. She pressed her ear against the door and heard Louise talking. She knocked gently, before twisting the doorknob open. "Hi," she sang.

Louise gasped with a smile. "It's Mommy!" she said, talking to Adam who lay in her arms, feeding from a small bottle of breast milk.

Kate crossed the room and joined them on the bed. "I'm so sorry about last night," she said. "I don't know what happened."

"It was nothing out of the ordinary, darling," Louise said. "Everyone—and I mean, everyone—needs a hand. It's not easy looking after a baby on your own. How was your sleep?"

Kate told her about how she'd woken thinking she'd smothered Adam.

"Don't get yourself worked up over it. You're doing all the right things and you're a great mom."

Kate burst in to tears. She'd felt it coming, but it was too strong to stop it. She wiped her face with the back of her hand. "I'm sorry," she sniffled and then laughed. "I have no idea where that came from." Kate rolled her eyes and wiped her nose with the top of her shirt.

"Cry, laugh, scream...it will all happen. Blame the hormones; you're allowed to. They are incredibly powerful.

Here,"—Louise passed the baby on to her—"take a look at this little wonder of yours." She stroked his cheek. "There we go." Her voice was soft yet confident.

"How do you always know exactly what to do?" Kate asked.

Louise laughed. "I've lived a lot longer than you, my dear. Give yourself some time and stop being so hard on yourself."

Kate looked at Adam as he lay in her arms. Her heart swelled at the pure sight of him. "Hi there, my love," Kate cooed, "hi."

Adam turned his head towards Kate's chest and opened his mouth, snorting as his head moved around looking for her breast.

Louise laughed. "Looks like he knows when the chef is in the room."

Kate had been trying every single day to get Adam to latch on, but to no avail. She was embarrassed and didn't want to try it in front of Louise—only to be rejected by her own baby.

"Why don't we give it a try?" Louise encouraged her.

Shyly, Kate lifted her top and held her breast out for Adam. Hungrily, he opened his mouth and moved his head around as trying to find Kate's nipple. "Here you go," Kate guided him, hoping that this time would be different. Adam's cries grew louder and Kate felt her panic rise.

"Just relax," Louise reminded her.

Kate took hold of her breast. She pinched the nipple between her fore and middle fingers in a bid to guide it into Adam's hungry mouth.

And just as her doubt had begun to set in, Adam latched on to her breast.

Kate gasped and watched as her baby fed from her. Adam gurgled and swallowed as he tried to keep up with the strong stream of milk coming from Kate's breast. Her chest rose, and she looked at Louise, who smiled back at her, and nodded approvingly. "We did it!" Kate beamed.

"Will you look at that..." Louise said proudly.

Kate stroked the top of Adam's head. "I love you," she whispered. "I love you so much." And when he wrapped his little fingers around her own, Kate fell even more in love. She looked at Adam—at the life she held in her arms. In that very moment, Kate knew she was finally *home*. Home wasn't in the Philippines...or in Carlton Bay. Home was where her heart was, and her heart was with Adam.

Chapter 42

Louise Delaney

Louise left Kate and Adam in the bedroom while she went down to prepare some breakfast. She was looking forward to a relaxing weekend and hoped to spend some time teaching Abby to knit—if she could get her interested in it. She thought it might be a nice way to connect with her.

She put the kettle on and took some mugs down from the cupboard, when she heard a knock at the front door. Louise wrinkled her brows and looked at the clock. It was early, and she wasn't expecting anyone. She smoothed her dressing gown and opened the door. It was Abby...with Sheriff Johnson standing beside her. "What's this?" She couldn't hide her surprise. "Abby! Are you okay?"

"'Morning, Louise." Sheriff Johnson tipped his hat. "I sure am sorry to be troubling you so early this morning, but I thought you'd like to know that Abby and—"

Abby pushed past Louise and ran upstairs, slamming her bedroom door behind her.

"I'm so sorry, Sheriff." Her mind was racing. "Please, come in."

The Sheriff put a hand up. "There's no need, ma'am. I just thought you should know that Abby and a friend were picked up early this morning."

"What for? Where was she?" Louise couldn't believe what she was hearing. "Who was she with?"

"She was with the Anderson boy." The sheriff motioned behind him.

Louise knew of the boy. The Andersons had moved into the small residential farm up on Dalefield Road some years ago, but no one really knew them. They were quiet and kept to themselves, farming sustainably with little need to go into town.

"We got a call from the caretaker at the cemetery this morning. It seems the two have been spending a lot of time in the grounds—sometimes, long into the night."

"The cemetery...did they damage—" Louise was baffled as to why Abby would spend time in a cemetery. And with a boy!

Sheriff Johnson shook his head. "Lots of things could've gone wrong—it's not a safe place, 'specially at night. Let's just say they were lucky they didn't come to any harm. Next time, they might not be so lucky."

"I'll make sure there isn't a next time, Sheriff." Louise thanked him and let him be on his way, presumably to take the Anderson boy home to his parents. She shut the door behind her. Eyes closed, Louise gritted her teeth and took a deep breath in. "Abby!"

Louise climbed the stairs and stormed in to Abby's room.

Abby whipped her head around. "Can't you knock? I swear, there's no privacy in this whole town!"

"Privacy is earned, Abby." Louise stood with her arms crossed over her chest. "Do you wanna tell me what that was all about."

Abby rolled her eyes and sighed. "No."

Louise walked across the room and stood in front of Abby, who was sat cross-legged on her bed. "After everything I've done for you, Abby, this is how you repay me?"

"Oh!" Abby's eyes were fierce. "Oh! So now I owe you—is that right? I need to repay you?"

"Do you have any idea how hard it was for me to take you in?" Louise couldn't hold it in. She'd kept her feelings in long enough, telling herself that it wasn't Abby's fault that they were in this situation. But this time—this time, she could not hold back.

"Because I'm the bastard child, isn't that right?" Abby yelled.

Louise didn't appreciate Abby's tone or volume. "You will keep your voice down, young lady. Don't push it."

"Or what?" Abby spat. "You'll send me away? Send me back to my mother? That's what you really want, isn't it? To be rid of me!"

"Abby!"

"It's true, isn't it?"

Louise held her tongue, warning herself to watch what she said.

"Just tell me how much I owe you and I will pay you back for all your—your—for *everything* you've done for me!"

"What is going on with you, Abigail?"

"Don't call me that!"

"Abby—where is all this anger coming from?" Louise was beside herself.

"Is everything okay?"

Louise turned to find Kate standing at the door, rocking Adam in her arms.

"Apparently," Abby said addressing Kate, "I owe her for everything she's done for me."

"Abby, that's not what I meant at all." Louise found herself on the defensive. "What on earth is going on? Your attitude sucks! First you get sent home from school. And now this? Do you even know that Anderson boy? You told me you were going to be with Shelby."

"I was with Shelby!" Abby yelled, tears in her eyes.

"Don't lie to me!" Louise found herself shouting too.

"I'm not lying! Why don't you ever listen to me?"

"Then why did the Sheriff bring you home with that Anderson boy?" Louise was livid.

"That's Shelby!" Abby cried.

"Abby, stop this right now!" Louise could feel her jaws harden.

"I hate you! I hate all of you!"

"Abby," Kate said gently, "is Shelby the Anderson boy?"

Abby nodded.

Kate glanced at Louise. "So, Shelby is actually a boy?"

"She doesn't want to be a boy." Abby wiped her face with the blanket. "That's why we call her Shelby. She's the only one who understands me."

Louise managed to find her calm. "Then help me to understand, Abby. I really do want to understand."

"Why don't—" Kate spoke tentatively, walking towards Louise. "Why don't you take the baby while Abby and I talk for a while?"

Louise stared at Kate in disbelief. Was it disbelief? She couldn't understand what was going on. She was much too old for this. "I never asked for any of this," she blurted and took the baby from Kate.

"Then I'll leave!" Abby threatened.

"Okay—Abby, that's enough," Kate warned with a confidence that Louise had not heard before.

Louise walked away. That was all she could do. She felt helpless—as if her life had been taken away from her. Everything was fine...until it wasn't. Lord knows, she'd tried to be a good stepmother. Maybe she just wasn't cut out for it. *I can't do this,* she thought to herself.

Chapter 43

Abby Delaney

As soon as Louise left the room, Abby slumped face down on to her bed. She reached for a pillow and placed it on top of her head.

"Hey..." Kate climbed in to bed with her. "Wanna talk about it?"

"No," Abby said, her voice muffled. She wanted to forget everything that had just happened.

"You know you've got it really good here, right?" Kate continued.

"Yeah, yeah, yeah." Abby turned over and laid on her back. She brushed her hair off her face. "That's what everyone says—that I'm so lucky that a good woman has taken me in. But they don't really know."

"What don't they really know?"

"What she's really like!" Abby stared up at the ceiling.

"Well, why don't you tell me what she's really like then?"

Abby took a lock of her hair and twisted it around her finger. "I don't know," she mumbled.

"Surely you must know—seeing as you're dead serious that she's the worst person ever."

“That’s not what I said.” Abby moaned. “Why do you guys always put words in my mouth?”

“Then say it, Abby! Louise doesn’t deserve a sliver of the crap pie you’ve been dishing out. Do you know even know what she’s going through?”

“Everyone thinks she’s so nice. She takes in the strays—”

“The strays?”

“Yeah,” Abby continued. “Like you and me. And then she takes on everyone’s problems and—”

Kate laughed. “I don’t think I’m a stray.”

Abby scoffed. “She saved you, didn’t she?”

“She helped me. That doesn’t make me a stray.”

“Then what are you doing here? Isn’t this the house of strays?” Abby spat.

“Just because I’m staying with Louise—who happens to be a very good friend of mine—doesn’t make me a stray.”

Abby laughed sarcastically. “If the shoe fits.”

“You know, you’re not making it easy for people to like you.”

“Oh, so now you don’t like me too?” Kate was the only adult that Abby liked. If Kate turned on her, then Abby would really be alone.

“If the shoe fits,” Kate said. She laid on her back and stared up at the ceiling too.

“Rude,” Abby said.

“*You’re* rude,” Kate countered.

“Why are you being so mean? You’re supposed to be on my side!”

"Believe it or not, Abby, I am—which is why I'm trying to help you open your eyes." Kate sat up and gently tugged at Abby's hair. "Look, why don't you really tell me what's wrong."

"I don't know...I just get...it's like—I don't know." Abby pulled her hair away and turned to face Kate. "I feel like she hasn't even tried to get to know me at all. And then Philip came around. And now, there's you and Adam...no offence."

Kate sighed. "None taken."

"Like, she acts like she's so nice and helpful, but it's all an act. She didn't even say happy birthday to me—or, or get a cake or something...anything!" The truth was, it wasn't just Louise. Even her own mom didn't call.

"Did you tell her it was your birthday?"

"No, but still," Abby said smugly.

"She's not psychic, you know."

"I know that—stop treating me like a child!" It frustrated Abby that she couldn't articulate herself properly.

"Then stop acting like one! Seriously, Abby. Life doesn't always give you what you want. You've got to play your part. Louise has taken you and given you a lovely home—you've given her nothing but attitude." Kate was angry. "And what's this business about you spending the night at the cemetery? Are you crazy? Something could have happened to you."

"I made her soup! And that stupid grilled cheese sandwich—she didn't even bother to try it. I worked so hard on that dinner for her."

Kate didn't try to hide her surprise. "Are you still on that? Abby, you've got to move on from that. Don't carry that with you—because trust me, if you keep at it, you're going to be carrying a heavy load of baggage as you get older. And I hate to say it, but life is not always gonna be about you. I know it's hard to understand right now, but take it as an opportunity to learn."

Abby didn't say anything.

"Abby...think about it for a moment. Louise just found out that her husband of thirty-seven years had an affair with another woman. *Thirty-seven years*," Kate stressed. "And she had no idea about you until you showed up on her doorstep."

"Yeah, because strays..."

"Stop it with the strays, because you and I both know that she could have turned around and shut the door on your face." Kate pulled Abby to sit up with her. "But she didn't. I hate to say it, but most people would have. She looked at you and she saw the daughter of a man she so loved; the sister of her daughters—"

"She only has one daughter," Abby corrected her.

"Well, that shows just how much you know."

Abby looked up in surprise.

"Louise lost her second daughter when she was just a baby." Kate said.

Abby shook her head.

"And there are lots of other things you may never know, but Abby, that's life." Kate took Abby's hands in hers. "Abby, Louise chose to take you. She chose *you*. Think about that."

Chapter 44

Sarah Gardner

Today was the day. Sarah was determined to turn her life around. She was going to get a job and take charge.

She got up extra early and did yoga. She wanted to wake the parts of her that have been asleep for the last year—both physically and metaphorically. After that, she showered and readied herself, then got the children dressed and packed them all into the car.

"Where are we going?" Liam asked.

"Mommy needs to find a job."

"I don't want you to find a job, Mommy," Noah said.

"It's going to be a good day, kids," Sarah looked at them from the rear-view mirror and slowly backed out of the driveway. "Today is going to be a good day."

Kids in tow, Sarah entered every shop along Lighthouse Road. She introduced herself and handed in a copy of her resume.

Eager though as she was, things didn't go quite as smoothly as Sarah had hoped. Liam dragged along behind, making it difficult to keep the pace. Noah complained that he was tired and hungry, even if they'd all been fed. Zoe cried in each store, every time Sarah told her she couldn't touch, have, or eat something.

Sarah's nerves were frayed, and she felt more and more desperate by the minute. In the end, there were no job offers—just grumpy kids.

Deflated, Sarah dragged the children with her to Chapter Five, where Louise looked busy behind the counter. She held the door open and used her foot to keep it from shutting. She pushed the children and the stroller in, snagging her purse on the door handle. Sarah felt like crying.

"When are we going home?" Liam complained loudly while Zoe wrestled with the straps of the stroller as she tried to free herself.

Louise looked up from her work. A look of mild amusement graced her face. "Well, what have we here?"

"A disaster," Sarah sighed. She felt clumsy and inexperienced.

Louise stepped out from behind the counter and undid Zoe's straps. She gave her a little hug and set her off in the direction of the kids' corner. The two boys waited for no invitation. They'd already made themselves comfortable. "What happened?" Louise asked.

"What *didn't* happen?" Sarah rolled her eyes.

"Oh no, no...don't roll your eyes, please," Louise said. "I get enough of that from Abby," she joked.

"I swear—the three of them make me feel like I'm a first-time mom." Sarah leaned on the counter and bowed her head. "You know, I used to be a good mom. I used to be in control." She sighed. "Now...it's like I've lost control. I have no idea who I am and absolutely no idea to how to be a mother. I've got no idea about anything! Was I really that dependent on Adam?" Sarah's eyes grew hazy from the tears that welled up inside.

"Sarah, you've got to give yourself a break."

She felt Louise's hand on her back. "Isn't that what I've been having all this time? A break? Caleb was a break, wasn't he? He helped with the children. And what about my mental health break? How many more breaks do I need?"

"Sarah, Adam hasn't been gone a year yet. You've been through a lot."

"So do a lot of other people." Frustration did not become her.

"What's got you feeling like this?" Louise asked. "Tell me...what happened today?"

Sarah crossed her arms and let out a breath. "I went around town—dropping my resume off. The children were horrible little monsters, who couldn't—no, would not—stay still."

"And?"

Sarah stared at Louise, wide-eyed. "And of course, no one gave me a job. Why would they? I couldn't even control my own children."

"Why didn't you leave the kids here with me? I could have looked after them. You know better than to take children with you while looking for a job—much less three of them."

Sarah sighed. "You're right. But I can't keep relying on others to bail me out. Today was supposed to be the day that I would turn my life around. The day that I would be on top of everything."

"Darling, that kind of thing—the whole being on top of the world thing...that only happens in the movies."

Sarah scoffed. "And always with such great background music."

"These things take time."

"I don't have time." Sarah bit the inside of her lips.

"Do you know something I don't?" Louise stood with her hands on her hips.

"The money's not going to last forever—Adam's insurance. I need to figure things out for the long term."

"Tell you what," Louise said, "why don't you leave the kids with me for a while." She glanced over at the play area. "They'll be fine. You go and get a breather—go for a walk. Clear your mind and start over. Think of it as a reset button."

"I feel like I've pressed the reset button more than I care to admit."

"That's what it's there for—to reset."

Sarah looked at kids. From a distance, the little monsters looked like sweet angels. Liam was reading a book. Noah was playing with a truck and running it along the edge of the play mat. His hair fell over his eyes and Sarah made a mental note to take him for a cut. And Zoe busied herself with a shape sorter. She sighed and looked at Louise. "I haven't even asked how your day's been."

"Don't ask," she said with a laugh.

"What's happened?" Sarah guiltily felt a tinge of relief that she wasn't the only one going through a tough time.

"Abby happened." Louise told her about the early visit from Sheriff Johnson and Abby spending the night in the cemetery with the Anderson boy who was actually Shelby. "Believe me,"—she pointed towards the kids—"they're much easier at that age."

"The cemetery...that's so weird." Sarah shuddered at the thought.

"Who knows what goes on in their minds?" Louise sighed. The bell rang as a customer came in to the store. Louise rubbed Sarah's arm. "You go on for a walk to clear your head. Take your time and don't worry about the kids. I've got to attend to a customer."

"Are you sure?"

"I'm sure," she nodded. "I'll see you later."

Sarah ducked quietly out the front, careful not to let the children see her.

SARAH WALKED AIMLESSLY until she neared the Village Park. From a distance, she could see the vicar. "What was his name?" Sarah mumbled to herself. "Benedict? No, that's the Pope. Francis?" Sarah shook her head. *Also a pope,* she thought. He looked up and waved Sarah over.

Sarah straightened her back and walked over to greet him. "How are you, Father?" she asked with a smile, pleased that she thought to call him 'Father' instead.

"The sun's out, the gardens are looking lovely—couldn't be better, I'd say," he said. "And yourself, Sarah?"

Oh no, he knows my name. Of course he knows my name! Sarah wondered if she'd made a mistake. *What if I should have been a nun?* she thought. *Then I would only have to love God and live by the rules. No big decisions. No big dramas.*

"Sarah?"

"I'm so sorry," she said.

"Whatever for?" he asked.

"It's just that...you're having a lovely day. And I'm...." Sarah paused and sighed. "I'm like a walking rain cloud."

The vicar laughed.

He was a nice man, the vicar. Sarah had known him for a long time. *Jordan!* she thought again. *No...Saul. His name is Saul.* Sarah tried it out. "It's really not so funny, Saul."

"Paul," he said. "And I didn't mean that."

"Sorry, I meant, Paul." *At least it rhymed.*

"If I may, Sarah, what is it that burdens you?"

What is it that burdens me? Burden—it's such a strong word. *But yes, I he's right. I am burdened.* Sarah shook her head.

"You don't have to tell me, of course," Paul said. "But, I'm here, even if only to listen."

They walked along in silence for a while. Sarah wondered how priests could always walk in silence, while her head...her head was always full; jammed to the brim. "I went around this morning—with the children—looking for a job."

"Oh, how very nice," he said.

"It wasn't, actually. They screamed and cried. They did everything to make it impossible."

"Whoever receives one such child in my name receives me, and whoever receives me, receives not me but him who sent me."

Sarah looked at Paul, dumbfounded. "I'm sorry, I don't understand."

"Children are gifts from God," he said with a smile.

Sarah wanted to scream at him. "Is that from the bible? Because not everything can be fixed by a verse from the bible."

"Did you manage to find a job?" he asked gently.

"No. Who wants to hire a widow with three children in tow?"

"Well, Mrs. Wilson, our church administrator, has just resigned." Paul kept walking; his hands clasped behind his back. "She's been with church for the last thirty years," he said almost wistfully. "If you like, you can have her job."

Sarah stopped walking. "Are you serious?" she asked.

"Of course," he chuckled. "You need help...and so do we."

"But, I—I haven't worked in a very long time. You don't even know—"

"I'm sure that you will pick things up in no time," Paul said. "Mrs. Wilson will be with us for another two weeks. She can show you the ropes, as they say."

Sarah couldn't believe it. She wanted to drop to her knees and kiss his feet. "Father..."

"And you can bring the children to work with you," he added. "Mrs. Wilson used to bring her grandchildren in. We're very relaxed. And there are children's activities that they can take part in. Do your children like soccer? We have a wonderful soccer team and the children enjoy it very much."

"I know the one," Sarah said. "Caleb used to stay with us before he got the job at the church. The children used to go to the practice sessions."

"Oh, very good. Then you know each other—wonderful."

"I don't know what to say."

"Well, for starters, you can say yes."

"Yes...yes!" Sarah said excitedly. "Thank you. Thank you so much, Paul."

"Come by tomorrow morning and I'll introduce you to Mrs. Wilson."

"I won't let you down," she promised.

"I know." He smiled.

Sarah stepped forward to give him a hug, but stopped suddenly. "May I?"

Paul laughed and embraced her.

For Sarah, it felt like she was finally being embraced by God. In her time of weakness and despair...God placed his arms around her and held her close.

Once again, her tears fell...only this time, they were tears of happiness and hope.

Chapter 45

Kate Morgan

After talking to Abby, Kate realized that she needed to pull her head in and provide a stable home for her son. She was grateful to be living in Louise's spare bedroom, but she needed a long-term plan. If not for herself—then at the very least, for Adam.

She stood in front of the mirror and gazed at herself. Lots of things have changed in the last few months since she'd had Adam. Her belly was still heavy, but she could feel it slowly—very slowly—settling. Kate ran a hand over the stretch marks that covered her stomach and sighed. Even her boobs were unrecognizable. They were huge. It was almost as if she was wearing someone else's pair. And they hurt. They hurt every time Adam needed a feed. It was like a timer...or a dinner bell.

Kate smoothed her sweater over her leggings and took a deep breath. *It's now or never*, she thought.

Kate turned to pick Adam up from his crib. "How about it, mister? You and I are going on a mission."

Adam gurgled sweetly as Kate carried him in her arms, his pearl-white skin glowed against her own.

Kate ran a finger over his wispy brown hair and looked into his big brown eyes. "Are you my handsome boy?" Kate sang. "Yes, you are," she said. "It's time to go."

KATE SHUT THE DOOR behind her and crossed the street to where she'd once lived with Evan. It was just after six o'clock and Evan would be home. Kate knew his schedule well—it was like clockwork.

When they were married, Evan liked everything on time, so Kate had made it a point to know his comings and goings. Breakfast on the table by 4:00am—bacon, scrambled eggs, soft and fluffy. He didn't like the way she made scrambled eggs. *Darned rubbery and flat,* he said. So Kate scoured the internet for the perfect way to cook eggs. She'd practiced recipe after recipe—*Jaime Oliver, Julia Child, Emeril Lagasse, Martha Stewart.* She later found that he liked Gordon Ramsay's recipe—butter, crème fraîche, and chives.

Dinner was always meat, potatoes, and two kinds of vegetables. Medium-rare steak, crunchy fried chicken, juicy roast beef. "*None of that adobo crap,*" he'd say later on in their marriage.

Kate took a deep breath and stood tall as she raised a hand to knock on the door.

"What do you want, Kate?" Evan said when he opened the door and saw it was her. He was never one for small talk.

He looked different. She hadn't seen him since that night he was drunk and violent. *He's lost weight*, she thought. "Can we come in?" Kate motioned at Adam, who she carried in a baby sling.

Evan glanced at the baby. He let out a heavy sigh and stepped aside.

Kate stepped in and waited for Evan to shut the door. She looked around—not much had changed. Her pink throw was still on the sofa.

"Do you want a cup of tea or coffee?"

The question surprised her. Evan wasn't a tea or coffee guy. He was a beer man...an *open-a-bottle-of-beer-and-sit-on-the-big-single-armchair* kind of man. "You have tea and coffee in the house?" Kate followed Evan to the kitchen.

"I quit the bottle." Evan turned the electric kettle on and grabbed two mismatched mugs from the cupboard, setting them down on the on the counter.

"You quit...what?"

"I quit drinking," he said. "Milk and sugar?"

Kate pulled up a seat and sat down, resting Adam in the crook of her arm. "Just black tea, please." Her eyes followed Evan as he moved around the kitchen. It was...weird. Evan didn't potter around. Evan never spent time in the kitchen.

He put a tea bag in Kate's mug and spooned some instant coffee and three heaping teaspoons of sugar in his. When the kettle clicked off, he poured the hot water in each mug and noisily stirred drinks. He handed Kate her tea and apologized when the string fell into the mug.

"It's okay," she said with a faint smile. "So, you quit drinking?" Kate hoped he couldn't tell that she was nervous.

"Yeah." Evan hunched over his coffee. Even when sitting down, he was a big man.

Kate could feel the table shaking as Evan shook his foot. "Why? I mean—if you don't mind me asking."

Evan shrugged. "I didn't like what it did to me."

Silence fell between them. While she was pleased for him, it saddened Kate that he hadn't thought to quit when they were together. "I'm happy for you," she said after a moment.

Evan sniffed and drank from his mug.

"Are you coping okay?"

"I go to these meetings." He rubbed his chin. "They help keep me on the wagon."

Brave. Kate wanted to tell him he was brave. But she held back.

Evan cleared his throat. "So—uh—why are you here?"

Kate looked at Adam and smoothed a finger over his cheek. "This is Adam."

Evan looked at the baby, nodded, and looked back up at Kate. "Looks like you," he said.

She smiled. "I thought he looked like you."

Evan shifted in his seat. "Kate,"—he rubbed his forehead—"I can't. I told you before. I'm not the fatherly type. There were never any children in my pl—"

"I know, Evan." Kate sat up straight. "I know, and I respect that. Believe me, I do. At first, I'll admit, I couldn't understand it. I was angry...and hurt."

Evan sighed.

Kate continued. "But like it or not, he is your son." Kate's mouth felt dry. Her nerves were all over the place. "And we need a stable place—a house of our own. We can't keep living in Louise's spare bedroom."

Evan didn't look at her.

"Evan, I don't have anyone else to turn to," she pleaded with the hope that by some miracle, he would understand.

"We can't live together, Kate. I don't want that."

"And that's fine," Kate said. "It's probably better that way. But you do have the farmhouse."

He looked up at her. "What are you saying?"

"I—I don't..." Kate faltered. She took a sip of tea as she stalled. "We have nowhere to go, Evan. And Adam...he needs stability, a roof over his head, a place to grow."

"I think you should go." He pushed himself up to stand.

Kate reached for his hand. "Evan, I have never asked you for anything before. Never. But now, I'm asking for your help."

Evan sat back down.

"When we're able to get a divorce—I won't ask for anything else. Nothing at all. You have my word."

Evan pressed his fingers against the temples of his head. "What else do you need?"

"Nothing," Kate said quickly. "I promise."

Adam let out a small cry. Kate rocked him gently, but Adam persisted.

"What does he want?"

"He's just hungry," Kate said.

"I—uh—I've got some milk in the fridge, if..."

Kate smiled. "It's okay," she said as she reached under her sweater and unclasped the front of her nursing bra. Kate lifted the left side of her sweater, revealing her full breast that Adam hungrily latched on to. She'd become more confident about breastfeeding as she accepted her son's need for feeding on-demand. Nothing would keep her from meeting Adam's needs.

Evan looked away momentarily.

They sat in silence for a while, with only the sound of Adam's gulps and gasps for air between them.

"Is he,"—Evan glanced at her—"always that hungry?"

Kate let out a small laugh. "He's a growing boy."

Evan nodded as if he was taking in information about a new crop. And when Adam's little hand reached out from under the baby sling, Evan leaned back and rubbed his chin, letting out a small grin.

"Would you like to burp him?" Kate asked when Adam was finished feeding.

Evan put his hand up. "Oh, I wouldn't know how—no, that's alright."

Kate slowly took the baby sling off. "Here,"—she stood up and carried the baby to Evan—"don't worry, I'm right here."

Evan hesitated for a brief moment. Eventually, he took the baby and placed him against the side of his chest, just by his left shoulder. He looked at Kate when Adam squirmed.

"Just keep a hand on his back and give him a gentle rub."

Evan did as he was told. His hand was practically the size of Adam's entire body.

Kate watched as Evan held his baby for the first time. Her heart warmed as the once fierce man turned into a gentle giant right before her very eyes.

When Adam finally let out a burp, Evan smiled from ear to ear and glanced at Kate. "That was a big one."

Kate smiled. "Now you can turn him over. Here, let me help you." She took Adam and slowly laid him into Evan's arms.

Evan looked into Adam's face and stayed quiet for some time. Finally, he spoke. "I'll move to the farmhouse," Evan said, breaking the silence. "You two can have this house."

"Oh, Evan—" Kate leaned forward and placed a hand over his. "Thank you."

"You're welcome," he said. Evan kept his eyes on Adam. "Kate?"

"Yes?"

"I'm sorry," he said. "For everything."

Kate smoothed her thumb over the back of his hand. "I know."

"I didn't deserve you. I *don't* deserve you."

Kate felt for him. She really did. Everyone does stupid things in their lifetime. Some are lucky enough to come away unscathed, forgiven...maybe even forgotten. Others, not so much. She did not want to be a victim. No. She was a survivor. She survived—his threats, his verbal abuse, and in the end, his physical abuse. She was a survivor. She *is* a survivor, and she didn't want to carry the weight of the memories or the hurt with her. She wanted to move forward; to keep going. So she forgave him—not for him, but for her own peace of mind.

She had the power and forgiveness was hers to give...and so she did.

Chapter 46

Louise Delaney

Things have been less than pleasant in the house with everyone walking on eggshells. Kate had moved out with Adam; and Louise missed them...even if they were just across the road. They had provided a break from the arguments and glaring stares of Abby. They helped keep the peace. But now that they were gone, it was just Abby and Louise.

Never in her life did she ever think she'd be afraid of a teenager. Was that the word? Afraid. No. Maybe not. In any case, Louise didn't like the drama. The mess. The constant bickering.

"I'm too old for this," she told Sarah over the phone.

"Perhaps she just needs a little more time," Sarah suggested.

"Time for what? She's got plenty of that!" Louise moaned. "I can't get her to do anything these days. She's either holed up in her room with head down on her phone, or she's out with Shelby."

"Have you met him?" Sarah asked. "I mean, her, sorry. Have you met her?"

Louise could hear echoes of cooking in the background. "Are you cooking? Should I call you back later?"

"No, no—that's alright," Sarah said. "I've got you on speakerphone. And besides, it's just scrambled eggs. Nothing too high-brow," she said with a laugh.

"Breakfast for dinner," Louise sighed. "Always a lifesaver."

"Only until the children start complaining about what they eat," Sarah laughed.

"You know what? I'm really proud of you." Now that Sarah was working, they hadn't been able to see each other as often as before. She missed their Tea for Three dates. But working at the church had been good for Sarah and Louise was happy for her friend. There was something about her that had changed. Sarah was calmer—somewhat more confident.

Sarah laughed. "Of me? Why's that?"

"You've really come around, Sarah. You're doing well at work. You're a fantastic mother. And an absolute gem of a friend." Louise meant every word she said.

"It's only taken a whole year, hasn't it?" Sarah joked.

"Oh, darling—it has been the craziest year. But the way you've come through is just inspiring."

"Well, I couldn't have done it without you guys. You and Kate are my lifelines."

It was true. They were each other's lifelines. One way or the other, they were all connected.

"Anyway, so have you met her?"

"Shelby? No. Abby hasn't brought her home or anything."

"Maybe you should meet her?" Sarah suggested. "Find out why Abby likes hanging out with her so much."

"Oh, I don't want to pry—do you think I should?"

"It's not prying. You're her mother."

"Step-mother," Louise corrected.

"Either way, you're the parental figure in her life."

Sarah was right. Louise really hadn't made an effort to get to know Abby's friend. "You're right," she agreed. "I should. She's just so—so—she can be so terrible at times."

"They don't call it the terrible teens for nothing," Sarah joked.

"I thought it was the terrible twos. No one told me about the terrible teens."

"Now I'm a terrible teen?"

Louise turned around to find Abby glaring at her. "Abby—"

"I knew it! You hate me—everyone hates me. I hate my life. I wish I was dead!" Abby turned on her heels and stormed off up the stairs. The door slammed just seconds later.

"I'll talk to you tomorrow," Louise said into the phone.

"She heard you?" Sarah asked.

"Uh-huh...and now I'm walking into world war three."

"Good luck."

"Thanks, I'll need it." Louise hung up and took a deep breath in. She walked towards the stairs and called out. "Abby?"

When Abby didn't answer, she tried again. "Abby—can we talk?"

Louise sighed. It was easier to just put her hands up in defeat. "This is ridiculous," she mumbled and headed to the garage instead. She needed time to think, and there was something she'd been meaning to do.

LOUISE STOOD IN THE garage with her hands on her waist as she eyed the boxed memories, each one with its own label: *Madison's Baby Clothes. Madison Grade School Artwork. Madison's Prom Dress Etc. Warren's Books. Louise's Books. Wedding Dress.*

She ran a finger over a box that said, *Amari's Things*. It was a box, considerably smaller than all the others. She opened it and inside it found Amari's baby blanket. Louise picked it up and put her cheek against it. It smelled old and stuffy, without life. Then she picked up a pair of baby booties. How small they looked in the palm of her hand. Louise closed her eyes and breathed in. Tears welled up in her eyes. It didn't matter how many years it had been since Amari had passed. No amount of time would ever erase the pain of the loss of her baby. Louise covered the box and replaced it where she'd found it.

She wiped her eyes and looked around. "Where did I put that thing?" she mumbled. And then she saw it. It was a medium-sized FedEx box; not much larger than 25kg. She never opened it, and it still had the original packing seal and paperwork attached to it. Louise took a rag and wiped the top of the box that was addressed to her.

RECIPIENT: Mrs. Louise Delaney
ADDRESS: 607 Mulberry Lane, Carlton Bay | OR 97476, USA
Contents: Personal Effects

SENDER: Dalefield Terrace Assisted Living
ADDRESS: 192 Dalefield Terrace, Carlton Bay | OR 97476, USA

Using a pair of garage scissors, Louise finally opened the box that contained her mother's last known personal effects.

One by one, Louise took the items out.

There was a bible. Louise had always known her mother to keep one by her bedside, even when she was still a child.

Next was an old hairbrush with a brass handle. Tears of guilt fell down her face when Louise saw the strands of hair woven into the bristles.

Louise sat cross-legged on the floor and wiped her nose with the top of her shirt. After Amari's death, Louise had pushed everyone away...including her own mother, who, in hindsight, had tried her best to be there for her only daughter.

The rift between mother and daughter had grown into a large black hole. Louise had never allowed her mother the chance to repair it...nor had Louise ever tried.

Louise choked on her sobs as she thought about her mother. "I'm sorry," she whispered. She allowed herself to cry the tears that she'd held back for so many years—tears of anger, sorrow, guilt, and pain.

When Louise managed to compose herself, something in the box caught her eye. It was a stuffed brown envelope.

Taped on the front was as folded piece of white paper that read, *For Louise.*

Louise wiped her nose once more before taking the envelope out of the box. She gently ripped the paper off and unfolded it.

To my dearest daughter, Louise

All I ever wanted for you was to be happy.

It is my hope that when you finally see this, you will understand why I did it.

I love you, my darling girl.

Always,

Mama

Louise's hands trembled as she picked up the envelope. It was sealed—held together by a string, wrapped around a button. She took a deep breath and held it in as she unwound the string. And when undid the last round, Louise tipped the contents out.

Tears welled up in her eyes as she rifled through dozens of unopened letters. Letters addressed to her...letters from Philip.

Louise laid down on the garage floor and curled up in a fetal position. And then she wept—softly, at first, until she could no longer hold it in.

Chapter 47

Abby Delaney

When her anger finally subsided, Abby sat up in bed and stared out the window. Kate was right. Louise chose *her*. She didn't have to, but Louise did.

Abby climbed back out of bed and went to Louise's room. She took a small breath in and then knocked on the door. When Louise didn't answer, she opened the door. The room was empty.

She went downstairs and headed straight for the kitchen. "Louise?"

Abby looked around the rest of the house—no one was home. But then she heard it. It was the sound of muffled cries. Abby put her ear against the door in the kitchen that led to the garage. She put her hand on the doorknob and slowly twisted it open. "Louise?"

Abby let out a soft gasp. She was not prepared for what she saw. On the floor, curled up and in tears, was the strongest person she knew. Abby decided to speak. "Can I come in?"

From where she stood, Louise still looked like a young woman. She wondered what life would have been like, had

Louise been her real mom. Snippets of visions whizzed through her mind.

"Abby,"—Louise sat up as soon as she realized that Abby was in the garage with her—"is everything okay?"

Abby sat down on the floor, next to Louise. "Are...are you okay?"

Louise wiped her face and nodded. "I was just—I wasn't feeling well," she said.

Abby looked at the envelopes around Louise. "I'm sorry."

Louise looked up at Abby.

"I'm sorry for everything," Abby said as tears filled her own eyes. "I don't deserve to be living here with you. I'm an awful person and I'm a waste of space."

"Hey...what's this?" Louise pulled Abby close. "Don't you say that, okay? You are not a waste of space. You are a bright and intelligent young woman with her whole life ahead of her."

With her nose clogged, Abby sniffled. "I shouldn't have come here. I ruined your life."

"Abby,"—Louise wiped the tears that fell down Abby's cheeks—"you didn't do anything wrong; you hear me? You did *not* ruin my life."

At first, Abby stiffened. No one had ever held her like that before. She closed her eyes as more tears pushed past her eyes. Before long, Abby was sobbing uncontrollably; her body shaking as she let herself be embraced by the only person in the world to ever choose *her.* "I'm sorry, Louise, I'm sorry."

"I have an idea," Louise said as she wiped the hair off Abby's wet face. "I'd like for us to start over again. Tell me where I went wrong."

"It's not you," Abby said. "It's me."

Louise smiled. "It sounds like you're breaking up with me."

Abby sniffed and let out a small laugh.

"How about you and I start over...we can both get to know each other?"

"You don't want me to go?" Abby asked.

"No, I don't want you to go, you silly goose."

Abby smiled. She'd heard other mothers call their kids a silly goose when she was in grade school.

"We can cook something together—you and I. And just have a nice...how do you say it these days? We can watch Netflix and chill."

"Eeew—don't say that...I don't think you know what it means," Abby said.

Louise laughed. "Okay then. We can have a nice evening. I can get to know your friend Shelby and she can get to know me too."

Abby sniffled. "No one likes Shelby, you know? We're the same."

"What do you mean?"

"We're the outcasts of Carlton Bay. No one understands Shelby, not even her parents." Abby pulled her hair into a ponytail, using a hair-tie that she wore around her wrist. "Do you know one time...Shelby's dad beat her up?"

"What? No, that's terrible."

Abby nodded. "He was trying to get Shelby to turn straight."

"To *turn straight*?"

"Yeah, her dad said that she was living in sin by being gay."

"And what about her mom?"

"She can't do anything. She turns a blind eye to everything."

"That's really sad, Abby."

Abby didn't say anything. She knew it was sad. It was their reality—nobody loved them. They only had each other.

"Abby...why do you think no one likes you?"

Abby shrugged. "I don't know." She chewed on her bottom lip.

Louise reached for Abby's hand. "Because that's not how I feel."

Abby slowly pulled her hand away. "You're always at work. Or with Sarah and Kate. Or Philip. I guess—I guess I feel like you don't have much time for me." Abby paused. "And I know I'm not your real daughter, so I don't blame you." Abby cast her eyes to the floor. "Even my own mom doesn't want to have anything to do with me."

"That's not true. I'm sure it's not true."

"She hasn't tried to contact me since I moved out." Abby scoffed. "She didn't even call me for my birthday."

"When was your birthday?"

Abby shrugged. "It doesn't matter."

"Of course, it does."

"It was last June." Four months ago.

"Oh, Abby. I'm so sorry." Louise took Abby's hand again. "I've been selfish, haven't I?"

"You didn't know...and I could've said something."

"That's true. But I also could have asked." Louise smiled. "So...what does Shelby like to eat?"

Abby wrinkled her nose. "Anything, I guess. But she likes pizza."

"How about we celebrate your birthday and order in some pizza?"

Abby felt her heart swell. It was a weird feeling—her tummy did a little turn too. "You don't have to do that."

"I want to," Louise said. "It was my daughter's birthday, and we missed it. That's so uncool."

Abby laughed at Louise's use of the word *uncool*. "When was Madison's birthday?"

"Not that daughter, silly goose."

"Whose birthday?" She didn't want to ask about her dead daughter.

"Yours!"

"But I'm not..."

"You're my daughter too, Abby—whether you like it or not."

"Yeah, I know, but you don't have to..."

"I want to be your mother, Abby—or stepmother, whatever. I want you with me."

Abby looked into her stepmother's eyes. "You mean it?"

Louise smiled. "I mean it."

Abby threw herself onto Louise and hugged her with all that she had. The best part was that Louise hugged her back.

Winter

God, grant me the serenity to accept the things I cannot change,
the courage to change the things I can,
and wisdom to know the difference.
~Serenity Prayer

Chapter 48

Sarah Gardner

The last few months had been incredibly busy, but Sarah was grateful.

It had been a while since she'd seen the girls for more than a wave across their front lawns. It was funny how even if they all lived so close to each other, time still had a way of slipping past them. They did however manage to keep up with phone calls and text messages. Kate had even set them all up on a group chat so that no one missed out on conversations with each other.

Sarah was glad when Caleb asked if he could spend some time with the kids over the weekend. They had a weird arrangement. It was some kind of *shared custody* of the children; the way families with two homes made it work. The only difference was that they weren't divorced—or even married. But they did have two homes, and they saw themselves as a blended family in a way that only they understood. The kids loved Caleb—as he loved them—and for the most part, it was an arrangement that worked. The only thing that Sarah had to be wary of was keeping her feelings for Caleb at bay.

Every time she saw him, her stomach still did a somersault—or two, or three.

Liam had started kindergarten, and Sarah had managed to follow a schedule that worked well. She woke each day at 5:30am and began her day with yoga and a hot cup of tea afterwards. Then, she would get the kids up, get them fed and ready for the day—dropping Liam to school, while she took Noah and Zoe with her to work.

Working at the church had been a huge blessing for the family and the truth was, she couldn't have asked for a better opportunity.

"Let's go, kiddos!" Sarah called out as she put her earrings on. After a long wait, she was heading out for an afternoon with Kate and Louise. She was eager to get out the door and enjoy some adult time—refusing to give in to any pang of guilt. Sarah had finally learned that caring for herself was as important as caring for the children. She needed nourishment—not just of the body, but also of the soul.

"Uh-oh," Sarah said when she walked into the children's bedroom. "What have we here?" Zoe had managed to get her dress tucked into her stockings. Noah undid his shoelaces. And Liam...well—Liam had become such a handsome big brother. It was cute to watch him take charge.

"Come on, Zoe," Liam said. "It's time to go now."

Zoe adored her big brother and followed him around everywhere. It was as if his absence during the day while at school caused her to miss him. "Not now, Liam. Not now," Zoe said.

"Now, Zoe," Liam said in his big brother voice.

Zoe pulled the pacifier out of her mouth to reply. “Okay, Liam, okay—just wait, okay?”

“Noah...” Sarah kneeled down in front of him. “Why did you undo your laces?”

Noah pushed his hair off of his forehead. “Uh—because it was *strangulizing* my feet.”

Sarah smiled, amused by the big words he’d been trying to use as of late. “You mean it was strangling your feet?”

“Yes, it was *strangulizing* me and my feet got angry,” he said with a hand on Sarah’s shoulder for balance as she tied his laces back up. “Mommy, when I am going to big school like Liam?”

“Very soon, darling,” Sarah said. Her heart swelled. The children were growing up and thriving right before her very eyes. And while she watched them with immense pride, there was a sense of longing that tugged at her heartstrings. A small part of her knew she would soon long for the times when they were little and looked at her as if she was the only other person in the world. “Alright,”—Sarah pushed herself up—“Caleb should be here any moment now.”

LOUISE AND KATE WERE already seated when Sarah arrived at the Dockside Cafe. She spotted them seated on the couches by the fireplace where a healthy fire was burning. Sarah unraveled her scarf and felt the warmth of the fire kiss her neck. “Great table, ladies!” she beamed.

“Aren’t we the lucky ones?” Louise agreed.

"Sarah!" Kate stood up and gave Sarah a hug. "It's been so long! I've missed our tea dates."

"I know, I have too." Pleased to see her best friends, Sarah returned Kate's hug. "I couldn't wait to get out of the house!" She told them that Caleb had the children that day.

"That's really something, isn't it?" Louise thought out loud.

"You mean with Caleb?" she asked.

"Yes—he's really fond of the kids, isn't he?" Louise said. "I mean, I know of lots of ways to spend a beautiful Saturday afternoon and it doesn't include babysitting." Louise threw her head back and laughed. "No offense," she said as she placed a hand on Sarah's knee.

"None taken!" Sarah laughed with her and leaned back on the couch. "Gosh, these couches are comfortable, aren't they?"

"You know, it's interesting..." Louise said, chin on hand. "Despite everything that's happened between you two—he's still there."

"I know what you mean," Sarah said.

"I agree! Like, why aren't you guys together yet?" Kate asked.

"Yes, why?" Louise asked in agreement.

Sarah sighed. "I guess you might say we blew our chance." She clicked her tongue. "The timing just wasn't right. And besides, it hasn't even been a year since Adam's passing."

"Truth be told," Louise said, "there really isn't a perfect time." She'd used her fingers to make air quotes. "No one else but yourself knows when *you* are ready."

"I don't know...I mean, when I first started seeing Caleb like...like *that* as a man, I think we can all agree that I was a bit crazy. It was an emotional time. I was on medication for depression and I just wasn't myself." Sarah had remained on her medication, and she'd come to be okay with that. People used medicines for a variety of reasons. *If it helps, then I will take it,* she'd decided. "I'm more...grounded now."

"Grounded..." Louise echoed her. "I like that."

"I do too," Sarah smiled. "I'm back on my own two feet. I have a career. And I'm a much better mom to the kids. I mean, that's big stuff, right there."

"It is and we're super proud of you, Sarah," Kate stated.

"Of me? We're so proud of you, Kate," Sarah said, thinking of everything Kate had been through as well.

Louise looked at Sarah. "Do you still like him, though?"

The question caught Sarah off-guard. She'd tried to steer clear of it, knowing that they could never get together. "Do I still like him?" Sarah sighed in response.

"Oh my gosh, you do." Louise threw her hands in the air.

"I think we all knew it." Kate smiled. "What's stopping you?"

Sarah threw her head back and groaned. "I don't know...I blew it."

"Blew it, schmoo-it!" Louise said. "Darling, life is too short for regrets. Think about it. You're young, absolutely gorgeous, and there's a kind, wonderful man—whose name is Caleb, in case that isn't clear—who adores you. A man who worships the ground you walk on. You, my dear friend, are very lucky. Not many people experience true love in one lifetime—much less two loves."

Sarah laughed nervously. "He does not adore me. I think that's a bit far-fetched."

"Not according to Philip, it's not." Louise said with a wink.

"What?"

"Sorry—I can't tell you...priest and parishioner confidentiality," Louise said.

"Then how come you know?" Sarah jokingly protested.

"Take it from me, darling." Louise tapped her nose with a finger. "The man's in love with you."

Chapter 49

Louise Delaney

"Oh, you should talk," Sarah teased Louise. "Does that mean that you and Philip are back together?"

Louise shook her head. "Mmm...no."

"Why not?" It was Sarah's turn to challenge her. "Did you tell him about the letters you found?"

"I did," Louise nodded with a smile.

"You know, I still can't believe it. All those years...and your mother knew." Kate sighed. "I just can't."

"I have to admit, I was very confused. Angry, actually," Louise said. "But then, I thought about it. If my mother hadn't done what she did, then I would never have had a wonderful marriage with Warren." Louise leaned back in the sofa. "I wouldn't have had Madison...or Amari. I wouldn't even have Abby in my life."

"Life's funny, isn't it?" Sarah mused.

Life was funny alright. It took a long time for Louise to accept what she'd lost—and even longer to appreciate what she'd gained. But she got there. "Whatever her reasons, my mother thought she was doing what was best for me—for her daughter."

"I would do anything to protect Adam," Kate said thoughtfully.

"Yeah," Sarah nodded. "I would tackle anything that threatens any of my kids."

"And I would do the same for any of my girls." Her girls—Madison, Amari, and Abby.

"What did Philip say?" Sarah asked.

"Well...we've waited long enough. What's another few walks around the block?" Louise joked. "Right now, I"—Louise put her hand on her chest—"am concentrating on being a good stepmother."

"And you are doing so, so well," Kate said. "Abby's been texting me and she's just a different girl, I swear."

"Has she?" Louise asked Kate and placed a hand on her arm. "I'm so glad she has you. I think she sees you as a big sister."

"How are things going?" Sarah asked.

"I think we're making really good progress," Louise sat up as the waitress brought their tea for three—English breakfast this time—along with three cheese scones. "Thank you, Jacqui." Louise looked up at the waitress.

"Anything else I can get y'all?" Jacqui asked. And when they declined, she said, "just holler if you need me," and walked off.

"That's good to know," Sarah said, picking up where they'd left off.

Kate picked up a scone. She sliced it in half and lathered each one with butter. She took a bite and sighed dramatically. "I missed this."

"Mmm, yes." Louise did the same.

"Have you met Shelby?" Kate asked.

Louise nodded, wiping her mouth with a napkin. "Yes, yes...she's a lovely girl."

"So they're not dating, right?" Sarah asked with a mouthful.

"No. Shelby identifies as a girl."

"Well, it sounds like you're raising Abby very well." Kate looked up from her scone. "From what Abby's told me, that's a bit of what connects them. Shelby's parents don't approve of her lifestyle. And of course, living in a small town like Carlton Bay, not too many of the kids at the high school are very accepting."

"And what about Abby?" Sarah asked.

Louise took a sip of tea. "Like Shelby, she felt like she didn't belong here."

Kate nodded.

"In the beginning," Louise explained, "Abby felt like I only took her in out of obligation. Then, being the new kid at school didn't help either. And then there were the stories about being Warren's love-child circulating the halls—she found it difficult to make friends. She and Shelby found comfort in each other."

"Oh, bless them both," Kate said with a hand on her heart. "Isn't that interesting? How they found each other?"

Sarah nodded in agreement.

"They spend a lot of time together at home—just hanging out, as they call it."

"And that's okay with you?" Sarah asked, picking up her cup of tea.

"Oh, yes," Louise exclaimed. "I'd much rather know they're safe at home. Shelby's actually a good girl. I wish there was something more I could do for her...talk to her parents or something."

"That's sad, isn't it?" Kate sighed.

"She has you," Sarah said. "They both have you."

"Well, as I've told them both—Shelby is as much a part of the family as everyone else."

Sarah blew into her tea before taking a sip. "That would make Abby happy, wouldn't it?"

"She's certainly come out of her shell. I feel like we're getting to know each other more." Louise took another bite of her scone. "You know, sometimes I look at her, and I see this young adult—ill-tempered and cantankerous. And other times, I see this little child—eager to please, wanting to be loved."

"You're an amazing stepmother," Kate said.

"Especially given the circumstances," Sarah added.

Louise knew Sarah was referring to Abby being the result of Warren's affair. But she was done with ruminating on the past. What's been has been. What's done is done. "I've decided to move on from that."

"What do you mean?" Sarah leaned back on the couch and crossed her legs.

"I've chosen no longer to dwell on what Warren did. Whatever the circumstances, whatever his decisions—it's done. What I have now is a beautiful stepdaughter who has given me a new sense of purpose in life. I mean, I know I have a life...I have the bookstore; I have you guys. And then there's Philip. But when I look at Abby, my heart beats a little bit faster. It clenches just a little bit tighter. Do you know what I mean?"

Kate and Sarah gazed at her. She wondered what they saw.

Louise smiled. "I finally have another daughter to love."

Chapter 50

Kate Morgan

Kate felt the words that Louise just spoken. "I know what you mean, Louise," Kate said. "With Adam...now that I'm a mother, I feel like I'm a different person."

Louise nodded. "I've noticed that."

"Have you?" Kate asked with a smile.

"There's this confidence about you. An aura, if you like. One that says, 'don't mess with me, I'm a mama bear!"

Kate laughed. "That's exactly how I feel. I used to just go with things and do whatever people told me I should do. But now, I make big decisions. I think about how it will affect my son. He's the center of my life."

"I think you're very strong," Sarah said. "Motherhood has a way of bringing out all our strengths. I can certainly see it in you." Sarah smiled.

"Where is Adam anyway?" Louise asked.

"You're not going to believe it." Kate smiled and covered her mouth.

"What is it?" Sarah glanced at Louise who'd also raised her eyebrows.

"He's with Evan," Kate said.

"What?" Sarah couldn't hide her surprise. "Why?"

"Because he wants to be more involved in Adam's life," Kate said. "And it feels right."

"Are you two..."—Sarah pointed at Kate.

"No, gosh no," Kate said. She knew what Sarah was thinking. "We're not back together. And we're never getting back together."

"Well, that's a relief." Sarah waved a hand. "What's changed? I mean, am I missing something?"

"After that night that he met Adam...I don't know. It's like I saw something in him. Last month, he invited us to one of his meetings." Kate told them about Evan's journey to sobriety.

"Did you go to the meeting?" Sarah asked.

Kate nodded and recalled the events of that night.

"MY NAME IS EVAN MORGAN and I'm an alcoholic," Evan said.

"Hi Evan," the room replied.

"I never thought I had a problem," Evan said, "until the night that the sheriff and his team pulled me off my wife and cuffed me." Evan paused. "That was six months ago."

Kate held her breath. Unsure of what he was going to say, she bit down on her lip.

"When Kate told me she was pregnant, I told her to get rid of it. I told her I didn't want a baby. I accused her of purposely getting pregnant and told her to choose. It was me or the baby."

Kate felt exposed; as if she was standing naked in front of a room of strangers.

"Kate chose the baby. And tonight, she sits among us, supporting me—even when I don't deserve it. Kate is now the mother of Adam. That's her right there," Evan said as he pointed at her. "She is raising the same baby I told her to get rid of—the baby I told her to abort. The baby that made me see red and raise a hand to my wife."

Kate blinked back her tears as she recalled the night that the police came.

"But you see, Kate is a strong woman." Evan paused for a breath. "She's the strongest woman I've ever had the chance of knowing. She didn't let no alcoholic break her. She didn't let him tell her how to live her life. And she sure as heck didn't let no alcoholic kill her baby. Kate stood up to me...and I'm glad that she did."

Unable to hold them back, Kate's tears streamed down her face.

"It's been six months that I've been sober. Six months since my last drink. It's been six months since I lost the two most important people in my life." Evan looked at Kate.

Evan held up his sobriety chip and read the words engraved on it. "*Unity. Service. Recovery. To thine own self be true.*" Evan looked up from the chip. "I'm glad that Kate walked away—because I was a monster. I *am* a monster. I want her to be safe and to give our son the life that I cannot give him."

"Kate?" Evan said to her. "Thank you. Thank you for being strong. For being the person that you are. And for being here for me this evening."

Kate wiped her tears and nodded.

"I'd like to read out a prayer that is inscribed on the back of this chip," Evan said. *"God, grant me the serenity to accept the things I cannot change, the courage to change the things I can, and wisdom to know the difference."*

"WELL, HE'S CHANGED. He's softer. Kinder," Kate continued after she told them about Evan joining AA and how he'd been attending his meetings regularly.

"That must have been so hard for him," Sarah said.

Kate nodded.

"That's wonderful to know," Louise said.

"And so now what?" Sarah asked. "I mean, with Adam."

Kate pressed her lips for a moment. "He wants to be more involved in Adam's life. We hadn't really gone into it. But right now, I'm being guided by how I feel."

"A mother's instinct is very strong," Louise said.

"Do you know, Evan refers to himself as Dada when he talks to Adam? I mean, there he is...this big, burly guy cooing to a baby the size of his arm?"

"People change." Louise voiced her thoughts out loud.

"The important thing is that I don't feel like Adam's in any danger when he's with Evan." Kate smoothed her dress over her lap.

"That's very important," Sarah agreed.

"You know, I really do believe that he's looking out for us."

"Who?" Sarah asked. "Evan?"

"God," Kate pointed upwards with her finger.

"It's been a tough year, hasn't it?" Louise said with a sigh. "For all of us."

Sarah sat up straight. "Well, I for one, could not have gotten through this year without you two."

"I feel the same," Kate said. She reached out for both their hands. "Without you guys, who knows what would have happened to me and Adam?"

"What are you gonna do now?" Louise asked. "About Evan, I mean."

Kate shrugged. "We're not getting back together. I told him I thought it wasn't a good idea," she said. "And besides, I didn't like who I was when I was with him."

"Good for you," Louise said with a soft clap of her hands.

"I think I'm good, you know? Me and Adam—we'll be just fine. And besides, who knows what tomorrow will bring?"

"What about Mark?" Louise asked. "The poor guy is truly smitten with you. I see it every time he comes to the bookstore."

Kate smiled. "Well, I'm really grateful for his friendship. He's amazing with Adam and I feel really lucky to have him in our lives." she said. "But *friends* is all we can be for now. And I've told him that too."

"What did he say?" Louise asked.

"He said there was no rush. That he'd be there...as a friend, a buddy, or whatever."

"I'm so proud of you, Kate," Sarah said.

"So you're happy?" Louise asked.

Kate nodded. "The happiest I've ever been."

Chapter 51

Sarah Gardner

The next day, they all went to the Village Park to watch the children's final game of the year. Little children aged two to five filled the field, wearing their too-big jerseys. Parents gathered on the sidelines as they chatted to each other. Some carried homemade pompoms cheering for the children, while others held up small posters with their child's name scrawled across. Excitement filled the crisp winter air, and it was contagious.

Sarah sat on the folding chair she'd brought from home. It was one of a set of four that she and Adam had bought when they'd moved to Carlton Bay several years ago, both promising to be more active and one with nature. She brought another two for Louise and Kate who'd come along to support the kids too. Funnily enough, it was the first time the chairs had ever been used.

Sarah pulled a throw over her legs and rubbed her hands together. "It definitely feels like winter now."

"Ah!" Louise exclaimed. "I have just what you need." She'd brought a thermos of hot coffee for them to share and another filled with hot chocolate for the children to enjoy after the game.

"Lifesaver," Sarah said as she was handed a paper cup of steaming coffee.

"Where are the kids?" Kate asked as she scanned the field. "Oh! I see them!" she said excitedly. "Look at Zoe—oh my gosh, she's so cute!! I love her little pigtails."

"She's a lot more confident on the field now," Sarah said with pride. "Especially since she knows her brothers are there with her."

"I can't wait until Adam can join them." Kate adjusted the beanie that sat snug over Adam's head.

"Get him crawling first, darling," Louise said with a laugh. "And quit hogging that baby," she said as she stood from her chair. "Come here, darling. Auntie Louise needs a cuddle."

"Hello ladies—it's nice to see you all here today."

They turned to a smiling Philip. He stepped towards Louise and gave her a peck on the cheek.

"Oh, just her?" Sarah asked, teasing.

"Ah, but there's more..." Philip obliged and greeted Sarah and Kate with their own kisses.

"So, last game of the year, huh?" Sarah turned to the field.

"It is," Philip said. "Time for everyone to enjoy the Christmas season."

"The kids will miss their training sessions over the winter break, no doubt." Sarah knew that Liam was upset about it. He'd gotten more serious about the game. Next year, he would be joining the school soccer club with the older kids.

"And we will miss them. It's always a joy to have the children around. Will you be taking a break over the winter?" Philip asked.

"You mean at work?" Sarah hadn't thought about it and suddenly felt a bit of panic. "I—uh—I haven't actually spoken to Father Paul about it."

"Well, there's plenty of time," Philip said, "whatever you decide to do."

"Who's that with Caleb?" Kate asked in a loud whisper.

Sarah looked up and saw a woman dressed in a two-piece tracksuit. "Is that velvet she's wearing?".

"Looks like Coach Caleb is popular with some of the moms," Louise chided.

Sarah's heart sank when the tracksuit lady put a hand on Caleb's arm. But she knew she had no right to be upset.

"I'm sure she's just wishing him good luck for the game," Philip offered.

"Oh, I don't know about that," Kate said. "Shouldn't she be wishing *her* kid good luck instead of Caleb?"

"You guys, stop it," Sarah said. "He can do whatever he wants to do." As if that wasn't enough, Caleb glanced in their direction. Sarah quickly looked away.

A whistle shrieked, and a voice came over the speakers. "Welcome, everyone, to the last game of the year. Let's give it up for our little boys and girls who are going to be giving it their all on the field today."

The crowd cheered just as Sarah took a sip of her coffee. She put her cup down and cheered for the children, shaking the image of Caleb and the velveteen mom from her mind.

AFTER THE GAME AND everyone had said their goodbyes, Sarah decided to walk over to the cemetery with the children.

It was hard to believe that just last year; she sat on the front row of seats, not quite believing that it was her husband that was being lowered into the ground. Today, she sat on the grass and ran her hand over Adam's headstone which read, *"Here lies Adam Gardner, much loved husband of Sarah, and father of Liam, Noah, and Zoe. Until we meet again."*

Sarah looked up, keeping an eye on the children, who had busied themselves picking dandelions. "Kids, please make sure you stay close by."

"I think we're going to be okay, Adam," Sarah said softly. She laid down on the grass alongside Adam's plot. "It's been a tough year and I'm still cross with you for leaving us, but I know that you've been looking out for us."

Sarah sighed as she told Adam about everything that has been happening with the children. "Liam's at big school now. You would be so proud of him, Adam. He's such an amazing little man. And Noah...he's just like you. He also loves corn on the cob like you did. Zoe's a little madam. I hope she doesn't get it from me," Sarah joked.

"Sarah?"

Sarah looked up to see Caleb. "Caleb, hi." She sat up. "Sorry, I was just talking to..." Sarah stopped herself. What was she going to say? That she was talking to Adam?

Caleb got on his knees beside her. "May I?" he asked.

Sarah nodded and Caleb sat opposite her, across from where Adam laid. "Good game today," she said.

"Sarah, I miss you," Caleb said. "I miss talking to you. Laughing with you. Playing board games—me, you, and the kids."

"Caleb...what are you doing? Stop..."

But he continued. "I miss our cooking experiments and competitions. And I miss you laughing at my jokes, no matter how bad they are."

Sarah looked away.

"I know, I'm not Adam—and I will never try to be him."

Sarah looked back at Caleb.

"I will always respect Adam for the husband he was to you. I know that he will always be the father of the children."

Tears threatened her eyes. She couldn't help it. She wasn't supposed to cry. This was not supposed to happen. She was supposed to be strong—loyal.

"Sarah...without you, my life is empty," Caleb said.

"Caleb, I know you love the children—"

"Give me a chance, Sarah," Caleb said. "It's not just the children I love."

Sarah bit her lips—as hard as she could. Her tears fell.

"I love you. I have always loved you."

She took a deep breath and took Caleb's hand when he reached for hers. "But... Adam...and the kids...I can't." Her mind was spinning, but as she looked into Caleb's eyes, Sarah felt her heart open. It was as if air had finally been let through. She closed her eyes and took a deep breath in. She was alive. She was *still* alive.

Sarah felt something on her hand. She opened her eyes—it was a butterfly...with two specks of black on each side. Sarah gasped, careful not to move as it sat atop her hand and Caleb's.

She blinked, and more tears fell.

And just as quietly as it had landed, the butterfly took off. Sarah kept her eyes on it as it flew towards the children.

"Look!" Zoe squealed. "A butterfly!"

The white butterfly danced above their heads for a few moments and then flew off.

Sarah looked up from behind her tears. She smiled ever so slightly and nodded.

Caleb took her into an embrace and Sarah fell into his arms. She closed her eyes as she felt a kiss on her forehead.

Before long, the children were climbing over the both of them.

"Mommy, we saw a butterfly!" Liam exclaimed.

"Mommy, why are you crying?" Liam asked.

Sarah laughed and wiped her tears.

"She's happy crying, silly," Liam said.

Caleb put an arm over Liam's shoulders. "Is this cool with you, buddy? Me and your mom?"

Liam nodded. "Yeah, it's cool."

Sarah laughed at how grown up he'd sounded. She pulled Liam into an embrace and kissed his cheeks.

"Mommy, you're embarrassing me," Liam said. But when Caleb joined in the embrace, he stopped complaining.

Noah climbed on Caleb's back. "I think it's cool! It's cool! It's cool!"

Sarah wasn't sure if Noah knew what was happening.

"I wanna cook too," Zoe cried.

Sarah laughed. "No one is cooking, my sweet girl." She stroked Zoe's head and pressed a kiss to her forehead. "Are you sure about this?" she asked Caleb.

"It's the most certain I've been about anything in my life." Caleb winked at her.

Sarah didn't know what the future would bring, but there was one thing that was certain—everyone she loved was there. And that was all that mattered.

And Adam? Adam was always going to be in her heart. There was no doubt about that. He wasn't going anywhere. Adam was her first love, and Sarah would always be grateful for the time they'd spent together. They were happy—truly happy.

Louise's words rang through her head. *'Darling, life is too short for regrets. You, my dear friend, are very lucky. Not many people experience true love in one lifetime—much less two loves.'*

She could see it now. Sarah could see how truly lucky she was—to have loved and been loved. And... to have the chance to love again.

"See?" Sarah could hear Kate's voice. *"I told you. He's looking out for us."*

Sarah threw her head back and looked up at the sky. She nodded slowly and smiled. "He really is."

The End

THANK YOU

Thank you for reading Tea for Three. I hope you enjoyed getting to know Sarah, Kate, and Louise as they journeyed through faith and hope during moments of despair; and learned about life, love, and true friendship.

If you enjoyed it, please consider leaving a review on Amazon.com.

If you haven't already, and you would like to receive updates on new releases and freebies, please visit **www.MelissaCrosby.com** and sign up to the Melissa Crosby Romance Newsletter

READ OTHER BOOKS BY Melissa Crosby:

Willow Oaks Sweet Romance Series

- **Book 1:** Love Me True ♥ Amy and Sam
- **Book 2:** Love Me Maybe ♥ Charlotte and Ben
- **Book 3:** Love Me Again ♥ Jenna and Dave

- **Book 4:** Love Me Always ♥ Mallory and Ethan
- **Book 5:** Love Me Timeless ♥ Mick and Carly

About the Author

Melissa Crosby lives in Wellington, New Zealand with her husband, two children, and their adopted rescue pets, Evie and Zuko. She enjoys writing inspirational women's fiction and heartwarming small town romance.

To be the first to get updates on new releases and freebies, sign up to her newsletter at www.melissacrosby.com.

Read more at https://melissacrosby.com/.

Made in the USA
Las Vegas, NV
29 December 2020

14972184R00204